BALBOA FIREFLY

Also by Jack Trolley

Balboa Firefly
Manila Time
Juarez Justice
La Jolla Spindrift

As Tom Ardies

Kosygin is Coming (aka Russian Roulette)
In a Lady's Service
Palm Springs

The Charlie Sparrow Series

Their Man in the White House
This Suitcase is Going to Explode
Pandemic

As Richard O'Brien

Storming Heaven
By Friends Betrayed

BALBOA FIREFLY

JACK TROLLEY

BRASH
BOOKS

ISBN-13: 978-1-7358517-7-8

Published by
Brash Books
PO Box 8212
Calabasas, CA 91372
www.brash-books.com

*To whoever invented the word processor
and discovered lithium.*

ACKNOWLEDGMENTS

My appreciation to Lynn Stanley, for introducing me to the Lindbergh Field glide path, and keeping me on it, and to Al Zuckerman for his wisdom and patience, and to Tony Lexier, for his help with thrifts and motor cars, and to Bill Robinson, who knows all about the San Diego Police Department

BALBOA FIREFLY

Sometimes, in his lunatic fantasies, he imagined himself a god. He was all knowing and all powerful and he could do anything he wished. He could reach into the sky and pluck the eye from a bird. If he wanted, he could catch the bird, crush it in his hand, the feathers flying. Not just a bird, either. He could catch a plane. The biggest plane in the sky. He could do that. So they had better watch out.

PROLOGUE

For Grenier, it all began here, on the other side of the world, in a place he would always think of as full of dark danger pushing inadequate seams. They were in a bar, but it looked like a butcher shop. It had a steel counter and glass display cases and bone-white tiles on the floor and all the walls. It was at once dirty and antiseptic and the lighting was too bright. To passersby, it promised warmth. Actually, it was cold. It was as cold as the rest of Moscow. The only warmth was in the vodka.

There were just the two of them, Grayson Grenier III, president and chief executive officer of the Pilgrim Tobacco Company, and Rudolf Pinsky, managing director of Zoltin Exports. They had made a deal that afternoon. Now it was night. The others had left. Everyone. Grenier wanted to leave, too. But not Pinsky. He wanted to drink some more. Grenier wondered where Pinsky put it. He must have consumed a quart of vodka, Grenier thought. Grenier also was drunk. But not as drunk as Pinsky. The fat Russian would soon be comatose.

"How do I know I can trust you?" Pinsky asked.

Grenier looked at him. A pig in a bad suit. There was that question again. Earlier, in the drafty boardroom at Zoltin Exports, Pinsky, pen in hand, had asked it sober, perhaps jokingly, perhaps not. You don't know, Grenier had said then, smiling, and everyone had laughed. So loudly that it echoed from the smiling cherubs carved into the vaulted ceiling. Now, Grenier decided, in view of the drunken circumstances, of the certainty that it was no longer a joke, perhaps he should reply differently, although of course there was no way he could cheat. It was a straightforward arrangement, price and quantity agreed, shipment against letters of credit to be cashed upon delivery. The most basic of transactions. Not to be repeated if anything went amiss. Only a Russian would look for treachery.

"You trust history, Rudolf," Grenier answered, hoping that didn't sound as pompous as he thought it did. He was a man of distinction, in appearance, bearing, and composure, and he had an aristocrat's fine good looks. The price was to sometimes seem too self-important. "My company is one of the oldest in America. It has been held by the same family for six generations. It is a dynasty."

"Dynasties don't cheat people?"

"Dynasties don't have to cheat."

"Nonsense. They do what is required."

Grenier felt himself getting angry, defensive. Yes, I suppose, he thought. The Pilgrim Tobacco Company probably was an excellent example of that. It was why he was here. Drunk in a Moscow butcher shop. Persisting with this conversation, he said, the vodka talking, "Yes, I suppose."

"What?"

"I do what is required."

Pinsky liked that answer. "Now," he said, "you're being honest." He unscrewed the cap of the new bottle. "You don't get to be a survivor—six survivors in a row, yes?—unless there is steel inside. I know you, you are a man of steel, Grayson Grenier."

Grenier smiled. Superman? Not quite. Actually, he was running scared these days. The Pilgrim Tobacco Company was in financial trouble. It was falling deeper and deeper into a hole being dug by the U.S. Surgeon General. The cancer scare—the cancer *reality*—was starting to take hold. Eventually, the company would be buried, he could sense that, see it, and so he was anxious to diversify, peddle a different poison. They'd never outlaw booze. They'd tried that and it hadn't worked. They wouldn't try it again. The booze business was safe, and the marketing strategies were the same as those for tobacco. He'd be on essentially familiar ground, applying tested, proven principles. Back in New York his marketing people already had the campaign mapped out. Stalvart. The Other Russian Vodka. If, as some suspected, there was a God, a God who rewarded good and punished evil, he was going to hell. Tobacco and now spirits. Both. That worried him sometimes, but only vaguely. He liked to think that he was very much his own man, in command of his own destiny, secure in his indifference to what, in the final analysis, were imagined forces. He could, and would, take care of himself. He was a loner, no family, the last of his line. He had associates, not friends. He had a woman he wouldn't marry and material possessions he couldn't let go. He lived in a manner and style which he intended to maintain, whatever the price. He wanted his salvation on earth. He would risk the other.

Pinksy filled their empty glasses. The liquor splashed on the table.

"Your turn," Grenier said, the vodka talking. "You tell me. What are you inside?"

"Me?" Pinsky stared with his bright pig eyes. "You get what you see. Outside, inside. It is the same." He took hold of his glass. "What do you see?"

Grenier hesitated. He was sorry he had been so careless as to provoke such a question. The truth wouldn't do now. This required a clever lie. He studied the Russian, who would be perhaps sixty, twenty years his senior, but undoubtedly stronger, tougher. He truly resembled some huge hog. Coming here, swathed in animal skins, making mock of his, Grenier's, camel-hair coat, his fine cashmere scarf, Pensky had taken most of the sidewalk. You couldn't walk with him and stay out of the gutter. You had to follow behind. You compensated by pretending to herd.

"I see a chess player," Grenier said finally. "No, a chess master. The world is your board. You move people on it. You move them to win." Grenier wondered if he was gilding the lily. A bit, maybe. Six layers and an undercoat. "You're a winner."

Pinsky stared at him. He said, "That's very clever of you, Grayson Grenier. You must be familiar with an international export company. You saw the board. You saw the world." He smiled. "You saw me moving my men?"

Grenier shrugged. He had seen no such thing. What he saw was a drunken pig. The Russian ought to change his name. Not Pinsky. Pigsky.

"I have many men," Pinsky said, slurring. "If you cheat me, Grayson Grenier, I will send someone after you. He knows America well, he has been there many times, so he will know how to find you, and he will tear your heart out."

Grenier had to laugh. "Really? Who is this animal?"

"An assassin for the KGB. Or, he used to be, anyway. Now he's unemployed."

"You know assassins?"

"We're all assassins."

Grenier was angered now. That was enough. Hours of catering to a slob. He pushed up from the table. "Excuse me, I'm going back to the hotel, Rudolf."

"Why?"

"I don't want to kiss your ass anymore."

"See?" Pinsky laughed. "What did I say? I knew there was steel inside." He tried to rise and couldn't. "I think I'm drunk."

"You are." Grenier looked around. All the other customers had left. There was just the owner, an old woman with a rag, staring fearfully. "Do you realize what you're talking about? Assassins?"

"I am talking about the unemployed of my country," Pinsky said loudly. "We have a great number of people without work. Engineers, scientists. Secret police. Spies. They used to make missiles, nuclear bombs. They used to arrest people and steal things. Now nobody wants them anymore. They have nothing to do. So they will work for anybody. Foreigners. It is a sad thing that has happened to my country. Mother Russia. A whore."

Grenier said, "You're drunk on your ass."

"Perhaps, but if you ever want anybody killed, give me a call," Pinsky said. His head slumped onto the table.

Grenier steadied himself. He was unaccountably angry. Outraged. "Give you a call? Me?"

There was no answer.

Grenier grabbed Pinsky by the hair. He pulled up his head so he could see the pig eyes. "Do you know who I am?" Grenier demanded, the vodka talking. "I'm a major player in the tobacco industry. I kill half a dozen people every day. I tear their fucking lungs out."

"Randomly," Pinsky muttered, unimpressed. "You don't choose them. You never see them."

Grenier let Pinsky's head drop. He was angry. He could barely control himself. He said, the anger talking, "What's this guy charge?"

"Who?"

"The assassin. What does he charge?"

"Dollars or rubles?" Pinsky asked.

CHAPTER ONE

If there was a precise moment of choice, of no return, it probably came at the crest of the hill, the old Mercedes hanging there, as if catching its breath for the plunge. The Canadian muttered, "Jesus, is this crate gonna make it?" and Joseph R. Foley, Realtor, wound tighter than a Mexican watch, was somehow suddenly at peace. The long wait was over. He knew, if he continued, that this was the day it was going to happen. Free choice. He could turn around and go home and pull the covers over his head and wait for the demons to pass. Or he could continue and welcome them.

"I mean, it *is* kinda steep, eh?"

For answer, Foley eased off the brakes, starting the long, rattling, unsure descent down Juniper Street, never to look back. He'd had his chance to stop. He wouldn't get another. And that was okay. He looked forward, actually. Finally, some action. They'd gone two blocks before his passenger relaxed a bit and managed a thin smile. "Reminds me of San Francisco."

"But better," Foley told him.

The man had an odd name, Parlan, Parlin, something like that, Foley hadn't gotten it correctly, which was unusual for him. Normally, he took the time to have the person spell it. People appreciated you getting their names right. But Foley had messed up this morning—the wild rush of events, eh?—and so he had pigeonholed the man as The Canadian. He hadn't said so, but he had to be a Canadian. They all said, eh? That's why there had never been a Canadian spy, Foley thought. They'd give themselves away as soon as they opened their codfish mouths.

1

"The view is beautiful," the man said, trying to be agreeable. San Diego Bay's North Harbor, shimmering in the morning sun, was set like an enormous sapphire. Sailboats sparkled like scattered diamonds. "I can see why you wanted to come this way. It's a real selling point, eh?"

"At least you can see it," Foley grumbled. Normally, he'd be touting Balboa Park over Hillcrest or Uptown, not fucking San Francisco. "We don't get as much fog. Or rain."

"Is that right?"

Foreigners, Foley thought. He turned sharply onto Curlew, two blocks up from State and Interstate 5. They were piling in like flies on a ripe corpse. The Chinese. The Koreans. The Vietnamese and the Thais. The Iranians. They were taking over everything. The restaurants and food markets, the gas stations, the dry cleaners. The 1-hour photos. They were taking over, and one of these days they were going to pull the plug. You wouldn't be able to eat or go anywhere and you wouldn't have the pictures to prove it. The 1-hour photos. Key to the plot.

"Made it," the man observed. He was breathing normally now and exhibiting some appreciation for the Mercedes. "How long have you had it?"

"Picked it up yesterday," Foley told him. "My first real run. The brakes seem to work."

The man regarded him unsurely. He wanted to say something but decided against it. Foley nosed the Mercedes into the curb in front of the Cypress Gardens. It was a '72 280SE 4.5, salvaged. He'd got it from a junk yard. It wasn't registered. The plates were off an old Monte in the same yard. The tags were mimeos off yet other plates. He didn't like fees, taxes. He hated politicians. The fucking pols.

The man was struggling with his door. "This is it?"

"It's got a cypress." There also was a FOR RENT sign.

Foley got out and waited for his prospect to extract himself. He needed the man to take the place. Not for the money, not for a lousy rental, the amount was trifling, but for the psychological lift. He hadn't rented anything for a month. He hadn't made a sale in three. The bloom was off the boom. More people were leaving than were coming to California and that was especially true of San Diego. The guts had been ripped out of the defense industry, and out of its workers, too. They couldn't find anything else and they'd given up. They were going to Oregon, Washington. They were going to Arizona and New Mexico. They were going to where the jobs were. The foreigners replacing them were moving in with relatives. The real-estate market was dead.

"You coming?" Foley demanded. The man had somehow got himself tangled in the seat belt. It looked like a typical Canadian trick. Foley waited, then led the way, limping. He needed a cane but refused to use one. He needed a new hip, but he had declined that, too. He'd never had a knife cut him. Not yet. He had endured the pain all his adult life. Thirty years of stoic suffering. It was like a nail in his side. A nail that fixed the leg to his body.

The man looked around doubtfully. "It's kind of rough." Cypress Gardens was a scruffy four-unit box, all one-bedroom, one-bath. Two on the bottom. Two on the top. The grass was dead. The cypress was dying.

Yeah, rough and tough, but wait till you hear the bad news, Foley thought. He scowled for answer. That usually worked with most people and did this time. It was a bulldog look, full of power, menace, impatience. Foley, when he looked in the mirror, saw a dark image of a glowering Winston Churchill, and he would recall what Churchill had said: "I know we are all bugs. But I like to think I'm a lightning bug."

#3 was top left. Foley went up the stairs at the right, moving painfully. The man followed at a distance. They got to the top of the stairs. Went past #4 on the empty balcony. Came, finally, to #3. Unlike the other shuttered apartments, #3 was a fishbowl, the blinds up, the drapes pulled open for show. Foley motioned with a flourish. The man peered through the big picture window. He made a whooshing sound.

"You like it?"

"Are you kidding?"

The man cupped his hands around his face and pressed against the glass for a better look. The neighborhood and building might be decrepit but the apartment was a glorious find. It was elegant and special and had a bright and airy open plan. He could see through it and out the rear picture window with its unobstructed view of the harbor. Four brass ceiling fans, the blades inset with woven straw, hovered over the gleaming dark chocolate plank floor, which was filled with rich reflections. There was a small fireplace, the mantel matching the floor, the yellow tile face mirroring the brass of the fans. There was a bar with a brass rail and a whole wall of bookshelves. The bar and the shelves were in the same dark chocolate gleaming wood as the floor. The place looked old, from another era, antique. It looked very inviting. You'd want to stay forever.

The man said, his tone changing, trying to sound casual now, "What did you say the rent was?"

"Four hundred dollars."

"Four hundred." The man pressed against the glass, reviewing the small gem, which was filled with expensive, tasteful furniture, including a shiny black baby grand.

"That's unfurnished, of course," Foley reminded him.

The man pressed harder. He seemed to be imagining his own stuff in there, and it still worked. "Why's the guy moving?"

"I don't know," Foley said, lying.

The man moved back and shook his head. "This kind of place? That cheap? He must have a damn good reason…"

Suddenly, behind him, there was a low rumble, growing louder. He turned and looked up at the sky. Now the rumble was a roar, boiling up behind the rooftops across the street. He stood, frozen, staring. A huge jet airliner exploded into view. Its engines screamed. The man stared, his face drained white, as the enormous aircraft passed directly over him, so near he could see the rivets.

"Jesus Christ," the man said, after the sound faded. "That was close, eh?"

"You get used to it," Foley told him, lying again.

The man said, "Lemme outa here."

Foley felt it then. It had been coming for years and today was the day. He'd known that, since the top of the hill. This was it. Somewhere inside, he snapped. He actually felt it, he thought, smiling. Hell, he even heard the twang.

CHAPTER TWO

Sgt. Tommy Donahoo stared at the scrap of paper left in tatters by his obsessive folding and unfolding. He carried it wadded in his wallet and opened it almost every day, looking for a miracle. One day, erased by the gods, the words wouldn't be there. That's what he wished for. But of course that never happened. Nobody got their prayers answered. Nobody he knew.... *the blood is on your hands.*

He had hundreds of threatening letters in his files. They vowed havoc on everyone and everything. Celebrities, politicians, judges, athletes. The President, the Governor, the Mayor. The whole County Board of Supervisors. San Diego Gas & Electric. The Pope. Home Savings. The U.S. Navy. Nothing was sacred.

Donahoo took them all seriously, to a degree. He was head of a small, elite San Diego Police Department unit which had the designation Squad 5 and was known, more popularly, as SCUMB, standing for Sickos, Crackpots, Underwear & Mad Bombers. One in five cases ended up having something to do with underwear. Panties, garter belts, stockings, some kind of underwear. SCUMB's job was to sift, to evaluate, to decide. To choose between the harmless cranks and the real killers. To make judgments that were based, finally, uncomfortably, on an uncertain mix of science and gut feeling. It was impossible to be absolutely sure about which threat to ignore and which to act on. But there wasn't the manpower to investigate them all. So—scary word in his profession—Donahoo had to guess.

He pushed away from his desk, feeling suddenly trapped in the small squad room fashioned, as an afterthought, from half of an adjacent storeroom. He went to the one window and the escape and freedom it lied about. He went to it often, like a prisoner in a cell. He was a big man, six foot two, two hundred and thirty, a bruiser. Big head, big hands, big feet, a physical throwback to tough shanty Irish, but he had a keen, probing, puzzle-breaker's intellect. He wasn't handsome, not anymore, the busted, pushed-in nose denied that, but he had an arresting look, helpful to a cop. He had steel-blue eyes under thick bushy eyebrows and a solid no-nonsense mouth. He wore his graying hair long; it fell over his collar, untamed. On the job, he was tough, as mean as required, and only as honest as necessary. He knew how the system worked and how to work it to his advantage. He knew how to kick ass and how to kiss it. He was softer off the job. He knew how to laugh then, and, sometimes, how to cry. He knew, on occasion, how to love.

Now, looking out at the city he was sworn to protect, he wasn't sure if he was capable of any emotion. The task never ended, it just got larger, more difficult, he thought. It was starting to drag him down. It was a killer.

San Diego had come of age in his lifetime. It had gone from dumb-ass Navy town to high-tech metropolis. It had big-city sky-crapers now, and culture enough, and even some sophistication, although it also remained forever cutesy. At almost every turn there was some enterprise with a name like Kung Food. The practice was an affliction as contagious as the graffiti, all part of a curious and sometimes frightening mix of conflicting values and goals. "America's Finest City," if you had a good job, could afford the right neighborhood. But on every side were problems that seemed beyond solution. Out-of-control violent crime and drug addiction. Massive, widespread unemployment. Untold hundreds of the dispossessed and homeless. An overwhelming tide of illegal immigration. We built it, and now we're losing it,

Donahoo often thought. And, if we lose it, we'll never get it back. All we'll be able to do is pick and defend small enclaves. What we're doing, essentially, now.

He had chosen his. He'd get there, maybe. A dozen blocks to the south, the Coronado Bridge, graceful as a swan, and as fragile, seemingly, as a rainbow, arched up, up and away from Barrio Logan and across San Diego Bay to the pot of gold that was Coronado. Donahoo looked at the island longingly. The place to live, better than Mission Hills, better even than La Jolla or Point Loma. It still had a village atmosphere, where people knew and cared about each other, where the houses were kept up and the streets were clean and the most threatening drive-by was the ice-cream man. A small toll charge away from the barrio's slums and the overflowing human sewer that threatened to engulf him. Donahoo sighed. Missed opportunities. There had been a time, years before, when he could have bought a home on Coronado, had he been willing to make the sacrifice. Or, more correctly, had he known, in time, it would be necessary. Now it was out of the question. A tiny house on a narrow lot went for half a million dollars. Only the rich could afford Coronado. Or the people who had bought there early. Donahoo turned away and back to the note. The lesson, if there was one, was to try not to miss again, he told himself, and it applied to all things. A man could carry only so many regrets.

Gomez was on the other side of the cramped, cluttered room, waiting for some sign. Donahoo frowned, which was enough. Gomez said, "Jesus, Sarge. Give it up, willya? There's nothing there."

Donahoo looked at him. Investigator Anthony Gomez, aka Spick, the upwardly mobile member of the celebrated team of Spick and Spook. Gomez and Montrose, a Mex and a black, had been named that the moment they became partners. They didn't like it at first, but now they did, it made them special.

"When are you picking up Hudson?" Donahoo asked, as if he didn't know what Gomez was talking about, the note.

Now Gomez was frowning. "Reading it, reading it. That's all you've been doing, Sarge. You're wasting your time."

"When?"

"Noon."

Donahoo looked back at the note. Yes, and time was life, he thought. He was painfully aware of the swift passage of life. At his age, pushing fifty, it hurtled by, a runaway train, no stops. You just became a wreck.

"Today, he always eats at Anthony's," Gomez said. "I thought we'd get there early. Be there, you know, when he comes in?"

"The Star of the Sea Room, I suppose?"

"Well, yeah."

Donahoo smiled. He could see the expense chit. Lunch at the Star of the Sea. Gomez, being upwardly mobile, was famous for his expenses. Once, he had listed PACR, $20. Which, upon investigation, turned out to be pissed away, can't remember.

"You coming?"

"No," Donahoo decided. "You and Montrose. He's your collar. You can bring him in." Hudson was the bag man for First Fidelity Trust. They had him for something else. Jury tampering. "But try to resist the lobster tail."

Gomez shot him a sour look and pushed up from his desk. "Whatever you say," he complained, preparing to leave. He was weighing the risk of a parting shot. "You really think you're going to solve that puzzle?"

Donahoo shrugged. "I don't know."

"A piece of paper, some words. That's all you've got."

"So?"

"So I worry about you. Jesus."

"Don't."

Gomez hesitated. He was considering the risk again. Finally, he moved off, shoving into his best jacket, the fake black suede, screaming for his partner, "Montrose!" Gomez with his slicked-back hair and thin string ties and shiny black patent-leather four-lace-holes ballroom slippers. The Beau Brummel Chihuahua. Lewis, who was Chief of Homicide, who could get away with it, had made him take one off in the Detective Parade Room. Lewis had looked inside and read what it said there. *Capistrano's. Dancing Since 1884.* "You gotta be exhausted," Lewis had said.

Donahoo shook his head and pressed the note flat. He didn't know why he had chosen this particular threat. He just had, that's all. Something told him this was real. Some inner voice beyond explanation or denial. The rationale came later. In the note's lack of specifics, in the long lead time, in the flat, emotionless form. *This is your last warning,* the note said. *You have six months to relocate the airport. Or the blood is on your hands.* No diatribe. No dirty words. No crude drawings. Just a neat businesslike let-ter, laser printer, copier paper, and mailed from the main post office with a patriotic, three flags stamp.

Try to trace that, Donahoo thought, as always, staring at the ragged scrap. The original was between protective plastic sheets in a fireproof steel filing cabinet. This was a copy, the second that he had made. The first copy had literally worn out. Yeah, try to trace that, Donahoo thought. Or fathom it. He'd been trying, all that time, and he had nothing to show, he'd come up empty, yet he couldn't, wouldn't, give it up. He knew something the others didn't know. A lifetime of police work told him this one was real.

There were six airports in San Diego. Lindbergh Field. The U.S. Naval Air Stations at North Island and Miramar. Montgomery Field. Gillespie Field. Brown Field. There were a lot of complaints about the noise caused by the Navy's jets, both at North Island and Miramar, but if one airport aroused outcry, it was Lindbergh Field. As an international airport serving a major city, Lindbergh was far busier than the two naval air stations combined, and it was unfortunately situated, on the north reach of San Diego Bay. Takeoffs shattered the residential quiet of Point

Loma, lowering property values in Ocean Beach and neighboring Fleetridge and Loma Portal. The landing glide path funneled a steady stream of descending jetliners just north of San Diego's downtown core and at a disturbingly low altitude over the residential area west of Balboa Park. There was never any relief. Only east/west runways existed. When heavy fog rolled in, requiring that the flight pattern be reversed, the takeoff noise was shattering over Balboa Park, which, in earlier years, had been prime property. Now real-estate values there were severely depressed. The once-proud neighborhood was slowly falling into ruin.

That was the other reason Donahoo carried the note in his wallet. Lindbergh didn't just annoy people. It stole from them. Tens, hundreds of thousands. For some, perhaps millions. So the hate was real. People, important people, had been lobbying for years for Lindbergh's relocation. It had been a popular political position, and football, for as long as he could recall. A smart pol could jump on the relocation bandwagon safe in the knowledge that he wouldn't be held to his campaign promises. There were too many forces working against it. Nobody had the money for a new airport, especially not in these hard times. Relocation to an existing facility seemed the only answer, but there were limited choices and formidable hurdles. Naval Air Station North Island, in the middle of the harbor, was as badly located as Lindbergh in terms of nuisance, and the Navy wasn't about to give it up, anyway. NAS Miramar, home of the Top Guns, was a workable choice, and it could become available as the base closure process moved ahead, but people nearby were vehemently opposed. A County referendum for moving Lindbergh there had split 52% for, 48% against. Relocating to Montgomery Field, the city's auxiliary airport, and also its busiest in terms of light-plane traffic, would just put the big airliners over different residential districts. Gillespie and Brown were too small. A proposal for a two-nation international airport at Otay Mesa had been scuttled by the Mexican government.

The pols, they played their games, Donahoo thought, and nothing happened, and nothing was going to happen until even more people died. California's worst air disaster had occurred on the approach to Lindbergh. A PSA jetliner had collided with a small plane over North Park. The combined death toll, on the two aircraft, on the ground, 144. It would have been much higher in a densely populated neighborhood. Fifteen years had passed and nothing had changed. The same danger still existed. Major international airport in the wrong place. So it was going to happen again, Donahoo thought. A similar disaster had been statistically reserved. It was as sure as dawn. No real argument on that. The only question was when.

The pols, the fucking pols, Donahoo thought. He imagined a jumbo coming down and ploughing through crowded apartment buildings in Balboa Park. When it did happen again, maybe a couple hundred more innocent lives snuffed out, then, and only then, would they move Lindbergh. Twice was the magic number. If you had twice, you could have three times, four. Twice and it finally sunk in. You didn't dare risk three.

Palmer and Cominsky came into the squad room. They were the other team of detectives who, with Gomez and Montrose, comprised, under Donahoo, Squad 5. They wore the same harnesses stuffed with .38 Colt Specials but all similarity with their fellow officers ended there. Gomez and Montrose, Spick and Spook, had been chosen for their excellent records and solid casework, and for their ethnic links to the city's large Hispanic and black populations. Palmer and Cominsky had been picked off the wall, where they were most of the time. It was Donahoo's theory, ravaged but intact, that it sometimes took a crackpot to catch one, and that they ought to be assigned in pairs. One on a team would be too stressful for the other partner. Palmer was small, pushy. He had a ferret's face and close-cropped pincushion hair. He walked around as if looking for a fight, chest pumped up, elbows bent. He moved like the featherweight boxer he was once was. Cominsky was tall, thin, gawky, weird. He wore a ponytail and checkered suits with wide lapels. He'd be attractive to Julia Roberts. Gomez had sent her Cominsky's picture. Pretty woman, dig this.

Palmer was still bitching about what he called the defecation of the Cabrillo Monument. Somebody had taken a dump on it.

"You gotta help me here," Palmer told Cominsky. "I want this report to be perfect. How do you spell it? Terd or turd? Is it t-e-r-d or is it t-u-r-d?"

Cominsky said, "Palmer, you don't know shit."

Cops, Donahoo thought. He stared at the note, wishing, a favored diversion, that some decent citizen, nerves rubbed raw, pushed to the limit, had mailed it to the Mayor. Perhaps the one irrational act of the guy's life. No real harm intended. Just wanted to get it off his chest, that's all. Was that possible? Sure. Anything was possible. And that was the trouble. Anything. The spectrum ran from decent citizen blowing steam to blood-thirsty lunatic plotting unthinkable carnage. With all the stops in between. Realestate syndicate seeking to create windfall and/or recoup losses. Radical environmental group intent on making an indelible statement. An old and bitter adversary fucking with his head...? Yeah, it could be anything and anybody, Donahoo thought. It was open to all faiths, colors, and creeds, and it could be all of the above. But he was betting, cop's intuition, psycho-path. Patient psychopath. He'd given them six months, and now time had run out. What Gomez and Montrose didn't realize, too busy with other, more pressing cases, the six months was up. Palmer and Cominsky didn't know it, either. Nobody knew the deadline had passed, and if he told them, they'd just look at him, like he'd been into the Old Crow again. Lewis, Chief of Homicide, he'd say, "Take it easy, huh?" Saperstein, who headed up Detectives, boss of bosses, he'd say, "Not now, Tommy."

Donahoo stared at the note. There was someone else who knew the deadline was up. The sonofabitch who wrote it.

CHAPTER THREE

He knew the city, he liked to think, the way a good man would know his woman. Every hill and valley and knoll and crevice. Every twist and turn. Every fault.

He had maps on his office walls, huge blowups, massive. He could read the street names from anywhere in the room without his glasses. A Av to Zurich Dr. From U.S. Naval Air Station Miramar south to the international border and Mexico. Torrey Pines Beach to the Tijuana Slough. East to Santee and El Cajon and Sweetwater Reservoir and down to Otay Mesa. A thousand streets. Two million people. All the cities and communities and districts and neighborhoods that were San Diego. Lemon Grove and Chula Vista and Del Mar. Coronado and Banker's Hill and La Jolla. Dozens more. He had prowled them all, every street and alley, mews and court. Day and night, relentlessly. All his life. He knew the sights and the sounds and the smells. Where the offshore winds died and where the smog settled and held. Where the traffic jammed. He knew where you were as safe as custard pie. He knew where you could get killed for no reason. He knew everything. Which part was black and which was brown and which was yellow. Lily white and redneck. Where the money was and where it wasn't. Where the most murders and rapes took place. The most burglaries. He could pinpoint the worst drug problem. The worst graffiti. The best toilet for fags and the best corner for whores. He knew where to buy a good cheap burrito and where the next freeway was going to go. He could tell you, eyes closed, not checking the maps, where a hundred invisible lines went, separating paradise and hell.

A telephone rang. He wasn't sure which. He had three of them. Three phones for three things. He used a different name for each. He also answered each as a different person. What he planned, he couldn't do alone, that was impossible, it was too intricate, but he also couldn't trust any element to anyone else. If, by chance, they were caught, they'd break. Everybody broke. Except him. He stood the pain. He never cried out. And so, the only solution, he had become three, a trinity. He was the power. The others did his bidding. On his right was the schemer and fixer. On his left was the instrument of death.

He concentrated, and when the phone rang again, he picked it up.

"Joseph R. Foley, Realtor," he said. "How can I help you?" The second phone rang. "Hold a minute, please." He picked up the second phone. "Mission Temporary Service." Now the third phone was ringing. "Hold, please." He got the third phone. "Farthest Star Productions. Please hold."

He surveyed his disaster. Well, now, look at this, will you? It never rained but it poured, and it wasn't all gumdrops being a god, either. It could keep you hopping.

CHAPTER FOUR

Donahoo went home to the Old Crow. An occasional but pre-dictable ritual. He drank in waves, starts and stops. There'd be long periods of calm, and then, like an ocean responding to invisible forces, he would begin crashing against whatever shore. He would rise up in anger and anguish. Spend himself, and retreat.

There were reasons for his binges. Reasons, not excuses, Donahoo thought, going immediately to the wheezing fridge. There was that important distinction. *Reasons,* and the main rea-son, number one, was the long departed and grievously mourned, not that she was by any means dead, Monica. The whiskey was in the freezer section. It was icy cold and didn't need ice cubes. No reason to dilute it.

He had only to turn around to be back in the living room. The apartment, like his office, was small and cramped, a stu-dio in an aging three-story stucco, The Arlington, which clung precariously to an Uptown canyon. The kitchen was a small bar fitted in between a bookcase/entertainment center and the door to the shower-only bathroom. On the plus side, it had a big, comfortable Murphy bed, a 10-foot high ceiling, a fireplace that worked, and a balcony deep enough to stand on. The canyon wall was dressed with the semitropical forest that marked the north parameter of Balboa Park. California 163 twisted below, distant enough that the traffic's noise was to reassure, not intrude. The rent was reasonable.

He had been there two years but was still regarded as the "new tenant" by the others. On the top floor, Barney, a spinster bookkeeper, was marking, as the longest in residence, her fifteenth year at The Arlington. She grew vegetables in a rooftop garden. She hung the harvest in plastic bags on Donahoo's doorknob. Cody, a Navy vet, and his wife, Vera, had occupied the next-door apartment for twelve years. Cody was a secret drinker. He would sneak over sometimes, share a nightcap. He never stayed long. Vera watched him like an owl.

Donahoo would have preferred something larger—if only to swing a certain cat—but he had expenses that took precedence. Monica, a shock, had claimed, and won, support. And there was also, even more unlikely, the monthly stipend he felt obligated to present to Father Charlie Donahoo, who had been forever banished, and correctly so, to St. Paul's Mission for Men in Desert Hot Springs.

Our father, who art not in heaven, Donahoo thought. He went to see him every other Sunday. He would be going this Sunday. Because the old priest's check was due, expected, needed. Because, otherwise, there'd be all that smothering guilt. He removed his jacket and laid it over the back of the cat-raked sofa. He sat down and kicked off his shoes and made flight preparations. Departing, parts unknown. The cat, Oscar, came by, rubbed him.

"Pussy," Donahoo said. That was when he noticed the feather in its mouth and the pile of them in the killing field under the coffee table. Yellow feathers. Oh, shit, where would it get a canary? Donahoo wondered. He hoped it wasn't from Martyr Mary in 2B. Monica, when she left, had left this, a cat that was such slime, maggots wouldn't eat it. It was also very smart. It somehow knew, as her only bequest, that it was safe from all harm.

For a while Donahoo sat thinking about Monica, so beautiful it made your heart ache. People would come up to her in the supermarket, tell her that. Excuse me, but ... Donahoo had a wish list. Monica was on it. Right after penile implant. He'd clean up the feathers later. First, the Old Crow.

The phone rang. He put it on speaker. It was Gomez, saying, "Sarge?"

"Yeah?"

"I just thought you'd like to know," Gomez said. "We finally caught up with Hudson."

Donahoo looked at his watch. It was almost six. "Now?"

"Well," Gomez said. "He wasn't at The Star of the Sea."

"But you had lunch anyway?"

"We thought he'd come in."

"Okay. And then?"

"We had to do the tour. The usual haunts."

"I don't believe you guys."

"You'll never guess where we found him."

"The Chee Chee Club?"

"No. Pure Platinum."

Donahoo sighed. "Is he behind bars?"

"Yes."

"Thank you and good night."

Gomez laughed and hung up. Donahoo opened the Old Crow. He poured three fingers. Spick and Spook. They arrest a guy for jury tampering. And they get him in a strip bar. Sure. Donahoo drank his whiskey. It had been his wish—how long? five, six years?—to nail Eric Victor Hudson. But not for jury tampering. For bribery. Hudson bribed politicians on behalf of First Fidelity Trust. He bought their votes on key issues involving millions of dollars. Zoning changes that made marginal land suddenly worth a fortune. The diversion of public funds into questionable investments that paid poor returns. He bought a lot of things that shouldn't be for sale. He was—let's put this in perspective—a menace to democracy. Saperstein had said that. Several times.

Donahoo drank his whiskey. Like Saperstein, he had wanted Hudson for a long time, predating Squad 5, but when the break finally came, it had nothing to do with buying votes at City Hall. Instead, doing the ultimate favor for his boss, Hudson had rigged a murder trial. He had paid a juror one hundred thousand dollars to vote not guilty in one of those toss-ups sliced so fine there's not going to be an appeal. He might have gotten away with it, too, except that Montrose, ever vigilant, wondered why his cousin, Junior Townsend, was suddenly driving a new 5.0 Mustang. Well, Junior said, all he ever wanted was a fast car and a reliable woman, or was that a reliable car and a fast woman? Gomez leaned on him and it all came out. A hundred grand to spare a banker's son from doing hard time for an act of passion. He'd come home to Goldilocks and someone was sleeping in his bed. What did he see? He saw red.

Anyway, not his collar, Donahoo thought. Six years invested, and it goes to Gomez and Montrose. Spick and Spook. It had been their pleasure—he could visualize it—to take Hudson by the scruff of his baggy silk suit. To stick the warrant under the booze-swollen nose and watch the realization take hold in the rheumy ice eyes. Sorry, old man, finish your drink, savor it. They don't serve Chivas Regal in Chino. No fat shrimp, no caviar. No hundred-dollar pussy. Oh, Jesus Christ, would he have liked to have told him that, Donahoo thought. But fair is fair and it wasn't his collar and it was like somebody was always saying. You win some, you lose some. And he, Donahoo, had won more than he lost, which made him lucky, although not in love. Donahoo drank his whiskey. He had been real lucky that first time. His first murder case, and it wasn't really his, and he wasn't a detective. The Purple Admiral Case.

Donahoo had every detail etched forever. Admiral Patrick "Fighting Smith" Smith, supply officer for the Pacific Fleet, found dead in an alley in the Stingaree, completely covered with purple spray paint. They had no idea he was in dress whites until they rolled him over. That's also when they found the bullet exit hole in his back.

There were a lot of theories and they all centered on a woman. Lipstick on his shorts. Small-caliber gun fired at point-blank range. Wallet found elsewhere with cash intact but photo pack ripped apart, one photo missing, they found just a small, torn section. Those were the clues. Plus the purple spray paint.

A woman. A jealous woman, Homicide thought. "Fighting Smith," they figured, had been seeing a lady of ill repute—a purple lady—in the Stingaree. He was an old sailor and he had become enamored. He talked about her and kept her photo in his wallet. That made another woman jealous. She stalked him and killed him and took the photo. She sprayed him with purple paint. But who was the other woman? "Fighting Smith" had a little black book that read like the Social Register. Homicide spent a week interviewing whores, visiting clerks at uptown hardware stores, calling on society matrons. The papers went apeshit.

Donahoo, he was a patrol cop then, got the idea to drive over to Barrio Logan. He cruised around until he found a building with purple graffiti. He found the kid who did it, the kid was twelve, Luis Hernandez. Yeah, man, Luis said, he did happen upon a corpse in an alley, and since he'd never done a body before, he did get carried away. Also, Luis said he may have seen the killer.

The police artist drew a sketch. It turned out to be a Navy officer, Lt. (jg) William Evans, who, when arrested, had the torn photo on him. The lady's name was Rita. She was a bartender on Guam. "Fighting Smith," his last trip, had taken her to bed, and she was supposed to be Evans's girl.

That easy. That easy and that lucky. And, after awhile, all anybody remembered was lucky. He was the luckiest cop in the world. He was promoted to detective and he couldn't do anything wrong. He solved a string of murders and he got his name in the paper and then his picture and pretty soon he was famous. The Babes in the Wood Murder Case. The Wayward Heart Murder Case. The Stardust Donut Shop Murder Case. He, Donahoo, he solved them all, those and others, and, mostly, it was luck. Pure luck.

Donahoo turned on the television. He went looking for a movie and found *Kindergarten Cop*. He hadn't seen it. He wondered what the plot was about. *Kindergarten Cop*. Maybe little Susie Jones gives Jimmy Smith a blow job?

Probably not.

Donahoo killed the TV and poured some more whiskey. It was time for the record. He put it on.

I wonder... who's kissing... her now.
I wonder... who's teaching... her how.
I wonder... who's looking... into her eyes, breathing
    sighs... telling lies.

Donahoo could see Monica. He had this perfect total recall of her. She was looking at him and she was smiling. She was smiling like she really meant it at this big lucky Irishman with a face that had been hit by a paddle. She was saying, you're full of shit, Donahooie.

I wonder... who's buying... the wine...
for those sweet lips... I used to... call mine.
I wonder if she... ever tells him... of me.
I wonder... who's kissing... her now.

It had been a while since he had solved a murder, Donahoo thought. He wondered if his luck had run out. He wondered where the guy was now. He'd written the note and time was up.

CHAPTER FIVE

Tonight, depending on one's point of view, he could be in heaven. He was parked on El Prado at the Sixth Avenue entrance to Balboa Park. The south side, which meant he wanted a blow job. The north side was for guys who wanted to give one.

It was nine-thirty, dark. He'd been there half an hour. He'd had a couple offers but had turned them down. The first guy had been too scruffy for his tastes. Two-day beard, wrinkled shirt, wearing about a cup of cheap cologne. The second guy had been kind of cute. But too big. He wanted, if possible, someone small.

Small beginnings, he thought. As in all things, one started small. He sat rolling a cigarette, an affectation. It gave him something to do while he waited, and he waited a lot. The nature of his new calling. In fact, that could be his job description, he thought, smiling. He was a waiter. Stryker, the waiter.

He didn't mind. It was a pleasant August evening. The temperature was in the mid-sixties, a drop of fifteen or so from the day's high, and an offshore breeze was snaking up from the bay, turning the eucalyptus into wind chimes. Their leaves tinkled faintly in the park's dark forest.

He wondered if anyone else heard them. Probably not. People, they were so busy with their lives, they hardly had time to live them. Sixth Avenue was a flash, flash, flash of hurrying cars. Lights blinked on and off in the windows of the apartment buildings. People coming, people going. Tasks, duties, obligations.

Hey, pick more daisies, he thought. This was a special evening. But then they mostly all were in San Diego. It had the best climate in the country, one of the best in the world. It was very even, the change of seasons hardly noticed, they just sort of melded. He could hear Frank Sinatra singing somewhere in his memory bank.

How did it go? Something about one day you turn around and it's summer. The next, it's fall. Something like that. Now, almost September, it was how he remembered April. The fall would be like spring. It always was. June was colder than November. That's when the fog came. Fog for lovers. January, February, they might be a little colder, too. The rain came then, sometimes. Sometimes it didn't. If it did come, it was welcome. That was the wonderful thing. Every day was welcome. As now, there was some humidity on occasion, but slight. Nothing like the East. Here, now and always, this was a very comfortable place to be, and it was really too bad that they were fucking it up.

A white Mazda pickup drifted by. The driver looked at him. He was a clean-cut blond, muscular, early thirties. Handsome in a bitchy sort of way. He almost stopped, then continued on.

Too big, too bad, Stryker thought. The Mazda made a U at the end of the median. It came back and parked directly across from him on the north side of El Prado. The headlights blinked off and the dome light came on. It bathed the driver in a soft, warm glow. He looked like a portrait. A work of art.

Too bad, Stryker thought again. A very interesting specimen. But he had to be careful. It wouldn't do to mess up, get caught. He lit his cigarette.

The Cadillac in front of the Mazda suddenly started up and drove away. A Chrysler near the entrance to the park quickly followed. That left just the Mazda on the north side.

Thee and me, Stryker thought, becoming uncomfortable. He was the only one on the south side now. They were alone.

Stryker smoked his cigarette. What he hadn't expected, he was afraid. The fear sloshed in him, threatening to spill out. He kept it down with effort. If he comes over, tell him no, that's all, he thought. It's our last freedom. We can still say no.

The Mazda's driver side door kicked open. Posing, every movement choreographed, the portrait came to life and got out and looked around, pretending that Stryker didn't exist. His body slowly turned full circle with the ragged rhythm of a bird on a spit. Then he leaned against the pickup's bed, his long muscular arms outstretched, looking up into the trees and smiling to himself.

Stryker stared, fascinated. The guy had to be an actor. He rolled his window down a couple inches for a better view. If he comes over, say no, he thought. Say no.

He came over. He was dressed in white. T-shirt, drill pants, sneakers. Even in the dark his skin was gold.

Stryker rolled the window down some more. The guy crossed the median with a few effortless skippy hops. He crossed the road like he was dancing. He stopped in midtwirl. His smile was dazzling. "Hello."

"Hello," Stryker said. He wasn't afraid anymore. He knew what had attracted the guy to him. It was because he willed it, he thought. Because, out of sheer inner power, he was transformed. He was interesting, and he exuded confidence, strength, and an air of mystery, and the guy couldn't resist. He stubbed out his cigarette. He thought he'd play with him. "Listen, did anybody ever tell you, you oughta be an actor?"

"No. But why don't *you* tell me."

"You can make an entrance out of an exit."

The smile faded, replaced by a pout. "You mean I should leave? Is that nice?"

"You looking for nice?"

"Not necessarily."

"Good. Because it's not here."

The guy's smile returned. "You alone?"

"Yes."

He looked in, confirming that. Up close, he was perfect. Fine, chiseled features. Pale-blue eyes. Firm, full mouth.

"I don't think I've seen you before."

"No. This is my first time." Stryker fell into the guy's ragged rhythm. "Here."

"You're not a cop?"

"No."

The guy considered, looking around the park, looking at Stryker. He wasn't quite sure. He looked at the Mazda.

"What happened to the gay abandon?" Stryker asked.

The guy turned back. He had been angered by the comment, it still showed on his face, but now—because he was an actor?— he was smiling. He leaned in close. A nice smile. "Would you like some company?"

"Sure," Stryker said, wondering what the hell was happening. He had intended to say no. Up until the last second, no. But then the controls got real mushy. He wanted this guy. Very badly. He popped the lock on the passenger door. "Let's do it."

The guy was all business now. He came around and settled in with a hitchhiker's eagerness. He produced a condom—his eyes saying, You don't mind, do you?—and tore open the pouch. He said, "Okay, where is that big thing?"

Rhetorical question. He'd already found it. Stryker sat silent, a little stunned, watching him put the condom on. The guy was so quick.

"Ooh," the guy said. "You … are … *wired*."

"Flatterer," Stryker told him.

"I mean it."

Stryker waited for him to go down. He'd never had a man suck him before. Then he opened the passenger seat's hollowed-out headrest and removed a snub-nosed revolver fitted with a silencer. He shoved the silencer against the guy's left temple and pulled the trigger. That close, soft slug, the guy's brain exploded in his lap.

Well, that was easy, Stryker decided. He had wanted to know and now he had his answer. It was easy. He wiped off the gun and put it back in the headrest. It was his purpose, in the not too distant future, his *assignment,* to kill a large number of people, and he didn't want everybody going to a lot of trouble and expense, all the planning, the logistics, if, in the end, he didn't have the balls for it. He carefully eased himself out of the dead mouth. Anyway, that was settled. It was easy.

CHAPTER SIX

Donahoo's phone rang a few minutes after two. He groped for it in the dark. His head hurt. "Yeah."

"Sorry," Frank Camargo said. "But you said call, no matter what time, if something came up. Something came up."

Donahoo wondered if he had actually said that. Anytime? He must have, though. For a cop, especially a Homicide cop, Frank Camargo went to unusual lengths not to offend. He needed all the help he could get. He survived by collecting markers. He could ask you a favor because he had done you one. Donahoo found the switch for the bedside lamp. He turned it on and looked at his watch. "Tell me."

"We've got a dead fag in the park," Camargo said. "Bullet hole in his left temple. Probably happened in a car. Like—this is Jelley's theory?—he was blowing when he got blown." A brief pause so that could be properly appreciated. "Also known as The Giving Head Can Make You Dead Theory."

"Tell me more."

"There was a note."

Donahoo pushed up, suddenly awake. "What kind?"

"Your kind."

"Read it to me, will you?"

"Sure."

There was another pause. Donahoo looked for his clothes. They were scattered on the floor. He wished he hadn't drunk quite so much Old Crow.

"It says," Camargo began. " 'I can do it.' "

"I can do it?"

"Yeah."

"And that's all?"

"Yeah."

Donahoo frowned. "What makes it my kind of note?"

"Well," Camargo said. "It's on a piece of copier paper, you know? Typed just the way your airport note was typed. And, you know, it's so simple. Straightforward."

Donahoo was thinking. The guy says he can do it?

"Maybe you have to be here," Camargo said.

"I will be," Donahoo told him.

There were five vehicles parked on a slow curve along Balboa Drive. Two black-and-whites, an unmarked detective, the crime lab van, and an ambulance. Donahoo pulled in behind and made it six.

Camargo came out of the night. He waited for the window to creak down on Donahoo's aging Olds Toronado. "That was fast."

"No traffic," Donahoo said. Actually, the short distance he had come, it would have been five minutes at the worst of times. He pushed out of the Olds, watching, uncomfortably, the ghostly shadows lurking at the farthest reaches of the flashing emergency lights. The night was still warm, but he felt a chill. The ghosts were the homeless, anxious for a free show, but at a careful distance. "You got the note?"

Camargo opened his attaché case and removed a sheet of white copier paper protected by a clear plastic casing. He moved into the ambulance's swirling amber standby lights before handing it to Donahoo.

Looking at it, Donahoo knew, beyond any doubt, that the same person had written both notes. He had hundreds on file and very few matched, in their simplicity, with such chilling precision. The same man had written both. He was absolutely sure of it.

"I, uh…" Donahoo didn't know where he was going. Six months and now he had a place to start. "Thanks for calling. I owe you one."

Camargo's expression was pained. He wanted to protest. He was owed several.

Donahoo almost smiled. He handed the note back. "Where is he?"

Camargo motioned. "Where he was dumped. We've been keeping him for you."

Donahoo followed Camargo to the black-and-white at the head of the line. The ambulance driver and uniformed cops were sitting in their vehicles, drinking coffee, eating doughnuts. Somebody had been to the 7-Eleven.

"What makes you think he was dumped?"

Camargo gestured vaguely. "Prima facie evidence."

Donahoo glanced back. Dimly, through the trees, he could make out El Prado, where it joined Sixth Avenue. A white vehicle was parked there. A pickup?

"It belongs to the deceased," Camargo said, anticipating Donahoo's question. "Fags, they meet over there…" He grinned. "You know all that shit?"

"Yeah. I know all that shit."

Now they were at a rectangle of yellow crime-scene tape guarding a black lump at the side of the road. The body was covered by a sheet of plastic. It looked, in the dark, smaller than a man.

Sgt. Ben Jelley, head of the crime lab, was sitting in the back of the first black-and-white, jammed in sideways with the door open and his feet dangling. He was so huge he couldn't sit in it any other way. He was chauffeured around in the back of the lab's van.

Chip Lyons, a Homicide investigator, off duty, was standing in the road, lighting a cigarette. He looked grotesque in the cupped flame. A glass eye and a nose that could stuff a turkey.

One of the homeless, a small, bundled man with a hurt face, was standing near him, waiting.

Donahoo pushed by wordlessly. Lyons's car was the one with the blinking hazard lights on Sixth. He'd have picked the call up on his private scanner. He'd have come over because he was in the neighborhood. He was combative, intrusive. He liked trouble. It worked for him. He'd shot and killed three suspects in eight years with the department. All three deaths had been ruled justifiable. He'd gotten a commendation in one instance. The fact, though, the rulings didn't change it, he was trigger-happy. He had the most kills on the SDPD. He was planning on staying ahead.

"Can we go home now?" Jelley said by way of greeting. He had all the charm of a tethered blimp.

"Thanks for waiting," Donahoo said. He motioned to the corpse. "May I?"

"Be my guest," Jelley told him. "We've got all we want."

"The pictures taken?"

"They're being developed."

Donahoo ducked under the tape and pulled back the sheet. Camargo shined his flashlight. Donahoo winced. Pretty boy with half his head shot away. An awful waste of a prime specimen in the peak of physical condition. Even in death, the muscles seemed to ripple, cut.

"What's his name?"

"David Garrett."

"Lived around here?"

"Hillerest."

"Employed?"

"We don't know yet."

"The way I figure it," Jelley said, drifting in on cue, "it's a random killing. The killer parks over there in Dateland. He sits and waits. Mr. Garrett here joins him. It coulda been anybody. Just a shuffle of the cards. The wrong guy in the wrong place at the wrong moment in history."

"Got it."

"They agree on a little joint ecstasy…" There was a pause. Cops, Donahoo thought. "And the cocksucker gets his fucking brains blown out for the sheer pleasure that brings."

Donahoo put the sheet back. "You find any semen?"

"No sign of any. We'll look closer at the morgue. But take a whiff now. What I think, the guy's mouth was wiped out with a powerful astringent, destroying—chemically altering—any semen that might be present. Ergo, no DNA. So you're looking for a belt-and-suspenders type. He's not happy with just a condom. He knows there's an off chance." Jelley waited. "A chance of it coming off? In the thrill of the moment?"

Donahoo frowned. "Why are you so sure about a condom?"

"There always is, these days. Nobody wants AIDS." Jelley grinned at the lump on the ground. "If you don't use one, that's an easier way to go, Tommy."

Donahoo went to Chip Lyons. The little bundled guy was still with him. "What have we got here?"

"Shortie," Chip Lyons said. "He may have seen the killer's car."

"That's good. Can he describe it?"

"Sure. Tell him, Shortie."

Shortie showed one tooth when he talked. He said, "It was old, black. It was classy."

"What else?"

Shortie stared. "It made me hungry."

"Write that down," Donahoo said.

Chip Lyons smiled.

Donahoo moved away. He got hold of Camargo. He wondered if Camargo had anything else. Camargo, he could have something, he wouldn't know it. He was kind of slow.

"You know, all this dirty talk, it's making me horny," Jelley was saying. "What say we go over to The Baths, have a shower together, Chipper? It'll be a cheap date. They got showers, three minutes for a quarter."

"Naw, you go yourself," Chip Lyons told him. "Here's a dollar. You can wash all four sides." He called to Donahoo. "You killed anybody yet?" He was always asking.

Donahoo headed downtown instead of returning home. There was no way he was going to go back to sleep. Not for a while, anyway. He needed to be around some humanity. If only a waitress and a couple drunks in a coffee shop. The four words, *I can do it*, were confirmation of his worst fear. There really was a sicko who hated the airport. A remorseless killer capable of killing again. Capable of killing... how many?

He slowed and then stopped at Sixth and Hawthorne. Faintly, from the direction of the park, he heard the noise of an approaching plane. He turned to look. A mix of blinking lights bore down on the park's eucalyptus canopy. The noise grew louder. Donahoo stayed stopped in the street, rooted. The huge jetliner passed directly overhead. The noise was unnerving. Donahoo looked at his watch. Two-thirty—middle of the night. Yeah, the guy could kill again, Donahoo thought. With good fucking reason.

CHAPTER SEVEN

Nicholas Valesy, coming in low like that, almost at rooftop level, imagined himself on a sneak attack, suicide run. This wasn't San Diego. It was Iraq, it was Baghdad. Tracers blazed randomly across the night sky. A barrage of ack-ack hammered from the banks of the Tigris. But they were shooting blind. They hadn't found him yet. Nor, at this stage, would they. Against all odds, he was going to succeed. The target loomed. Saddam Hussein's personal quarters. If intelligence was correct, Saddam was there now, all of his top aides. They were the men coming out on the balcony to see what the noise was all about. In another moment, he, Valesy, struggling with his explosive-laden old Spitfire, barely able to keep aloft, would join them there. He was going to accomplish what the American war machine and twenty billon dollars had failed to do. This was going to be the mother of all assassinations. The Spitfire was beyond the point of changing path.

"Fasten your seat belt," the stewardess said, a third time.

"You're talking to an old hand here," Valesy reminded her, but he did as instructed. The Trans World MD 80 was seconds away from touching down.

Unsmiling, the stewardess grabbed a seat across the aisle from him in the otherwise deserted first-class section. At first, she had found him amusing, or had pretended to. But several hours of crude courtship had soured her on him. Now, she found him a bore, and she wasn't hiding the fact. He was at the top of her no list. No, she wasn't going to have a drink with him. No, she wasn't going to have dinner with him. No, she didn't care if he committed suicide.

"Is this your first trip to San Diego?" he asked pleasantly.

"No, but my last with you, Mr. Hand," she told him.

Nicholas Valesy laughed. The stewardess was a very attractive woman. He could imagine himself in bed with her just as readily as he had imagined the suicide run. And it gave him just as much pleasure. He closed his eyes and she was struggling in his grasp as he exploded in her.

The wheels touched and they were down at Lindbergh. He slipped out of the belt's restraint and pushed up to his feet. "You are to remain seated," the stewardess began. Valesy pulled down his garment bag, his only luggage. "If I did that, you couldn't kiss my ass," he said, smiling. "I'll remember you."

But, in a week or so, despite her dislike, she wouldn't remember him with any degree of accuracy, he thought. She wouldn't recall what was foreign about his speech. He'd just be an annoying question mark. She'd remember the incident, but she'd forget him. What made him forgettable, what perhaps kept him alive, was his being so very plain and ordinary, so utterly average in all respects. He had a face that was not unusual or different in any feature or element. He had a physique that could have been taken from a textbook drawing of Homo sapiens. He looked—what a mockery—bland.

He had arrived two hours late. There'd been a delay changing planes in Phoenix. Valesy waited another half hour and then went to a terminal pay phone. He made a two-second phone call. "We have begun," he said simply, and then hung up. It was an overly dramatic act, but then he was an overly dramatic man. Drama was an inherent part of his heritage and culture. He had suffered more than most men. And had caused more pain than most, too. He was trained in the art.

There was a sign. WELCOME TO AMERICA'S FINEST CITY.

He smiled. Not when I get through, he thought.

Grayson Grenier hung up his phone with conflicting emotions. He was paranoid about security and that had been an unnecessary call. On the other hand, he was elated to have received it. We have begun, he exulted, imitating, part of the thought process, Nicholas Valesy's rough Kazakh accent.

Grenier found a pack of Pilgrims. He knocked one out and lit up. He had to smoke. An example for his fellow executives, and, of course, for the Pilgrim Tobacco Company's employees. If you asked people to smoke—to treat the health risks as groundless—then you had to demonstrate that you were unafraid, too. Hell, life was short, and difficult, either way. So why not grab some quick, easy pleasure? Lighten up and light up. Or, light up and lighten up. He made a mental note to talk to Marketing about that. Maybe just, Lighten up? He smiled, aware that it was all a crock. The truth, he knew, and there were a hundred studies to back it up, the Surgeon General's warning ought to be changed to read, "We make our living killing."

We have begun. Actually, Grenier mused, the beginning, the real beginning, could be traced to that last night in Moscow, when he got drunk with Rudolf Pinsky. Or, actually, when he returned to New York and opened the Golden Hill letter from crazy Joe Foley. One or the other. Referral to KGB assassin or proposal from California Realtor. Did it matter which?

Ruby mumbled, "Who was that?"

"Wrong number."

"On a private line?"

"Unlisted," Grenier said. "But that doesn't stop wrong numbers."

"Then what does?"

You pull out the fucking phone, Grenier thought, but he didn't say that, nor was he annoyed. Ruby might not be the brightest girl in the world but she had other attributes. For one thing, make that two things, Ruby Slippers was born wearing a bra. He called her, an endearment, lung lady.

He sat smoking his cigarette, thinking that he didn't want a brain, he wanted the world's best pair of knockers, and also thinking about Colonel Nicholas Valesy, who, by now, was in a taxicab, headed for downtown San Diego. The Colonel was going to save his precious Grenier ass. Maybe.

"What time is it?"

Grenier didn't have to look. "Six-ten."

"*Six?*" Old habits were hard to break. Ruby had been a Vegas showgirl. Showgirls didn't get up at six in the morning. That's when they went to bed.

Grenier smiled ruefully. He had some old habits, too. Like eating. He took a last drag and stubbed out the cigarette. He had more to lose than most men if it all came tumbling down. This penthouse overlooking Central Park. A flat in London, a ski chalet in Switzerland. A Porsche that could do 200 and a Mercedes stretch limo that could sleep four. Plus, what he treasured most, *Endless Summer*, an eighty-five-foot Hatteras MY equipped to cruise the world. He could lose them all. Hell, if it got bad enough, he could lose Ruby Slippers.

Maybe he ought to marry her, bind her to him that way, he thought. It was what she wanted, to be "legal," not for the money, but for how, in her eyes, she was perceived by others, as a whore. Once a year, as faithful as the calendar, his attorney, Kilpatrick, called her, had her sign a new agreement. Her monthly allowance. What she would get, and what she would not get, if, for whatever reason, she left. Why, in the event of his death, she got nothing.

Grenier couldn't imagine being without her. She was a prized possession, like the flat in London, the Hatteras. The only human being he really cared for. That's why he owned her.

He lifted the pillow burying Ruby's tousled blond head. "I need a hug," he said.

"A half hour more, okay?" Ruby mumbled. "Then I'll do any-thing you want."

Grenier thought that would be the hardest part. When peo-ple stopped saying that. And it could happen. Very easily.

He got another cigarette. It all depended on The Colonel. The first task, simple enough, was to erase any connection between him, Grenier, and Joseph R. Foley, Realtor. That ought to be simple enough. There had just been the one letter, followed by the one meeting, no one else present. It ought to be easy. Child's play. Yet Grenier wondered about Valesy. He didn't trust him completely. The phone call, for example, had been kind of dumb. As if he wanted a gallery to play for. Had some strange need for applause in a profession where it was forbidden. But, like Ruby, the guy had other attributes, Grenier thought. Compared to Valesy, Attila the Hun was a nun.

CHAPTER EIGHT

"**M**y mind tells me not to worry," Saperstein said. "My dick says it's the Holocaust." The Assistant Chief, Detectives was talking to no one in particular. He was saying it for Donahoo's benefit. "This is the stuff of nightmares. This is what wakes you up screaming."

Donahoo didn't say anything.

"It's got all the earmarks," Saperstein said. He adjusted his tight-fitting tailored vest, then rolled up his shirt sleeves, two precise turns. He positioned three freshly sharpened pencils next to a yellow legal pad. He was ready for work. "I can see it exploding. Totally out of control."

"Yeah," Lewis agreed. "It could be a bitch."

Donahoo still offered no comment. He was admiring Saperstein's organization and mobility. He had joined them in the trenches with a few quick moves, and, if required, he could just as swiftly revert to general officer status. He was never more than seconds away from fitting back into the pinstripe coat that was waiting beside him on a thick wooden hanger.

Saperstein looked at Donahoo. "What do you think?"

"It could be a bitch," Donahoo told him.

"Yeah, well, you start thinking," Saperstein ordered. In many ways, he was more manager than police officer. Impossibly, he had come up through Purchasing. When his talents were recognized, they started moving him around, all the departments, grooming him for bigger, better things. Impossibly, he had arrived here without ever personally solving a crime. He administered the process, often brilliantly, but he had never, ever worked the sewer. He stayed at his desk, surrounded by the diplomas and awards and citations that proclaimed his qualifications, the United Way and Little League certificates proposing that he was a concerned, giving member of the community and, possibly, a human being.

Camargo came in with the coffee. Black for Saperstein and Lewis. A plop of milk for Donahoo. His own so sweet it was like chocolate.

"Close the door," Saperstein said.

Camargo looked around helplessly. He had a full tray. Nobody moved. Reluctantly, watching Saperstein, Camargo shut the door with his foot, banging it closed.

"You got hands?" Saperstein said.

Camargo didn't answer. He passed the coffee around. Donahoo thought that Camargo must hate these meetings. There were four of them crowded into Saperstein's small, utilitarian office. In his position, Saperstein could have a much larger one, but he was trying to make a purchasing agent's point. The more money you saved in office space, in fewer trappings, the more cops you could put on the street. There was a desk, filing cabinets, chairs. The stuff on the walls. That's all. No sofa. No rubber plant. No place for Camargo to hide.

"Who all knows?" Lewis asked. The Captain, Investigations was Saperstein's complete opposite. Saperstein was tall and thin and scholarly. He wore dark horn-rimmed glasses. He always dressed like a corporate lawyer. He wanted to be Chief. Lewis was a beefy wayward tank who survived on instinct and looked like he slept in his clothes. He lived an old cop's contradiction. He wanted to put his time in. He also wanted out.

Donahoo waited, briefly, for Camargo to answer Lewis's question. Then, taking his coffee, Donahoo said, "Who knows the note matches?" He paused. Camargo was oblivious. Donahoo said, "Frank, he found it. Ben Jelley, of course. His crime lab techs. Me." He looked at Camargo. "That's right, Frank?"

"Who do you mean?" Camargo said.

"You didn't show it to the black-and-whites?"

"No."

"Good," Saperstein said. "You get to stay with us." He said, "Where did you find it?"

"In the deceased's hand. It was folded into his hand. His left hand."

"Maybe the deceased wrote it?"

Camargo looked at Donahoo. He gave him a is-this-guy-real? look. Donahoo didn't respond. "I don't think so," Camargo said finally.

"Too bad," Saperstein said. "The deceased writes the note, we've got nothing to worry about, you can all get outta here. The killer writes the note? We're in deep doodie." Now he was looking at Donahoo. "Give us a hand here, Tommy. Did you write the note?"

Donahoo took a sip of his coffee.

"I was just thinking out loud, this is such a great note for you, Tommy," Saperstein said. "How long has it been? Three or four months ... ?"

"Six months."

"Even better. Six months. Everybody thinks the first note is a hoax. Everyone except you. Because you're a dumb stubborn sonofabitch. But now we've got a second note and we've got a deceased to go with it. So now you're smart and the rest of us are dumb. That's why I'm saying it's such a great note for you, Tommy."

"Oh. I thought you were saying I killed the fag."

"No. Camargo here did. You guys are in this together." Saperstein tried to smile, but it wasn't there. "The first note. Did anyone evaluate it?"

"The Three Wise Men," Donahoo told him, only one of them was a woman. He regularly used a psychiatrist, a psychologist, a social worker. None of them had ever been of any particular help. "A mixed bag."

"What the fuck is a mixed bag?"

"Well, in their opinion, he's got a personality disorder if he's not a schizo if he's not a manic depressive."

"They can tell that from one lousy paragraph?" Camargo asked.

"No," Saperstein said. "It's from the rag content in the paper."

Lewis said, "How much of this do you want out?"

"For the moment, nothing," Saperstein told him. "We don't want panic in the streets. People running around thinking the sky is falling down." He was trying to establish priorities. "We advise the port authority, airport security, the feds. On the QT. That's all for the moment. I'll tell the Chief and the Chief will tell the Mayor. That way our ass is covered. Otherwise, I want a lid on this, understood?"

"The Mayor's office is a sieve."

"The chance we take. First rule, we cover our ass."

"Okay. But it's gonna leak."

Saperstein glared. "Tomorrow the killer blows up the airport. The Mayor calls the Chief. He says, 'Did you have any idea this might happen?' That's what you want?"

"Okay." Lewis shifted uncomfortably. He said, "I thought we'd keep Camargo on the case. He took the call."

"What for? The note takes it out of Homicide. It goes to Squad 5."

Lewis was going to protest but changed his mind. Camargo's face shimmered with disappointment.

"Let Frank stay on," Donahoo said quietly. "I'll need all the help I can get."

Saperstein considered for a long moment.

"We're in this together," Donahoo reminded him.

"Okay," Saperstein said. "Make sure you are. Total communication. Nothing falls through the cracks." He looked at Lewis. "I want daily reports from both of you. Now get the hell out of here."

They all got up to leave. Donahoo thought that he'd go anywhere with these guys. Lewis, the tired old pro who'd seen it all, who didn't have to think, who operated on instinct. Camargo, who was too dumb, too afraid, to get in the way. And, beloved leader, Saperstein, smarter than all of them together, but, because he'd never been there, could be dumber even than Camargo. He, Donahoo, he was with them, but he was running free.

"Tommy. Stay a minute."

Donahoo remained behind. Saperstein waited for Lewis to pull the door shut.

"What's your theory?" Saperstein said then.

Donahoo shrugged. "It's a little early for theories."

"Bullshit," Saperstein said harshly. "You've had six months. I want to hear it."

"A psycho," Donahoo said. "He lives, or owns property, somewhere on the approach or takeoff path. The planes are annoying him. Or they're knocking the shit out of his property values."

"So it's greed? He wants money?"

"Or peace."

"If he wants peace, why the fuck doesn't he just move out?"

"Maybe he can't," Donahoo said. "Some of us, we get pushed so far, we get pushed in a corner, there's no way out. We're trapped. That's when we're the most dangerous."

"That's your theory?"

"Yeah."

Saperstein said, "This is a fucking nightmare."

CHAPTER NINE

Officially the area was named Horton, after one of the city fathers, but nobody called it that anymore. They called it downtown, because that's what it was, downtown, and Horton's memory was preserved in Horton Plaza, a tiny square that used to be in lawn but was now planted in chicken-wire-covered flowers to keep the bums off. It fronted an artfully concealed shopping mall of the same name. Up the hill, north of the curving Interstate 5, the area was called Balboa Park, because it ran parallel to the park as far as Banker's Hill.

Donahoo cruised it with Gomez and Montrose.

The murder had narrowed things for him. He'd always thought that the airport in the note meant Lindbergh Field. Now he was just as certain that the killer lived or owned property here in Balboa Park. He could have killed anyone, anywhere. A whole city. Yet he had chosen the park, and there had to be a reason for that. Donahoo thought he knew the reason. When the killer wrote, *I can do it*, he was, in a sense, protecting his ground. Territorial imperative. That was Donahoo's theory and it narrowed things for him. He could forget Point Loma, with Ocean Beach and Fleet-ridge and Loma Portal. He could focus on this one relatively small area. Actually, smaller still. On the glide path that crossed over it.

After an hour of driving in circles, watching the descending planes from all angles, carefully checking the noise levels, Donahoo felt confident about highlighting a "check zone" on his street map. Elm north to Laurel. Sixth Avenue, which bordered the park, west to State. Six blocks wide. Eleven blocks deep. Sixty-six square blocks, but subtract some of those, to allow for the approach angle, say—round number—fifty square blocks. Somewhere in there they'd find their killer. Or the clue that would lead them to him.

Gomez didn't think so. Earlier, setting out, Gomez had said, "It could be a trick," meaning he thought the killer was smarter than that, and he hadn't said anything since to indicate he might have changed his mind. Gomez operated on emotions. What it said in his heart. Typically, Montrose hadn't expressed an opinion. He was short on theories and long on facts. If he didn't have a fact, he didn't have anything.

Donahoo wasn't about to change his mind, either. Until this morning, he hadn't toured the area with a lender's eye, looking for all the things that were wrong. All the things, big and small, that translated into depressed real-estate values. Now he saw them, and they confirmed what he always knew, but hadn't given much thought to, that yet another fine old neighborhood was in ruins. If you lived here, if you owned property here, the planes, the noise, could start overwhelming you, he thought. And, if your lid was loose anyway, you just might blow. The theory held. The killer was around here someplace. Somewhere in a fifty-block slash of jet whine.

Also, Donahoo realized, again for the first time, the immensity of the financial disaster that the airliners imposed on property owners. This was the natural place for the downtown district's growth. Here was where the new skyscrapers ought to be built. The site surpassed the existing downtown. It was higher, more commanding, and free of the growth restrictions imposed by water on two sides, dreary inland slums on a third. But you couldn't put skyscrapers in the path of planes. Building sites that normally would be worth millions were going begging.

"You seen enough?" Gomez asked. It was getting near lunchtime and he was miles from the nearest taco stand.

"One more run," Donahoo told him.

"When are we supposed to eat?"

"Soon."

Gomez rolled his eyes and jammed the Chev. He was permanent designated driver. His request. Mexicans, he said, acquired, in this order, a woman and a car. If they got really lucky they went straight to car.

"I'm starving."

"You're always starving."

"It's part of my culture."

"You know what I read?" Montrose said sympathetically. "There's some scientists in Mexico. They're doing research with insects. They're gonna make 'em a food source."

Gomez stared at him in the rearview. "Yeah?"

"Yeah," Montrose said. "This is gonna be a big change for you guys. You don't hafta be beaners anymore. You can be buggers."

"What is your problem, nigger?" Gomez asked. "Your peanut brain or your watermelon lips?"

"Boys," Donahoo said.

"He started it," Gomez said.

Donahoo thought fuck it and let it go. Their bickering was harmless, a release. Actually, in their own strange way, they were brothers, they respected, even admired, each other. They were like soldiers in that they protected each other. He in turn respected them. He couldn't think of two other officers he'd rather have assigned to him. They were about as capable as he was ever going to get. He hoped they thought equally well of him. He wasn't sure. He wasn't good at command. He didn't have the taste, or the time, for it.

They were at Albatross and Ivy. Gomez slowed, almost stopped. Donahoo made a gesture. Down the hill, circle around. He was looking for something. He wasn't sure what. He hadn't found it.

Montrose said, "How about sushi?"

"Why do you fuck with me?" Gomez demanded.

Donahoo had vague memories of a better place. His stepfather, Mike, would bring him here as a boy, on Sunday expeditions that always excluded his mother, Kathleen. She preferred to stay home and cook. They'd drive down from Solano Beach on Pacific Coast Highway. The old Nash chugging, they'd come up here, take a wistful look at how the other half lived, in the fancy houses with the manicured yards, then go to the park and the zoo. Balboa Park and neighboring Banker's Hill, they were very toney addresses then, Donahoo remembered. They sat alone in their Victorian splendor, high above the drunken sailor-downtown, isolated from the bayfront melee. The prop-driven planes drifting over would have been a minor annoyance at most. Donahoo couldn't even remember their presence.

Then, almost overnight, it all changed for Balboa Park, he thought. The advent of jets. Suddenly, the noise was alarming, impossibly loud, a banshee's howl. The planes kept getting bigger, and, if that was possible, lower. They came in at rooftop. They came all day and into the night. They turned a peaceful neighborhood into a raucous bedlam and brought it down. They destroyed it.

Donahoo, drifting by a boarded-up house, remembered the way it was, in his young mind the grandest of all possible places. It probably died slowly, he decided. He could imagine how it went. The big money moved out, and then the smart money, too. The grand old rococo high-ceilinged apartment buildings slowly transmogrified into welfare shelters and flophouses. The Victorian homes with their hideaway towers and banks of bay windows were partitioned into cheap rentals. The place lost its style and ambience. It lost its class. Men of distinction and means disappeared, and, with them, their pampered women. The sleek black autos went, and the nannies pushing their buggies, and the prancing dogs on the long leashes. Neglect set in. The grass died and the paint peeled and the graffiti spawned. The homeless roamed the streets, picking through the garbage, rifling parked cars. It wasn't safe alone at night. Menace lurked in the shadows. New investors shied away. Every day it became more like a slum. FOR RENT, the signs said. VACANT.

"Where are we going here?" Gomez asked.

To the zoo, Donahoo wanted to say. They'd go to the zoo, like he did with Mike. See the monkeys. Maybe they hadn't changed. Maybe they still begged for peanuts, popcorn. He could remember them begging. So distinctly. Their little hands reaching. Like little people. You gave them the peanuts. But you kept the Cracker Jack.

"You remember when they put real prizes in the Cracker Jack?" Donahoo said. "Whistles that worked, and little paper flowers, you put 'em in water, they bloomed."

"Huh?"

Donahoo came back from his memories. Back to the foot of Kalmia, dead-ended at San Diego Engine Company No. 3, where the planes came in lowest before passing over Interstate 5.

He put a hand on Gomez's shoulder. Gomez stopped.

A woman was walking down Kalmia. She was tall, slim, dark, very beautiful. She had olive skin and long black hair hanging almost to her waist. She was wearing an embroidered vest and a clinging paisley skirt. She was in sandals.

"I saw her first," Montrose said.

"No, you didn't," Donahoo told him.

The woman went up an outside staircase on the two-story tiled-roofed stucco building set flush to the sidewalk at the corner. When she reached the landing, a huge airliner bore down, jets screaming. She turned and smiled and waved at the Eskimo painted on the tail. Or was it the passengers on Alaska Airlines? She went inside.

"Very nice," Gomez said.

"Yeah," Donahoo agreed.

"That ass," Montrose said. "Stuck up there like it was designed in a wind tunnel."

The lower level of the house was commercial. It had a coin laundry, ECONOMY WASH, and a fortune teller, MADAM ZOLA.

Donahoo wondered if the woman was Madam Zola. She had that certain what...? Air of mystery?

"You think you gotta shot with that?" Montrose asked, sounding incredulous.

Donahoo looked at him. Montrose, who was better looking than any movie star, and who knew it. Gomez accused him of being Jamaican.

"Maybe you could leave just one for me?" Donahoo asked.

Montrose stared back at him. There was amusement, and something more, in the calm, confident, matinee-idol eyes. He wasn't going anywhere. "I don't know why."

"We'll divide this up," Donahoo announced, angered by the challenge. He deserved...What? Consideration? He almost said something. He barely caught himself. "I'll work the murder with Camargo. Montrose, you look at property records, we won't need you here? Gomez, you go door-to-door, I've got it marked. I figure, roughly, fifty blocks."

"Fifty blocks?" Gomez complained. "You know how many people live in fifty blocks?"

"You're never satisfied," Donahoo said. He folded the map. "Yesterday it was the world."

CHAPTER TEN

Nicholas Valesy prowled the Gaslamp Quarter. He had gone there straight from the airport and checked into a flophouse. The Yale Hotel, on F at Eleventh, where the historic district's slow, spotty restoration had yet to reach. It was convenient, though. There was a trolley stop around the corner at Twelfth and Market. Small, spare, dingy room. Bath down the hall. $8.50 a night, $45 a week, $160 a month. He paid for a week.

The Gaslamp Quarter, and, within it, a four-block stretch known as the Stingaree, dated to the 1850's and the founding of San Diego. It was too soon for heroes then, no one to name streets for, so they were named A, B, C, D. The same for the avenues. First, Second, Third, Fourth. The Quarter had gone into decline but was making a comeback. A hundred or more turn-of-the-century ornate brick buildings had been restored. They housed an eclectic mix of enterprises. Hotels and work/live lofts. All kinds of shops and boutiques. Cafes, bistros, art galleries, bookstores. Professional offices, lawyers, architects, engineers. Produce warehouses and farmers' markets. Antique shops and thrift stores. Fine restaurants that spilled out onto the sidewalks. Fio's, Croce's, La Strada, Sfuzzi. The Bayou Bar & Grill.

The streets thronged with people. Sightseers, shoppers, office workers, tourists, Navy personnel, and, everywhere, the homeless. This had been their place before the restoration. They didn't want to leave. They had no place to go.

Valesy enjoyed the sharp contrasts and the brazen energy. He came upon whole buildings painted as murals. He also found pleasure in the knowledge that it was an uncertain re-creation. Several hundred more old buildings stood vacant and waiting. They could be torn down to make way for the gleaming towers that were intruding from all directions. In time, restored or not, all of the old could be swept away, reinvented.

He could have stayed anywhere, the finest hotel, or rented a waterfront home. He had a small fortune in his money belt. Another waited for him in a safety deposit box a few blocks away. He could go anywhere and do anything, but that, for this venture, would be out of character. Monied pleasure must wait. Not that he really minded. There were, after all, other pleasures.

He had a late breakfast at the Sun Cafe on Market. The #4. Two eggs, sausages, hash browns, wheat toast, coffee. $2.15, and not bad, either. Two days before, in Paris, he'd had a rough equivalent, hard little dog terds substituting for the sausages, and, with tip, it was $20. The world, he thought, was going topsy-turvy. No wonder so many students were coming from Europe to study in America. They might not get good educations. But at least their bellies were full.

After breakfast, he went to the Goodwill. He bought an old business suit, two pairs of pants, several shirts, all a size too big for him. He bought a huge topcoat that hung on him like a shapeless tent. The homeless favored them. They served as blankets at night. He chose two pairs of shoes that did fit, black oxfords, rubber-soled deck shoes. He also picked out a garish multicolored tie. $24 altogether. No tax. He got it all stuffed into plastic bags and went back to the Yale.

There was a new clerk at the desk. A younger man with puffy little eyes like warts on a bad complexion. He stared sullenly, almost contemptuously. Valesy showed him his room receipt. The clerk threw the key on the counter.

"You been shopping?" the clerk said then.

Valesy nodded. "What does it look like?"

"Goodwill."

Valesy wondered. He smiled. "How would you know that?"

"The bags," the clerk said, contemptuous again. "The blue plastic. That's Goodwill."

Valesy went up the stairs to his room. That had been a mistake, he thought. Not a serious one, but a mistake, nevertheless. He should have put his purchases in different kinds of bags. Now the wart-eyed clerk knew he had purchased a whole wardrobe of used clothes, *all at once,* from the Goodwill, and, perhaps, he was wondering why. Why does a man wearing a perfectly good suit buy so many old clothes? One or two items, maybe. But three bags full? That might set the clerk to wondering. He might mention it to someone else. The new guy, he's strange. You think he's strange? Then there'd be two, possibly three—who knows how many?—wondering about him.

He locked himself in his room and spilled his purchases on the bed. Was he losing his edge? A year ago, it wouldn't have happened. Six months ago. But lately? Valesy shook his head. A fortnight before, in Rome. He'd made a small mistake then. He'd worn the wrong kind of crucifix. "You're not …" the monsignor had started to say, alarmed. He had been forced to kill the old priest earlier than planned. Because his research had been sloppy. A little thing like the wrong kind of crucifix.

He knew better. Boris Yuschev, his superior, instructor, and mentor, had told him a hundred times, screaming and pounding the table. Nicholas Valesy! We don't die by the sword! It's the little things that bury us!! Chastised, he would return to his English lessons, to learn that when nature called, it meant you had to piss. It wasn't the wild wind beckoning.

Under ordinary circumstances, he would have purchased the old clothes in New York, brought them with him, but the one thing that he truly feared, it was having his baggage searched, even on a domestic flight. He might be singled out for some reason, and a suitcase full of old clothes could raise suspicions. He might be subjected to further search. They'd find the money belt. They might even find the key.

He threw himself on the bed atop the loose bundle of old clothes. He'd sleep the day, he decided. Tonight, the wart-eyed clerk gone, he'd check out, find another place. The night man wouldn't wonder why. He was an ancient stick, barely alive. He didn't have any more questions.

Valesy stared at the intricate design on the pressed-tin ceiling. This would be his last job. Finally, he had enough money, more than he could reasonably spend and not attract undue attention. Oddly, he had not made much money as the KGB's most relentless, perverted killer. The rank of colonel came at the end, a meaningless, but still appreciated, gesture. He liked to be called that. During his tenure, he didn't have a rank, he wasn't official. He made a soldier's salary, that's all, although there were, of course, perks. Travel. Clothes. Open expense accounts. He could see the sights and eat well and he could buy women. He had enough. But only adequate to the moment. Ahead, if one was to grow old, and one might, there was an inadequate pension. He would have died hungry if it were not for the collapse of the Soviet Union. He had thought, oh, it's over, only to discover that, in the free world, he was a valuable commodity. Rudolph Pinsky, a brother-in-law of his mentor, Boris Yuschev, became his agent and began exporting his skills. It was like a circus then. Free agent, he had offers, incredible offers, a lot of them, and this—the last—was best of all. Two million dollars. One million down. The other—what was the term—on delivery?

He had a farm picked out. A ranch, actually. Five thousand hectares in the softly rolling hills south of Alamos, Sonora, Mexico. Forty dollars a hectare. He had a mozo chosen, Juan. Two hundred dollars a month and housing. He had a woman arranged, Natalia Krasnitskaya. No charge. He had found her name and address on a small card posted on a bulletin board in a grubby market in Bucharest. Her cousin had posted it there for her, amid other cards that offered items for sale or exchange, advertised rooms for sharing, and appealed for lost animals.

EFFECTIVE LADY, 32/185/73, green eyes, dark hair, educated, w/sense of humour, optimist, seeks an intelligent, considerate, tender, energetic man for marriage. Small boy. Pls write w/ photo to: Natalia Krasnitskaya, post. rest. St. Petersburg, 195067 Russia.

He had met, and taken to bed, Natalia. He had played with the boy, Mikhail. He'd given him a piggy ride. At first, the child had cried. Later, he enjoyed it.

Nicholas Valesy closed his eyes and tried to think about something else. He thought about the key up his rectum that opened the storage locker that held enough firepower to bring down an airliner. He thought about his small electronic Personal Organizer with the coded names and addresses of the four people he had to kill. He thought, especially, about Joseph R. Foley, Realtor, who, supposedly, according to Grayson Grenier, was crazy as a shithouse rat, and also a genius, and who lived amid the roar of the jet airliners hounding Balboa Park. He thought about the airliners. He thought about the stewardess. He knew her first name. Gloria.

CHAPTER ELEVEN

It looked like a single-family home, but it had two units, one upstairs, one down. The entry to the upstairs unit was hidden around back and required almost a full circle to reach. You went through an iron gate, down the side of the house, then all around the rear, and then halfway back up the other side, which couldn't be approached from the front sidewalk. The way was blocked by a high retaining wall.

Illegal apartment, deviously accessed, Donahoo thought. A bad start. David Garrett had probably demonstrated similar traits in other matters. He might be hard to get to know.

Camargo hammered on the door. "Police!"

"Okay, okay." Palmer, already inside and waiting, pulled the door open for them, a Coke in hand. "Christ, you don't have to knock it down, Camargo. I've got a sick man in here. Delicate condition. He needs rest."

Donahoo went in. "Where?"

Palmer motioned with the Coke. "Bedroom. He's so shook up he can't talk now."

"It was you who broke him the news?"

"Yeah."

"Then I don't wonder."

Palmer grinned. "Hey, I was gentle."

Donahoo crossed a small, low-ceilinged living room, into an even smaller, shedlike bedroom. There was barely space for the double bed. Camargo had to stay in the doorway. Palmer remained in the living room.

A man was sprawled facedown on the bed. He had a good body, tall, muscled. He was sobbing into a pillow.

"What do we have so far?" Donahoo said.

"Positive ID," Palmer answered. "This is Purdy. Garrett's Significant Other."

The man on the bed screamed, "Lifetime partner!"

"Purdy made the ID. We just got back from the morgue. That's why he's so upset."

"Yeah, well, that's only natural," Camargo said. "A guy loses his partner."

"Oh, it's not why he's crying," Palmer said. "He's crying because the sonofabitch was cheating on him."

The man on the end of the bed had another spasm of sobbing.

"Leave us for a while," Donahoo suggested. He closed the door and sat down at the foot of the bed. "Purdy. That's your name, huh? A purdy guy with a purdy name."

"Fuck you."

"Maybe, after we talk," Donahoo told him. "First we talk, maybe dance a little. But first we talk. It's very important that we talk, Purdy."

"I can't talk now!"

"Here, or downtown."

Purdy turned to face him. Donahoo was struck by how much he resembled Garrett. The same bitchy good looks. His eyes were red-rimmed. "You're gonna arrest me?"

"Yeah, for murder," Donahoo said. "You've got the motive, Purdy. Your boyfriend is sucking around on you. You find out, you pop him. It sounds good to me."

"Fuck you."

"No, no. Fuck *you*, Purdy. I can arrest you. The charge may not stick. But I can arrest you. You ever been to jail?"

"No."

"Well, don't be in a hurry to book a trip. You come back, you're gonna have a larger asshole, faggot. You'll be able to put your Christmas tree up there without bending a branch."

Purdy pushed up into a sitting position. He wiped at his eyes and tear-streaked face. The defiance was gone, but he wasn't afraid, just resigned. "You're a jerk."

"I know." Donahoo got up and opened the door. "Purdy is gonna talk to us."

Camargo and Palmer did the questioning while Donahoo picked through the apartment. He was never out of earshot. Occasionally he asked a question. For the most part, though, he just listened, content with how Camargo and Palmer were handling Purdy. They were doing good cop, bad cop. Camargo was the good cop. "Yeah, I can appreciate how you feel," Camargo kept saying, and Palmer would say, "Can we cut the bullshit, please? A man is dead here."

Donahoo listened and let Purdy's answers paint a portrait of David Garrett. They had lived together for six years. Garrett was the one on the bottom. He didn't have a steady job. He worked at whatever came along. He was an actor, mostly. He was pretty good. He appeared in some productions at The Globe. He played Oscar in *The Odd Couple*.

Donahoo found a good photo of Garrett. "Can I take this?"

"Yeah," Purdy said. "Who gives a fuck?"

"I can appreciate how you feel," Camargo said.

Donahoo kept working the apartment. Documents, personal papers, books. He kept listening to the questions and answers. There had never been any indication or hint of unfaithfulness. Yes, of course they argued, that was normal, everybody did, but there was absolutely no suggestion that he was cheating. They were married in the truest sense of the word and they were saving to buy a place of their own. They had almost four thousand dollars in a joint account.

Donahoo found the bank book. The balance was $3,846.52. Enough for a burial. He put it aside and stood listening. They were going to move out of Hillcrest, to Kensington, or maybe Lemon Grove. Garrett liked the idea of Lemon Grove. He wanted some room. He wanted to keep pigeons.

"He liked pigeons?"

"Doves, actually."

Camargo looked over at Donahoo.

"I'm through," Donahoo said.

"You think it was random?"

"Yeah, random," Donahoo said. He was quoting now. "Just a shuffle of the cards. The wrong guy in the wrong place. The wrong moment in history."

Purdy stared at him with his red-rimmed eyes. "That doesn't make it any easier."

"No, it doesn't," Donahoo admitted. "It makes it harder."

CHAPTER TWELVE

Nicholas Valesy waited in the shadows of an old boarded-up house. It had been gutted by a fire started by the homeless. There was a big FOR SALE sign on it, but there had been no offers, and none were expected. It wasn't worth fixing up, and it wasn't worth tearing down, either. It was in the glide path to Lindbergh Field.

To look at him, Valesy was one of the homeless. He was wearing some of the old clothes he had purchased from the Goodwill. He also had a shopping cart piled high with the junk and trash he had gathered coming here from the Gaslamp Quarter. Bottles, aluminum cans, old newspapers. Some battered pots and pans. A rusted-out toaster and an empty picture frame. The stuff of pennies for the next sandwich.

The small, plain house across the street had a carved wooden sign next to the door. JOSEPH R. FOLEY, REALTOR.

Valesy had been waiting for hours but no one had paid any attention to him. That's what the homeless did. They waited. You saw them pushing their carts. Or you saw them waiting. One or the other. You saw them and you kept going. Out of fear, or guilt, you hurried away, without a glance back. Valesy knew that. It was the same everywhere.

Foley came out of the house across the street. He stood for a moment on the small, cramped porch, a hand raised against the sun, getting used to it. He looked angry, but maybe it was just the sun, now directly overhead.

Valesy stirred. Grenier had provided him with a business card with a photograph. Joseph R. Foley, Realtor. It was a bad photograph—they always were on business cards—but even at a distance Valesy knew it was Foley. He had a distinctive bulldog face, square, jowly, pugnacious. He looked like a fighter.

Foley limped off the porch and went to an old Mercedes parked on the lawn. He took something off the windshield, a flyer, or perhaps a parking ticket. He looked at it, crumpled it up, tossed it down. He changed his mind and picked it up. He got into the Mercedes. He started it up and it belched white smoke. Briefly, the car disappeared, lost in its own camouflage.

Valve job, coming up, Valesy mused. It would cost three times what the car was worth. He wondered why Foley drove it, or, for that matter, why he lived here, right under the howling planes. Grenier was right. He had to be crazy.

The Mercedes backed off the lawn and across the sidewalk and into the street. It sputtered away.

Valesy watched it go. 1972 280SE 4.5. License plate 2MRX007. A Realtor's car? It vanished around a corner. Valesy crossed the street. He went straight up on the porch. He took out a pick and inserted it in the lock. He was in the house in five seconds.

Inside, he was a cat, silently checking each room, making sure the house was empty. Satisfied, he went to the office, a large room at the rear. It was as big again as all the other rooms together. Huge maps of the city covered all the walls. Colored tacks were stuck all over. Red, green, yellow. It was like no real-estate office Valesy had ever seen. The colored tacks probably meant listings, escrows, sales. But the immensity of the layout suggested something vastly more important was in progress. The room looked like a command center.

Valesy glanced around. There was a word processor next to the bank of telephones. He would start there. He pulled on rubber gloves. One of the telephones rang. An answering machine switched on. "Joseph R. Foley, Realtor," a recorded voice said. "I can't come to the phone right now. But your message is important to me. Please leave a message at the signal. And I'll get right back to you."

Valesy was sorting through the word processor's disk storage bin. Your message is important to me. How did he know that? It could be unimportant.

"I was calling about your ad in the paper," the caller said. "The fixer-upper in Clairemont." He left a name and number. "Thank you."

Valesy went through the disks. He couldn't find a GOLDEN HILL. There was nothing labeled RESTORATION. Shit, he thought. He'd have to check every one. He'd be here forever. He'd be at risk. Then he saw a disk marked PROPOSALS. It sounded like a good bet. He turned on the processor and inserted the disk. He punched up the menu. He went down the list. TOWERS, LL, MORENA, GH. Bingo. He called up GH. It was Foley's letter to Grenier proposing the Pilgrim Tobacco Company's restoration of Golden Hill.

Never happened, Valesy thought. He erased the file and checked the others. Totally different subjects. No mention of Golden Hill. But there was still a possibility of a hard copy. He turned off the word processor and put the disk back in its bin.

One of the phones rang again. A different answering machine clicked on. Foley again, but in a strange voice, altered. He sounded British. "Farthest Star Productions. This is Mark. If you're calling about the acting job, that's been filled, I'm sorry." The caller waited for the beep anyway. He said, "You don't know what you're missing," and hung up.

Valesy frowned. Mark? Farthest Star? The firm's name was Joseph R. Foley, Realtor. It was on the card. It was on the door out front. Why was Foley pretending to be British? What the hell was Farthest Star Productions?

"He's crazy," Valesy said aloud, again reminding himself of Grenier's assessment. He pulled open a filing cabinet's PQR drawer. He located a file labeled PROPOSALS. He went through it and couldn't find any copy of Foley's letter to Grenier. He frowned, feeling the uncertainty return, the apprehension. Where would it be? He tried to think. He struggled with his inadequate English. Plans? He looked. Nothing. Ideas? Again, nothing. He steeled himself. He had to think clearly. He went back through the drawer, more carefully this time, willing himself to be patient. He found a folder that had slipped down, off the tracks. It was marked PROJECTS. Relieved, he fingered through it, quickly found Foley's letter to Grenier. He ripped it up and stuffed the pieces in various pockets. He'd scatter them later.

Now. Valesy opened a small fingerprint kit. He dusted the objects on the desk and found several good prints. He lifted them with a special tape. He put the kit away. He looked for a photo of Foley. He found one in a silver frame. He removed it. He got out a small camera with a built-in flash bigger than the rest of it. He took several pictures of the photo. He put it back in the frame. As he did so, he noticed, on the back, hardly visible, the engraved initials JRF. He checked the underside of a nearby stapler. It, too, had the initials. He turned over a small metal index card case. There they were again, JRF. He smiled. That was helpful.

A plane roared overheard. The house shook with the closeness of it. The sound died and suddenly someone was in the front hall. The plane's bedlam had masked their entry. Valesy had picked up a hypodermic at just that moment. He risked another to smell the contents. Morphine.

The third phone rang. Valesy lunged for the rear door. As he pushed outside, the answering machine clicked on, but he only heard a portion.

"Mission Temporary Service," the voice on the machine said. Foley again, but he wasn't British this time. He sounded Slavic and oddly sinister, cold, calculating. He sounded, strange coincidence, like Valesy's old mentor, Boris Yuschev. "This is …" Valesy didn't hear the rest.

CHAPTER THIRTEEN

Grayson Grenier waited by a pay phone in Central Park. Any moment now, the phone was going to ring, forever changing him, and also the course of his life. He'd known for months that this moment was coming. There hadn't been a day, an hour, that he hadn't thought about it, agonized over it. The moment when, everything in place, Nicholas Valesy was going to say, words to this effect, "Shall we proceed?"

To begin, that had been one thing. To proceed? He recalled Rudolph Pinsky's drunken dismissal of the lung cancer toll exacted by the Pilgrim Tobacco Company, and, therefore, by him. The fat Russian wasn't impressed. *Randomly*, Pinksy had said of his victims. *You don't choose them. You never see them.*

Grenier looked at the graffiti-scarred booth and its taped-together phone. When it rang, that critique no longer applied, he thought. The four names on Valesy's list were certified flesh and blood to him. Eric Hudson, the white fox, he knew him, quite closely. He had spoken to another, and he had seen the other two. He had carefully considered the pros and cons of listing them. He had assessed the value that their deaths contributed to the grand scheme. He had personally chosen them. It wasn't done randomly. Nor at a distance. So, now, to proceed, that required ... well, steel.

He was dressed as a jogger, a smart blue velvet outfit with maroon piping, new Adidases, and had, in fact, been running. He was tired, close to exhaustion. He hadn't paced himself properly. He wasn't used to running—normally, he worked out in a gym—and his legs hurt. Different muscles, he thought. Running was natural. The machines were machines. To stay fit, he ought to do more things that were natural. Look at animals. They ran free. Only gerbils ran in a machine. And not by choice.

The telephone rang. Grenier looked at his watch. On the minute. They had worked out a detailed schedule of contacts. Times, days, places, always a different pay phone. This was the first on the schedule. The call to his apartment had been an aberration. It still annoyed him.

The phone rang again. Grenier picked it up, wondering how many pay phones there were in New York. Thousands, probably. Perhaps tens of thousands. He had chosen seven of them, widely scattered. There was noise and music in the background. It sounded like a bar. "Hello?"

"First step, completed," Valesy said dramatically. "Disk, erased. Letter, destroyed. You're king of the hill."

Grenier felt a surge of restored power. King of the hill? That was nice. For all their boorishness, the fucking Russians, they could turn a phrase. Or, in this instance, use a tired one appropriately. "Good. Very good, excellent."

The music swelled. Someone was singing, off-key. Grenier waited for some sort of response. He felt exhilarated, but there was a hurdle here that he had to get over, to be pushed over. He said finally, "No problems?"

"No." A pause. Grenier thought he could see Valesy changing his mind. Normally, there was no hesitation; The Colonel cut through, a razor. "This is probably nothing. You said you thought he was crazy?"

"Is there a problem?" Grenier asked.

"You said he was crazy?"

"I said, is there a problem?"

"Perhaps," Valesy admitted. "It's like..." Another pause. "He seems to be three persons."

"I don't understand."

"He's—how do you say?—schizo?"

"Schizophrenic?"

"Yes. I heard him on his answering machines."

"Machines?"

"Yes, three. Three voices, two, maybe three names. I didn't hear it all. But I would guess three names."

Grenier said, "Jesus Christ. Not schizo. Split personality."

"Whatever. You were right. He *is* crazy."

Grenier was trying to think. He was too far in to consider stopping. He said, "It doesn't make any difference, does it? I mean, the crazier, the better. It's what we want, really, isn't it? He's that much easier to blame."

"Yes, I suppose."

Grenier was trying to think. The music was pounding. "Does it make any difference?"

"Only in fee," Valesy said loudly, talking above the music. "We agreed on four. Now there are six."

"What?"

"There are six!"

"Very amusing."

"So," Valesy said loudly, talking above the music. "We proceed as planned?"

"Of course," Grenier told him, not thinking now, it was anticlimactic. He said, "Start killing." He hung up.

Grenier returned to an empty apartment. Keebler, the cook, had the day off. He'd forgotten. Ruby would be picking up Chinese. She'd also be renting a video. Her idea of a night at the movies.

He showered and changed into slacks and a sweater. He kept wondering what kind of bars Valesy frequented. Nude bars, that would have been his guess before, but not now, after hearing the music, the singer. It sounded like karaoke.

He liked bars. The quick intimacy of them, and the easy dis-
entanglement. You never needed to continue with the new confi-
dant you had made. You could just walk away. No obligation. He
had a full bar in the penthouse. It took up a room that formerly
had been a library. Ruby had supervised the renovation and she
had been thorough. "You don't read Shakespeare, you quote
him," she had said, and the books, all of them, had gone to some
charity. There were bottles on the shelves now in what Ruby had
christened SMOKEY'S. There was a neon sign with neon smoke.

Grenier poured himself a double shot of vodka and drank
it in one gulp. He poured another shot, belatedly aware that it
was his brand, Stalvart. Normally he didn't drink it. The quality
was uneven. Sometimes he detected a trace of diesel fuel. His
chemists said no, he was imagining things, but he could taste it,
and there were complaints from consumers, too. The enormous
start-up costs and staggering advertising expenses hadn't paid
off. American vodka drinkers had failed to embrace The Other
Russian Vodka. The solution had become part of the problem.
Stalvart's market share was nil.

The fucking Russians, Grenier thought. Their country was in
a shambles. They produced shoddy goods at inflated prices. They
didn't have any quality control. He had hired a colonel with a
corporal's tastes. Karaoke, for God's sake.

He drank his vodka and poured another shot. He felt calmer
now. What did it matter, really? Poor taste. It was everywhere.
You couldn't avoid it. Even at your own dinner table. Chinese
was coming.

He drank his vodka and remembered the fateful night in the
desperate little butcher-shop bar in Moscow. Pinsky, drunk on
his ass, saying, "Dollars or rubles?" He hadn't needed an assassin then, but when he got back to New York, there had been
an equally fateful letter waiting, from Joseph R. Foley, Realtor.
Private & Confidential, the envelope had said, and even though

she was his confidential secretary, Mary Harper had not opened it. Grenier was grateful for that. He liked Mary Harper.

The letter, which no one else had seen, just him, Grenier, would have been tossed in the wastebasket in normal times. But when it arrived, precisely timed, in the depths of the recession, it had been accompanied by the bleakest in-house forecast Grenier had ever read. The Pilgrim Tobacco Company was going in the toilet, on his watch. Sales were down, markets were dwindling, the competition was cutthroat. The company was suffering major losses. It was going to go down and take him with it unless he found some way to turn it around. His private fortune was at stake in company loans he had personally secured.

He had been appalled. Much of the impending disaster was his fault. He hadn't been minding the store. He'd been flitting around London, he'd been schussing down the Alps. He had picked up *Endless Summer* after it had been refitted in Long Beach. He'd taken it to Hawaii. He'd been away from corporate, for months at a time. He hadn't been to the plants in years. He was listening to yes men in a Manhattan tower. North Carolina? He'd almost forgotten what the place looked like.

Oh, Jesus Christ, what have I done? he had thought, putting the chilling forecast aside. Then he had read the letter from Foley. *This is to propose a public relations program of truly exceptional potential for your corporation. It could be called PILGRIM RESTORES AMERICA. It could bring an enormous amount of positive national attention. And, while nonprofit, it could be, to large degree, self-sustaining.*

He had almost stopped reading there, at the nonprofit part, but he had been intrigued by the catch phrase, Pilgrim Restores America. He could imagine his marketing people jumping on it. He wondered if it might be the miracle he needed.

The letter continued: *Apart from reducing the national debt and creating more jobs, rebuilding our inner cities is perhaps the most important, and daunting, task facing this country. It is a slow, uncertain process at best. In many places it has been abandoned. By establishing PILGRIM RESTORES AMERICA, the Pilgrim Tobacco Company, with its financial resources, could provide the private sector leadership that is so desperately needed to turn this situation around and begin, by example, a nationwide mobilization for renewal.*

Again, Grenier had almost stopped reading. Pilgrim's financial resources? If the truth were known, its shares would be selling even lower. Still, he had remained intrigued.

There are hundreds of places suitable for a demonstration project. I am proposing the historic Golden Hill district of San Diego. Golden Hill is typical of the blight that scars America. It formerly was one of the finest neighborhoods in the city. Now, although grand homes and buildings remain intact, ripe for restoration, much of the district itself is a crime-ridden slum. Some private and public-assisted renewal has taken place. A house here, an apartment there, now a commercial structure, but it is spotty and not in concert. There is a brave hope—but no guarantee—that a complete rehabilitation can be accomplished at some distant date. What slows and may halt the process is the uncertainty that accompanies it. Very few people, be they ordinary homebuyers or seasoned developers, are prepared to make a substantial investment in such a high-risk situation. But what if, for the most part, the risk was removed?

Grenier had been hooked then. *Enter PILGRIM RESTORES AMERICA. The Pilgrim Tobacco Company forms several corporations that quietly buy up as much rehab property as possible in a designated section of Golden Hill. Once the parcel has been assembled, Pilgrim, with appropriate fanfare, puts the property back on the market, offering it at cost and at very favorable terms to a broad mix of buyers, ranging from ordinary citizens to experienced rehab specialists. The financing arrangements provide the funds for renewal and require that it be completed within a specified time period. Now, within this designated area of Golden Hill,* the "risk" is removed. People can buy property there knowing that all (or almost all) of it is earmarked for immediate renewal. They can look to swift and substantial appreciation in property values. What was once a risky purchase is probably the best buy in the city—thanks to PILGRIM RESTORES AMERICA.

That was it, except for the close, where Foley had made a modest pitch. If this is of interest to you, I would be happy to go into much greater detail, providing statistical information, etc. I own some, but not much, property in Golden Hill. My hope is that, should you go ahead, I might find a place in what, to my mind, would be a very special endeavor.

Grenier had picked up the phone and booked the next available flight to San Diego. It was familiar territory. He'd had a few business dealings there, handled by First Fidelity Trust, and he'd gotten to know their bag man, the white fox, Eric Hudson. He'd gotten politically connected. He'd met the Mayor, Gordon Fletcher. He'd had lunch with Fletcher's aide, an ice queen, Faye Stuart. For a time, not normal for him, he had also kept a woman there, a young, almond-eyed boat girl, Honey Ngo Bing. That was over, but he still went there often, most recently for the America's Cup. He could see the potential there for Pilgrim Restores America.

He had spent the afternoon touring Golden Hill with Foley. He had returned, that same night, to New York. He didn't make a deal. Joseph R. Foley, Realtor, wrote a great letter, but he made a lousy presentation. Foley had already lost interest in Golden Hill. He had another grand scheme, this one a secret, not to be shared. He wanted it all, whatever it was, and he was slippery as a buttered weasel. He'd hint at it, eyes bright, smoldering, and then, questioned, he'd twist away. He had complained bitterly about Lindbergh Field. The airport had ruined him, he said. Destroyed him. Grenier had decided the pissy bugger might be certifiable. One scene was vivid in his memory. Foley standing in front of his tacky office/home in the glide path. Foley, wild-eyed, shaking a fist, shouting at a big jet swooping noisily overhead, "You're coming down!"

The threat—a nut case threat—had disturbed Grenier. Later, on the flight back to New York, it had given him an idea. The thought, criminal but brilliant, that here was a way out of his mess. Here, if he had the balls for it, a way to make an enormous sum of money, guaranteeing him a safe, secure, all-the-toys future. He could dump Pilgrim. He could stand alone.

Grenier had always admired the famous New York developer William "Big Bill" Zeckendorf. In 1945, as World War II was ending, Zeckendorf optioned the Swift & Wilson slaughterhouse on the East River, then quietly bought up adjoining parcels over a fourteen-block area. He next suggested that the Rockefellers might want to donate the slaughterhouse site to the United Nations for its permanent headquarters. John D. Rockefeller, Jr., agreed, paying Zeckendorf a handsome profit, and he went on to make a fortune on his adjacent holdings.

Grenier smiled and patiently waited for the vodka to take hold. Zeckendorf must have been patient, he thought. It must have taken a lot of time to buy up all those slums around the slaughterhouse. Quietly, very quietly, buy up all those awful slums, and then, voilà, get rid of the slaughterhouse.

Brilliant, simple, daring. People still talked about him. The legendary Zeckendorf.

So simple, Grenier thought. Or at least he hoped so. Lindbergh Field was his slaughterhouse. He couldn't buy it. But he thought he had come up with a way to get rid of it. Nobody liked Lindbergh where it was. Everybody agreed that it was badly, dangerously, located. The PSA crash, 144 dead, proved that, and it was only a matter of time before yet another major tragedy occurred. It was a ticking bomb and it was going to go off. The only question was when.

Grenier felt a chill. He'd been on a plane when he first posed that question to himself. Open question, he remembered thinking, and it would stay open, because nobody knew the future. That was why there wasn't the political will to get off the stick and relocate Lindbergh. A gamble on the unknown was permitted. But not anymore. He was going to adjust the odds. No more gamble. Sure thing. Another plane was going to fall out of the sky and wreak havoc below. And, when it did, they'd move Lindbergh. It would be the shove they needed. When the smoke cleared, they'd know it wasn't an accident, that it was a criminal act, and they'd know, because of how the glide path was situated, low over many blocks of housing, impossible to fully secure, that it could be easily repeated. Unless they moved Lindbergh, it could happen again, and again, and again. There were all those places to hide in the glide path's sprawling warrens. It would be so simple to slip in with more rocket launchers. They fit in a car's trunk. They took but seconds to set up, aim, fire. Not much longer than to spray some graffiti. So they would heed that lesson. There was graffiti everywhere, it was a plague. But the elusive shadows who sprayed it, they were seldom, hardly ever, caught. It wasn't a fight you expected to win.

The clincher, though, and he wouldn't have gone into this otherwise, Lindbergh truly was in the wrong place. All of his careful research supported that. He'd made up his mind when he came across a Letter to the Editor in the *San Diego Union,* which, at the time of publication, was separate from the *Tribune.* The letter was from a commercial airline pilot. His letter said he had flown into almost all the world's major airports, and it said, commenting on the PSA crash, the toll of 144 dead, "No other airport is so dangerously and obnoxiously located."

Reading the letter, that had made up his mind, Grenier remembered. Normally, governments didn't respond to blackmail, or not for long, but in this instance, they were wrong, dead wrong. They had a busy international airport in the wrong place and they knew it. Most other large airports were situated ten to twenty-five miles away from city center, but Lindbergh Field was, quote, "dangerously, obnoxiously," at San Diego's heart. So he was going to cut it away and gain enormously by it, and if anybody got suspicious he had the perfect alibi in Golden Hill. He was a public-spirited developer who quietly bought up deteriorating neighborhoods for renewal. Golden Hill was one. Another, Balboa Park. How could he possibly know he would profit from a horrific tragedy in Balboa Park? How could anyone?

He smiled at himself in the mirror behind the bar. He liked what he saw there. A man who had come to terms with his limited choices. Daring enough to try. Wise enough to quit. If he got away with it—the legendary Grenier. If he failed—he'd blow his brains out.

Ruby came in. She was carrying an enormous brown paper bag. The Chinese.

"Hi," she said. "I got a movie. *Cronos.* You seen it?"

No, he hadn't. "What's it about?"

"Murder."

Grenier poured himself another drink. He looked at Ruby. Tits on a stick. The woman who knew nothing. He wondered if she somehow knew something. He also wondered—it had been in the back of his mind, festering there since the phone call from Valesy—about Joseph R. Foley, Realtor. So Foley was three persons now? Initially, Grenier had thought that made it easier, more proof that the man was a looney, but he wasn't so certain now. Three persons? Three *different* persons? That sounded terribly complex. Grenier could imagine them running off in all kinds of directions. He could imagine one of them doing something that the other two opposed. Then what? Grenier could see them fighting with each other. Might that happen? Well, one thing for certain, Grenier decided. If you framed one, you framed them all.

CHAPTER FOURTEEN

Donahoo was in his favorite downtown hangout, The Waterfront. He was one of the regulars, coming in two or three times a week for the happy hour, often staying for a hamburger-and-fries supper. It was where he watched Monday Night Football, and where, as now, unable to face his small apartment, he could waste, with some measure of company, the night's long, empty hours.

The place was a supposed landmark, a low, one-story brick building facing east on Kettner Boulevard, away from the actual waterfront, which was several blocks farther west, at Pacific Coast Highway. It claimed to be the oldest, or longest operating, restaurant in San Diego, and there was evidence of that. It was uneven, worn, scarred. It looked like it might be held together by the fishnet decor, and it offered an outdated milieu. A long belly-up bar took most of the front section. The dining room, and the pool room, together as one, shared the back. There were a lot of faded photographs on the walls. San Diego when it was a few primitive buildings. Dusty, unpaved streets. Horse and buggy. Mixed in were a lot of photos of heavily muscled commercial fishermen displaying enormous billfish. They'd been caught, most of them, off Peru.

Donahoo was just inside the front door, perched on a stool at the first of the cramped bar-high tables that were attached, like a row of ironing boards, below the narrow casement windows looking out on Kettner. It was his reserved seat, when he could get it. The window was never closed, or at least not in his experience, and it afforded him, with little effort, a clear view of the street, both directions, south to Grape and north to Hawthorne. He could keep an eye on his car. Also, with the door so close, he could exit, if required, in the time it took to swing around. Thus far, a decade of faithful patronage, no emergency had arisen to demand that kind of swift response, but he was prepared.

He was drinking coffee, he didn't want to go to bed yet, he certainly didn't want to go to sleep. His mind was still on Garrett's murder, on the note that said, *I can do it.* What the hell did that really mean? he kept asking himself. What, exactly? It wouldn't let him rest. He was browsing the *Union-Trib,* what remained of it, what he had gathered, scraps of it from the bar, a couple tables. No sports pages. No financial. But they had left him the classified.

CRAZY TEXAN [Donahoo was reading this]. Richard Widmark lookalike, young 53, 5'10½", 162 lbs., blue eyes, likes most anything if I'm with an attractive, intelligent lady, legs are a winner, any age if well preserved. Businessman from Texas, history is similar to a character from a Harold Robbins novel. Ad #3159.

"You find anybody?" Ginny wanted to know. She was the night manager/cook/bartender/waitress.

Donahoo pushed his cup at her. "Yeah. This guy."

"Too late," Ginny said. "I've already written him."

Donahoo shrugged. That was okay. There were others. MR. RIGHT [he was reading this]. I know you're out there. SWF, happy, 50's, seeking D/SWM, 45–60, ready to feel the chemistry…

Ginny asked, "Who you got?"

"Will you give me a minute?" Donahoo said. He wanted to feel more than chemistry. Maybe he ought to put in his own ad. Where was that code for abbreviations? B, black. C, Christian [he was reading this]. D, divorced. WW, widowed. J, Jewish. M, male. F, female. W, white. S, single. H, Hispanic. N/S, nonsmoker. N A, Native American.

He found a pen and piece of paper. Let's see. He'd be a DWM. Seeks SWF. Oh, and N/S. He'd put that in. But maybe it needed a little more ooomph?

Camargo came in, came over. He looked tired, spent, but he had to have something, Donahoo thought. He wouldn't be here otherwise. He'd be home in bed with the fat and warm Marie.

Donahoo took off his glasses and pushed his ad aside. "What you got?"

"A present."

They had split up after talking to Purdy. Donahoo had spent the day talking to Garrett's friends, his odd job co-workers, people at the places he frequented regularly, an estranged sister, the lovely Rebecca Frostmeyer, who couldn't condone *that* kind of relationship, and who was presently on her third marriage. Everybody said the same thing. The boys were in love. Even Frostmeyer had to admit that. So that confirmed, if confirmation was needed, today's theory. It was random. And random was hardest. If there was any sort of rationale, you could predict, maybe, where a killer was going to strike next. If it was random, you just had to wait, that's all. Wait, and hope for a break. But he couldn't rest.

"Let's see it," he said.

Camargo pulled a plain white #10 envelope out of his coat pocket. He ripped it open and dumped out a small plastic Baggie. He opened the Baggie and shook out two small black sticks into the palm of his hand.

"What is it?"

"I dunno."

"Matchsticks?" Donahoo said. He retrieved his glasses, put them on. He picked up one of the sticks and held it between thumb and forefinger. He still thought it looked like a burned matchstick. But the texture was wrong. It was hard, brittle. "What the hell is it?"

"A clue," Camargo said this time. "Jelley gave them to me. When they were undressing the body, they found a bunch of these things, nine altogether, sticking to Garrett's clothes. His pant legs, his T-shirt. Left side."

Donahoo stared at the slim little stick between his fingers. It was like a twig, except that it was too straight, too hard. He didn't have any idea what it was.

"I knew you'd be here," Camargo said.

Donahoo made a small motion, good. "What does Jelley say?"

"He says it's very hard rubber."

"What else does he say?"

"He says it broke off of something flat and partially ribbed. Maybe some nonskid flooring material? What you're looking at is a section of rib. It snapped off sideways and broke into smaller pieces."

"Why flooring?"

"They found some sort of cement on the underside of some of the pieces."

Donahoo turned the little stick in his hand. "Can we keep these?"

"Sure," Camargo said. "Jelley's got lots." He put the stick he still had into the white envelope. He folded the envelope and returned it to his pocket. "I already signed you out for it."

Donahoo sat staring at his stick. It might be nothing, and it might be everything, he thought. Sometimes, this was all it took. The tiny shred of physical evidence that linked killer and victim. The first straw. You got it, and then, remorselessly, you got others. They piled on, heavier and heavier. They formed the great weight of evidence that justified the charge. Donahoo got his Baggie. It was just a little stick. He'd seen men go to Death Row on less.

"Well, I gotta go," Camargo said.

Donahoo nodded. The fat and warm Maria.

"We'll get on it first thing tomorrow?"

"Yeah."

"What I think," Camargo said. "Fags, they keep pretty clean, huh? You see them around. They're clean. So what I think, Garrett wouldn't have gone to the park with stuff sticking on his clothes. He'd have noticed, brushed himself off. So the odds are, he picked the stuff up at the scene of the crime."

"I'm way ahead of you," Donahoo said. "He picked it up in the killer's car."

"That's what I was gonna say."

"Yeah. But were you gonna say European car?"

Camargo looked at him.

Donahoo didn't know it was Europen, he was guessing, it was a hunch, that's all. But the rubber was so dry and brittle he was sure that it was old. "*Old* European car."

Camargo was still looking at him. "You know your cars, huh?"

"Hey, many years ago, I had the first passenger-side airbag."

"Yeah, well, I gotta go," Camargo said. He made a gesture and moved off. "Marie. She's waiting."

Donahoo put his stick away. He could be a real idiot at times, he thought. He called after Camargo. "Frank?!"

Camargo turned at the door.

"Listen, thank you."

"Sure," Camargo said. He was gone.

Donahoo sighed and retrieved his ad. He ought to go home, but there was no one waiting. Not anymore. Ginny came over with more coffee. She was like Marie. A big woman. Fat, warm. She could comfort. Sometimes, not all the time, it seemed she wanted to do that, and there were times he would have gladly accepted. It was a draw. They were friends. No-fuckee friends.

He wanted magic, he wanted Madam Zola, Donahoo thought. He remembered how he felt when he saw her walking down Kalmia. He wanted to reach out, touch the long black hair. Make it spark. But Montrose was probably right. He didn't have a shot. He was too late for Coronado, and he was too late for magic. He said, "Help me write this ad, will you?"

Ginny turned it around so she could read. "You're really looking for a woman? Someone your age? What are you telling me, Donahoo? You can still see shadows? Smell pussy?"

Donahoo said, "On a clear day. Help me with the ad."

"Sure," Ginny said. "Where have you got so far? What's this? UFOO?"

"Under forty, ovaries out."

Ginny looked at him. "You can be a real idiot, know that?"

"Yeah," Donahoo said. "I do."

CHAPTER FIFTEEN

Stryker would wait until the dead of night. They had to sleep sometime and they would be asleep then. They wrapped themselves in folds of rags and huddled under crude tents formed by blankets stretched between shopping carts. They camped—their sanctuary—on the Date Street steps of the First Presbyterian Church. They bedded down early, as soon as night fell, but it was doubtful they went to sleep then. The street was busy with traffic off the freeway. The planes still rumbled in the glide path.

He went there at three o'clock. He parked a block away. He approached on slippered feet. He had his revolver and the silencer.

There was no sound when he came upon them. He had thought they'd be snoring, some of them, or coughing, making guttural noises. But they were as eerily silent as a cemetery. It was as if they were already dead.

Only the wind moved, and the fallen leaves it touched. It pushed them along the road, into the gutter. It swirled them over the curb, against the church steps, onto the silent encampment.

"Hello," he said, but very softly, only he could hear it. "I'm back."

He pulled the gun from his coat pocket. He switched hands and held it at his side while he got the silencer from the same place. He fitted them together, not having to look at what he was doing. He had practiced this many times in the dark, in bed late at night, waiting for sleep.

Routine, he thought, and he wondered if that's what this would be, even though he would be taking more victims. Having killed once—the fear, the suspense, the excitement, the pleasure—would he experience that kind of rush again? That incredible rush, and, afterward, later, the calm, the release? Like he was flying away on an avenger's wings, and the world was better, safer. He cleansed it.

Time to find out. Stryker went into the wandering leaves and down the line of crude makeshift tents. He fired at what he thought were heads. He couldn't be sure and it didn't matter. He didn't necessarily want all of them. Just enough.

He emptied his revolver and stuffed the note in the rags wrapping his final victim. That's when it came. On contact with a corpse. The rush.

The note said, *Talk to me.*

CHAPTER SIXTEEN

Saperstein crumpled his copy of the note. He rolled it into a tight ball and threw it across his office. It bounced off the wall, off the Little League photo, and into Camargo's lap. Camargo, incredulous, let it sit there.

Donahoo took the crumpled wad and put it on Saperstein's desk. He did it in the kind of deliberate way that suggested it shouldn't be thrown again. He had his own anger to contend with. Three more murders in the Balboa Park district. Three poor homeless bastards killed at random. He was angry because he hadn't seen it coming this fast and because there wasn't a damn thing he could have done about it.

"We've got a problem here," Saperstein complained, being very specific about the geography, *here*. "This kind of slaughter to force a political decision?" He was looking at the wadded note. "Fags. The homeless. Who the hell is next? Citizens?"

"It could come to that," Donahoo said.

"You're not amusing."

Donahoo shrugged for apology and sipped at his coffee. The meeting, like most meetings, was wasting time, he thought. He didn't need to sit here and be told they had a problem here. They'd known that—they'd all known that—before they sat down. They had a Class A, eyes closed, hard ride, kick-in-the-ass dick-puller going here, and it wasn't going to be solved by throwing paper around. It might not be solved at all—might not be solved in time—if they didn't get out and get on it. He wanted, *needed*, to be out on the street, at the crime scene, talking to the church janitor who discovered the bodies, checking with the first cops to show up. He wanted to be in the lab, examining the note, the original, not a copy. He wanted to hold the spent slugs found on the church steps. He wanted hands on. He also wanted, if this would ever start and finish, to take Camargo's little hard stick out to some wrecker's yard, to find what he could find.

"If I wanted comics, I'd buy a paper," Saperstein said.

Donahoo looked at him but didn't respond. He went back to his coffee, wishing that he had a better, easier rapport with the brilliant and complex Assistant Chief, Detectives. He wished he liked him. He respected him, he had to, because of his intelligence, drive, and dedication. But he didn't like him. The man was too... What? Fucking distant, remote, Donahoo decided. If you went looking for the real Saperstein, you'd never find him. He was too far away. And, Donahoo knew, this was in his heart, not worth the journey. He didn't like him. Not at all.

He asked, "Can we do this?"

As if asserting his rank and obligation, Lewis pulled closer to Saperstein's desk, easing just ahead of Donahoo, establishing himself as a better target. He made a production of getting his notes together. He looked for permission.

"Yeah, go ahead," Saperstein said. "Tell me how wonderful you are."

"I've talked to Patrol," the beefy head of Investigations said. "They've agreed to double their manpower in Balboa. I've talked to Traffic. They're gonna get tougher in that area. They're gonna pull over for any violation. They're gonna find excuses to search vehicles."

Saperstein stared at him flatly. "You talk to a psychic?"

Lewis didn't understand.

"Ask him what's next?"

"There's that Madam Zola," Camargo volunteered, a reminder for Donahoo.

Saperstein said, "Jesus Christ."

"The note is a match," Lewis went on. "We know that even without the lab report. The slugs look the same. I think we can bet money." He sifted through his papers. "Our guy wasn't as precise this time. Head shots, but all over the place, hit and miss. I guess he couldn't see too clearly. The victims were wrapped like mummies."

Saperstein, his mind elsewhere, said, "Huh?"

"They wrap themselves in rags."

"Rags?" Saperstein seemed offended by the idea. "What a way to live." He seemed embarrassed. "Any witnesses?"

"No."

"What do the survivors say?"

"Nada. They didn't see shit."

"Nobody saw anything?"

"Nobody. We got an old lady, she lives in the next block, she claims she saw flashes in front of the church, sometime in the night, but that doesn't make sense, the guy used a silencer. She just wants her name in the paper. Flashes in the dark, she says. Like a dance of light. It makes a good quote."

"You think so?" Saperstein said. "We've got a problem here. Two cases, and nobody saw anything. Bang, bang. He disappears. A fucking phantom." He turned to Donahoo. "The fag killing? How are you doing on that?"

Donahoo glanced at Camargo. He waited, then said, "The lab found some little sticks on the victim's clothing. Little bits of hard rubber. Frank thinks they may be from the killer's car. We're gonna check that out this morning."

"Frank thinks?"

"Yeah."

Saperstein looked at Camargo. He apparently didn't believe it. "Anything else?"

"No."

Saperstein frowned. He looked at the wadded paper. Lewis, ever alert, moved into a half crouch, ready to leave. Donahoo finished his coffee.

"'Talk to me,' huh?" Saperstein said finally. "I don't think so. I don't want to hear what the sonofabitch is gonna say. He wants us to shut down Lindbergh. *Or else.*" His voice was suddenly oddly querulous. "How do you respond to this kind of blackmail? How do you shut down an international airport?"

Nobody answered.

"You, Tommy," Saperstein decided. "You're the lucky one. You talk to him. Who knows? Maybe you can arrange a meeting. That would be nice, the two of you get together." He said, "I know how you like meetings."

Donahoo said, "Is he gonna wear a tie?"

Saperstein retrieved the wadded paper. He rolled it in his hand, making it smaller, harder. Donahoo wondered if Saperstein would throw it. He wondered what he would do if Saperstein did.

"Get the fuck out of here," Saperstein told him.

CHAPTER SEVENTEEN

Valesy conjured up the name of the first victim listed in his electronic Personal Organizer. The tiny screen flashed DQHB GTCRNM. Valesy unscrambled the code in his mind. Add one letter of the alphabet for each character. D became E. Q became R. And so on. He was going to kill Eric Hudson.

Ordinarily, Valesy could have remembered that name, and the scrambled information that followed, too. The address. The description. The pertinent facts about family, friends, occupation, car, etc. The places he frequented. His habits. But Valesy had more people to kill than Eric Hudson. There were three others. That was a lot to remember. Too much. So he had this list.

DQHB GTCRNM. NBWJT GBSSPX. KPIO MBTTJVFS. UPNNZ EPOBIPP.

If a dump cop found it on him, he'd think the device was broken. All the entries were gibberish. It obviously was out of order. Some more Texas Instruments junk. If a smart cop found it on him? Well, that was the chance he took, Valesy thought. He took a lot of chances and that was one of them, no larger, no smaller, than the rest. He lived in a glass world. One false step and it would shatter. Crash!, and there would be nothing, just a thousand scattered shards, impossible to repair. It was unnerving at times. Possibly why he had started making mistakes. Why this job was his last. Why he had looked for another way to spend his remaining time.

Larisa. He said her name as her face replaced the image of the broken glass. He would be joining her soon. Larisa Krasnitskaya, effective woman, green eyes, dark hair, educated, with a sense of humor, optimist. She had lied, but only about the hair, it was flecked with gray. The eyes were green and they did laugh. She obviously was educated. She didn't pronounce the *w* in answer. An optimist? Well, all Russians were optimists, he thought. Those that weren't had slit their own throats a long time ago. This was his last job.

Valesy showered in the bathroom down the hall. He had moved to a different hotel, the Drake, at Fifth and Island. It was in a better area and slightly more upscale but still in the Gaslamp Quarter. It suited his purposes just as well. When he left, depending on how he dressed, whether or not he had showered and shaved, combed his hair, he could be perceived quite differently. He could be a solid citizen down on his luck but still bearing up bravely. He could be one step away from the haunted mob who were the homeless. He could go either way.

Today, he was bearing up, Valesy thought. He was going to try to look his best. He was going to put on his suit and his brave smile. He was going to take the trolley down to Chula Vista and he was going to blow the heart out of DQHB GTCRNM, aka Eric Hudson, the bag man for First Fidelity Trust. Eric Hudson, who knew too much, and who had become too greedy. Eric Hudson, who wasn't satisfied with being a millionaire, he wanted an even larger wedge of cake.

There was a newspaper rack outside the hotel door. The headline said, THREE HOMELESS SLAIN. Valesy smiled. He had picked the right time to switch roles. Three, huh? That made them an endangered species. He started down the sidewalk and then something changed his mind. Yesterday, he had been one of them. He wondered—how close? He went back and paid his 35¢ and yanked out a copy of the *Union-Tribune*.

Valesy stood on the sidewalk reading the story. *Police are investigating the murders of three homeless men found shot to death early this morning on the steps of the Balboa Park district's First Presbyterian Church at Fourth Avenue and Date Street. All three victims died from a single bullet fired into their heads from close range while they were sleeping. Two other homeless men camped on the church steps were wounded. Police said there were no witnesses and they have no clues to the killer's identity. "It seems to have been a random thing," a police spokesman said. "It was a drive-by. Only in this case, the bullets fired from point-blank range, we may have a walk-by. Nobody saw a car."*

The First Presbyterian Church. He had passed right by it, pushing his junk-laden shopping cart, on his way to erase the Golden Hill letter at Joseph R. Foley, Realtor. Three homeless men shot in the head. For no apparent good reason. Just random killings?

No, Valesy thought. There was always a reason. Even a psychopath killed for a reason. If the police did their job properly, they would find it, the explanation, and hence the solution. The answer to the question, why?

Valesy read the rest of the story. There was nothing more of interest. Police were withholding names of the victims pending notification of next of kin. That might prove, for obvious reasons, a lengthy procedure. Police were stepping up patrols in and around Balboa Park. The homeless were being advised to seek space in designated shelters.

Balboa Park. That jogged Valesy's memory. There had been a story in the paper the day he arrived. A homosexual had been found murdered in the park. He, too, had been shot in the head, a single bullet, fired at close range. Was there a connection?

Valesy folded his paper. Four murders in two days. All very close to the glide path to Lindbergh Field. His territory, so to speak. The four people on his death list were all connected, in various ways, with Balboa Park. Was somebody competing with him? Was that possible? And, if so, for what reason?

There was that question again, why? With a disturbing difference. It wasn't a puzzle for the police to bumble with. It was something he personally had to solve.

Valesy wondered what he should do. Suddenly, he was at an impasse, not sure which way to proceed, or even if he should proceed at all. The strange business at Joseph R. Foley, Realtor. The answering machines with the contrived accents and the different names. That also disturbed him. So did the hypodermic smelling of morphine. What did that all mean? Foley was crazy. That was the easy explanation. But now Valesy hesitated. Was there another answer? Something more sinister? He wondered, a dark thought, if, somehow, these were greasy strings being pulled by his employer, Grayson Grenier. He didn't fully trust Grenier. He was sure that was mutual.

Well, he had to find out, Valesy decided. He had to take the time to do that. Until he did, he risked the danger, however slight, that all these things were linked, and that they also connected to him. He had to find out. Otherwise he was working blind, a fool.

He made that decision—to scout the minefield before crossing—but it didn't sit well. He had been looking forward to a nice day. It was a shame to cancel by giving DQHB GTCRNM a stay of execution.

No, that wasn't right, Valesy told himself. This was planned. He had a schedule. He ought to stick to it. If he didn't, Grenier might wonder, get suspicious, be on guard. If, as was possible, Grenier planned some treachery, it would be unwise to alert him. It was better to go ahead as if nothing was amiss.

First, he'd kill, Valesy decided. Then he'd check out the competition.

CHAPTER EIGHTEEN

onahoo drove with Camargo out to Wonder Wreckers in Jamul. *Top Dollar Paid for Junk Cars*, according to the Yellow Pages. *Specialists in Foreign Vehicles. Largest Junk Yard in Jamul.*

Camargo liked to drive. Like Gomez, it was a power thing for him. It put him in command, even as he was receiving instructions. "Turn here," Donahoo would say. "Okay, go now." Or, usually, "What are you waiting for?" And, sometimes, "For Chrissakes, Frank."

Mostly, though, Donahoo was enjoying the trip. It was a nice day and they were chasing puff clouds. Donahoo was a native, he was born in Solona Beach, and what he liked most, even better than the ocean, was the puff clouds. Once he had written a poem for Monica. It went, in part,

Now we're on the mountain
Puff clouds, eagles high
A wild wind is calling
Saying climb.

He thought it was pretty good. Monica? Well, who knows? She smiled, though. Donahoo remembered that. Monica reading it and smiling.

Camargo didn't complain. He was aware of his reputation for being a dumb cop. He compensated by sucking up. By doing everybody favors. By laying down a ton of markers. It had got him on Homicide. It had kept him there. A struggle, perhaps, but at the end of the day, there was always the fat and warm Marie.

"What are you gonna call the case, Sarge?" Camargo asked, sucking up.

Donahoo, thinking now about Madam Zola, said, "Huh?"

"Your cases," Camargo said. "They all get names, don't they? The Purple Admiral Case. The Babes in the Woods Murder Case." He looked at Donahoo. "Those are great names."

"Some of them," Donahoo admitted.

"So let's give this one a great name."

Donahoo almost smiled. "Frank, if we're lucky, this case won't last long enough to get a name, and anyway, the papers name the case. Some reporter comes up with it. Not me."

Camargo gave him another look. "Yeah, but you could name the case if you wanted, right? It's your case. You can name it."

"I suppose."

"Then what are you gonna name it?"

Donahoo sighed. "Jesus, I dunno, Frank. What do you want to name it?"

Camargo didn't know. "Well, Balboa ought to be in there, that's a great name, and maybe the little old lady who saw the flashes of light? How about—you ready?—The Balboa Flash?"

"I don't think so," Donahoo said.

Wonder Wreckers was way out in the boonies, on a rutted trail leading off of Campo Road, twisting into the Jamul Mountains. There was a faded sign, WRECKERS, a gutted Volkswagen bug below it, and that's all. The Wonder part had fallen off and the name on the rural mailbox had also disappeared and the dirt road stretched into a dusty infinity.

"Yeah, turn here," Donahoo said.

Half an hour from the coast and it was another world. They moved between low, dung-colored, boulder-strewn hills. The trees, desert growth, mesquite and chapparal, were small and dry. The sky seemed lower now, and oppressive. Crows flung themselves across it in ragged formation. The air was still.

Donahoo felt in his pocket for the Baggie and its little black stick. It was such a small, slender, fragile clue, and he held such high hopes for it. He didn't have anything else, not yet, anyway. The morning's fresh killings had offered up an empty box. Yes, it was the same gun that killed Garrett, but that didn't help. Yes, the same daisy wheel typed the new note, but it didn't get him any closer to the wheel. It was a Brother, pica, 10. It worked on thousands of word processors that could have been purchased anywhere at anytime. He had the little stick, that's all. If he couldn't connect it with a specific make of car, he had nothing.

Maybe half a mile in, past another sign, GUARD DOG, PROCEED AT OWN RISK, a ramshackle house came into view, looking like an antiwar poster. A picker's shack expanded by lean-tos, it was situated on a slight rise, presiding over an automative Armageddon. Wrecked cars were stacked all around in a haphazard and seemingly endless maze. Every make and model of foreign car imaginable. Donahoo immediately felt better. They had come to the right place, he thought. He'd find what he wanted here. Or it didn't exist.

There was a thin, dark, vacant-eyed girl in the yard, smoking a cigarette and pretending an interest in a little boy playing nearby. A small mongrel snoozed beside the steps—he opened one eye, then quickly closed it—and a crippled crow lurched about on one leg.

Camargo stopped the Chevy. Donahoo got out and walked over. "Anybody home?"

The girl stared at him blankly, her mind, if she had one, somewhere else. She didn't try to answer.

"She doesn't talk," somebody said then, and when Donahoo looked at the screen door, he could see parts of a woman, showing where her body touched the screen. "Just up and stopped. Nothing else to say."

"That can happen," Donahoo said.

"And should more often. Butch is away."

Donahoo stood in the hot dusty sun, looking at the impression she was making on the screen, and wondering about the one she was making on him. The screen was like a full-length veil. It gave her an air of mystery. He was into mysterious women these days. He kept thinking of Madam Zola.

"You a dick?" she wanted to know.

"Why would you ask?"

"That's either a gun or a bitch of a tumor."

"It's a colostomy bag. We wear 'em high in the Big City."

The door pushed open and she came out on the porch. She was barefoot and her hair was loose, butterscotch tumults that hung to her waist, and she was wearing a yellow polka-dot halter and white shorts.

"Okay, you're not a dick, you're a weirdo," she said, moving closer and hanging on the rail. Donahoo thought that the effect was almost scary. Dirigibles at war. "Maybe I can help you. What do you want?"

"I need a ton of parts for a '58 Corvair."

"Bullshit. The Corvair came out in '60. I *knew* you were a dick."

"Yeah, and I was just testing you."

"Sure."

Donahoo laughed and sat down at the foot of the stairs, wondering if all the cops she knew were stupid, and guessing probably. Up closer, she was even better, with a big splash of pumpkin freckles, marvelously liquid green eyes. "Okay. You made me." He looked around. There was nobody else but the girl and the boy and the dog and the crow. And Camargo in the Chevy. "I suppose you're Wonder Woman?"

"How original."

"Yeah, but what's important, do you know cars, WW?"

"Does a gynecologist know pussy?"

"Old European cars," Donahoo said. "I'm guessing here—a gut feeling?—but that's my bet. Mercedes, BMW. Maybe French. The Peugeot? This is a hunch. It could be Swedish. A Saab. Or Italian or British. I dunno. A Rover, huh?"

"You're losing me."

Dunahoo got out his Baggie with the little stick in it. He removed it and took her hand and turned it palm up. He placed the stick there carefully. "You know what that is?"

She looked at it. "No. Do you?"

"No."

"Can I go now?"

"Gimme a minute," Donahoo said. "It's probably off a car, okay? Broken off of something bigger. Maybe a floor mat."

She looked at him. "This is a restoration project?"

"Come on, gimme a minute," Donahoo said. "This is important. You could help solve a murder. So what do you think it is? Take a guess."

"What kind of murder?"

Donahoo decided to lie. "A little kid. They found this stuff sticking to his clothing. When they, uh, found him."

"Shit."

"Yeah."

She took a closer look at the stick. "I dunno."

"Take a guess."

"It's broken off of something?"

"Yeah."

"Like a floor mat?"

"Yeah."

"Maybe it's from the step plate that covers the rocker panel," she decided. "Cars now, they've got metal plates, aluminum. In older cars, the sixties, the seventies, they used plastic strips. Before that, it was metal. Now it's metal again. You figure it."

"Plastic?"

She handed the stick back. "Okay, rubber. This is rubber?"

"Yeah. Rubber." Donahoo put it in the Baggie. "Older European?"

"That's a start. Why don't you take a look?"

"Thanks. Now the rocker panel is ...?

"The doorjamb. It's where they hid the dope in *The French Connection*. So the cops take the whole fucking car apart, it's in pieces, and a body shop guy says, 'Gee, I dunno, we've looked everywhere except the rocker panels,' which is where they shoulda looked first, they're hollow. You remember what Gene Hackman said?"

"No."

"Neither do I."

She looked at him, disappointed. "Anyway, the step plate is on top of the rocker panel, okay? That's where they put the brag tag, Body by Fisher."

"Got it."

She went into the house and returned with a map. She passed him on the steps and went down to the Chevy. Her perfume clung for just an instant. Sugar plums. It could be sugar plums.

"Would you like to leave this?" she asked, looking the Chevy over, or maybe Camargo. "It would save a towing charge."

They drove, with her directions, X marks the spot, down several rows of wrecked cars, piled three and four high, sorted by make and year. The first six rows were Asian. Then the European makes started. The British first, Jags and MG's, Austins and a Morris Minor. A couple Rovers and one totaled Rolls or possibly a Bentley. The grill was gone.

"That *French Connection* case, it was fucked from the start," Camargo said. "It was star-crossed."

"Yeah, but it had a good car chase," Donahoo said.

Camargo parked and they got out. They went systematically through the stacks of British cars, checking all the rocker panels, looking for step plates with ribs that matched their little sticks.

Nothing came close. Either the material was different or the pattern didn't match. It was the same story with the rubber floor mats fused into the carpeting. They went through them all and drew a blank.

The French cars were next. Peugeots mostly, and a few Renaults, and an old Citroen. Again, nothing that matched. The Swedish wrecks, Volvos and Saabs, also produced nothing.

Donahoo began to wonder. He'd been so sure he'd find something here. Some easy match on some rare old car that would make his life simpler. He started on the Germans. The BMW's first, the largest presence, with reason. The old ones were so crappy, he thought. They looked like Yugos. Not much better than the early Hondas. He came to a stack of Mercedes Benzes. He went through them, ready to quit, disappointed. He clambered up to the top and to an old, faded black sedan. He got the door open.

Hello, Donahoo thought. There was a black rubber ribbed sheathing over the step plate. It had broken away in places. Little pieces of the ribbing—*little sticks*—clung precariously. He picked one up and compared it with the stick in his baggie. Exact match.

Donahoo opened the glove compartment. The manual was still there. Year, 1971. Model, 280SE 4.5.

Camargo was working on another pile. Donahoo called to him. "Frank!"

Camargo rose from the rotting casket that used to be a mustard yellow convertible. "Listen, Sarge," Camargo said, his face shining. "I got a name for the case. You're gonna love it. The Balboa Firefly."

CHAPTER NINETEEN

Oceanside. A military town, and there were three bars in this one block of Pacific Coast Highway. Rusty's, Lancers, and Duggan's North, all of which looked dreary. They were fitted among a dive shop, a hamburger joint serving out of a sidewalk window, a used furniture store overstocked on futons, and, on the corner, in what was once a service station, racks of used motorcycles proclaimed to be special bargains. The signs along the block said CHECKS CASHED and E-Z CREDIT and MILITARY WELCOME.

Mark Stevens, Marky to his new film friends, Mr. Stevens to aspiring porno queens, thought it was a long way to come to be offended. He parked and went into Duggan's North.

A young Marine was sitting in a back booth nursing a Bud. He was unmistakably a Marine. He had a Marine haircut and he was wearing a khaki T-shirt that showed off his Marine mucles. He also had that special look—a kind of cowed insolence—that is almost a badge of honor for a Marine PFC.

Stevens spotted him immediately. PFC Charles Kirk Robinson, attached to Company G, 3d Battalion, 7th Marines, Camp Pendleton. He was twenty-two. From Iowa. That might be corn in his ears.

Nice, Stevens thought. He hefted his portfolio case and moved directly to the booth. "Charles?"

The Marine looked up, surprised. He obviously had expected someone different. Stevens didn't mind. It happened all the time.

He wasn't the film producer type. He didn't have any varoom. He walked funny. Bad leg. Pain. "Yes. You Mr. Stevens?"

"I am."

Stevens shoved into the booth and got out his wallet and removed a business card. He pushed it across the table. The card said, Mark Stevens, Producer, Farthest Star Productions. Stevens let the Marine read it and then took it back.

"That's my last one," Stevens explained. "I've been handing them out like crazy." The Marine released the card readily. He didn't object, nor, more importantly, show any sign of suspicion. Passed the first test, Stevens thought. "You been waiting long?"

The Marine grinned and lifted his Bud. "It didn't matter."

"Yeah, well, I'm sorry I'm late," Stevens said, studying him. Actually, he didn't care what the kid looked like, but it was part of the routine, they expected it. "I had an interview on the way up. Solona Beach."

That did provoke a flicker. "I guess you got a lot of calls, huh?"

"I guess," Stevens said. He'd gotten a ton. The ad had read, HELP WANTED. Stud for porno movie. Good money. Pleasant work. Military man preferred.

"It's still open, though?"

"Why I'm here," Stevens said. "You want to do that again?"

"Sure."

Stevens excused himself and slid out of the booth and went to the bar. He ordered two Buds. The kid might work, he thought. The other two guys, they were too sharp. They were all over him like a bad paint job. They were places where they weren't supposed to be. But this kid? He was an innocent. He was waiting to be used.

The girl behind the bar brought the beer. "Two Bud, two bucks."

Stevens looked at her.

"It's Happy Hour."

"Hey, you're right, it is," Stevens said.

The young Marine had a bunch of photographs spread out on the table when Stevens returned to the booth. They were all of himself. He was shirtless in most of them. They had been taken in various locales. The beach. Camp Pendleton. Saudi Arabia.

"I thought you might want to look at these."

"Yes, please," Stevens said. He took a slug of his beer and then a long time examining the photographs. He said, "You're really buffed up, bloke. You must work out a lot."

"Some. Is that an English accent?"

"You noticed?" Stevens picked out the best photograph and put it aside. He didn't pocket it or anything. He just took temporary possession. "I try not to advertise. Well…"

"Uh, what do you think?"

"Why don't you tell me something about yourself?" Stevens suggested. "Tell me the kind of things you'd want me to know. Don't be shy. Let me hear the good things. All right?"

The Marine looked at him unsurely. "You mean personal?"

"Absolutely."

"Yeah, well," the Marine said, grinning. "Like I told you on the phone. I got a pretty big one." He hesitated, getting up his courage. "You're talking to an eight."

"Eight is good," Stevens said. "What else?"

"What else is there?"

Good question, Stevens thought. He drank some beer. He wondred if this was the time. Probably not.

"The girls seem to like it," the Marine said. He was still grinning. "That's what they say."

"There's a lot to like?"

"I guess."

Maybe now, Stevens thought. He picked up one of the photos taken in Saudi Arabia. It confirmed what was casually mentioned in their telephone conversation. The Marine standing alongside a rocket launcher. It was fairly small, portable. It looked like one guy could fire it without assistance. Maybe it would require two guys. Stevens was guessing. One or two. It could be jerry-rigged for one, though. He was pretty sure of that.

"That your weapon?" Stevens asked, putting the photo back.

"Was."

"What is it?"

"It's a TOW. We call it The Breaker."

"What's it break?"

"A tank."

"You're kidding."

"Uh uh. In half."

"Yeah? How accurate?"

"Well, put it this way, if there was a crow out there, it'd go straight up its ass."

"It sounds like something I could use," Stevens said, smiling. "I'm making a film now. We gotta blow up a circus bus."

"Why blow up a circus bus?"

"We're just clowning around."

For the first time, a shadow of doubt, faint, but nevertheless there, passed over Robinson's face.

"We'll think of something," Stevens said quickly. He unzippered his portfolio. "I guess you'd like to see the girl you'll be working with." He pulled out a large manila envelope and opened it. He removed an eight-by-ten color photograph of a nude woman. "What do you think?"

The Marine took it.

"Well?"

"Jesus," the Marine said. "She's, uh …" He stared in disbelief. "Beautiful."

Stevens said, "Yeah, and she's hot, too."

The Marine couldn't take his eyes off the photograph. "Gee, I don't think…" He finally looked up. "I don't think I've ever seen a girl this pretty."

Stevens said, "Yeah, but the important thing, she's hot, Charles. She's gonna make you a ten."

"You mean it?" the Marine asked. He couldn't believe it. "I got the job?"

"Absolutely," Stevens told him, taking the photo back. "We've got big plans for you, Charles."

"My friends call me Kirkie."

"Okay. Kirkie. And you can call me Marky, Kirkie."

CHAPTER TWENTY

They were crowded into Donahoo's office, eating cheese-and-bean burritos, a compromise. Gomez had wanted Carnitas Fantasticas. He had mentioned, several times, that while they were called cheese-and-bean burritos, they were really bean and cheese. He had suggested that they would probably find the killer before they found the cheese.

Donahoo was on one phone and waiting for the other to ring. He was on hold, listening to hold music, Montavani. He'd been to Mercedes Benz L.A., he'd been to Mercedes Benz College Park, Georgia, and now he was in Montvail, New Jersey. He was waiting for a guy named Gus in Customer Service at Mercedes Benz of North America. Gus had said he'd be a minute.

"I'm gonna need an army." Montrose said, complaining to Donahoo. "Maybe computers." He had spent the morning checking property records. He had just come in and he hadn't had a chance to share. He knew more than he wanted to know about Balboa Park. "You know what I'm talking about?"

"Not yet."

"Yeah, well, the trouble is, there's been a shitload of activity in that area, but it's not people."

"It's elves?" Gomez asked. He was still pissed about the burritos.

"It's corporations, Sarge," Montrose said, ignoring Gomez. "Mostly corporations, and they're not just California corporations, there's other states, other countries. Korea, Japan, China. You're not gonna believe this. Bulgaria."

Camargo said, "Bullshit."

Montrose got out his notebook. "Fortune Holdings, Inc., Sofia, Bulgaria. They own a vacant building at Front and Juniper."

"Bulgarians?"

"That's what it says."

Camargo said, "Bulgarians, are they still Communists? You should check that. How can Communists own property?"

Gomez said, "Yeah. The state owns everything."

"Is there any sort of pattern?" Donahoo asked. He was listening to Montrose. He was listening to Mantovani. "Love Is a Many Splendored Thing." He was waiting for his other phone to ring. Come on, ring.

In the *Union-Trib*'s afternoon replate, the story about the three homeless being slain, there was a brief insert. *In an unusual development, Sgt. Tommy Donahoo, head of the police department's Squad 5, has been assigned to the case, working with Homicide. Donahoo said he had reason to believe that someone with personal knowledge of the incident was trying to establish confidential contact with authorities. He said they should call him directly at police headquarters. Squad 5 normally deals with threats against public property and government institutions as well high-ranking personages. Officials declined comment on the seeming contradiction.*

"Pattern? You mean somebody owning more than one piece of property?"

"That would be a pattern." This from Gomez.

"Not really," Montrose said, ignoring his tormentor. "In some instances, the same person owns several properties, ditto for corporations, but nothing major. No one big player."

"Unless the same person owns a bunch of corporations?"

"Exactly," Montrose said. "Which is why I'm gonna need an army."

Donahoo was still listening to Mantovani. He said, "Never mind the fucking army. What I want you to do, talk to an investment broker, Montrose. Find out how it works. You buy property and you wanta hide the fact. How does that work? Have him take you all the way, go offshore. Hire him if you have to. He's an expert. Pay him his rate. Put it on Gomez's expense account."

Gomez almost choked. Beans went flying.

Donahoo said, "Did you lose any cheese there?"

Montrose asked, "Can I have a computer?"

Gus came on the line. Donahoo waved Montrose off. "Okay, the 280SE, 4.5," Gus said. "That was a two-year car, '71 and '72. Worldwide, they made 13,507. Not too many around."

Donahoo wrote the number down. He asked, "Would any other Mercedes have that kind of step panel?"

"Uh huh. The SEL, the same two years. But the part may not fit. The SEL is longer."

"That doesn't matter. It's the 280SEL, right?"

"Right."

"How many of them?"

"Lemme see. You're looking at 9,802."

Looking *for,* Donahoo thought. "Thank you, Gus. I really appreciate it." He wrote down the second number and did the addition. Total, 23,309. "I've only got a couple more questions. I need a bible."

"Mercedes Benz Production Models, by Nitzke."

"I need fanatics."

"The Mercedes Benz Club of America. You'll also find some in *Hemming's Motor News.*" He gave the telephone numbers. "Anything else?"

"Yeah. I love ya."

Donahoo hung up and glanced again at the total number. That wasn't too bad, he thought. He was looking for a car that was a quarter century old. There couldn't be that many still running. And, out of the whole world, there couldn't be that many in San Diego.

"May I finish?" Montrose said. He had a kid's expression. He had saved the good part for last. "I ran across an old friend. Listen up, okay?"

They all went on alert. Donahoo was going to pass the numbers to Camargo. He paused to listen.

"GP Investments," Montrose said proudly, reading from his notebook. "I found this just as I was leaving. GP Investments owns four adjacent buildings. The legal descriptions look like it's maybe half a block altogether. Hawthorne and Albatross. Center of the glide path."

"Okay. You gonna tell us who owns GP?"

"I think Eric Victor Hudson. He's listed as president on one of his business cards. I saw it when we booked him."

"Center of the glide path?"

"Right in the middle."

"Whoa," Camargo said, trying to sound wise. "This case, it's got two trains. One track, two trains."

Donahoo was thinking aloud. "Why would Hudson buy that shit?"

Montrose shrugged. "I dunno. But he picked it up about a year ago. For practically nothing."

"He owns stuff all over town," Gomez said. "So he's got some shit. That's natural."

Camargo said, "We know where he is. Why don't we ask him?"

"Yeah, why don't you do that?" Donahoo suggested. He indicated the door. "If you hurry, you'll have it done by five. You're home to Marie."

"Alone?"

"Yeah. By yourself. Montrose, he's doing the financial, and Gomez, you're going to the DMV. I want a printout. Everybody in San Diego county who owns a 1971, '72 Mercedes Benz, 280SE, 280SEL."

Camargo's face pinched with the hurt. "I should be doing that."

True, Donahoo thought, but he didn't want it screwed up, so it was going to Gomez. He gave Gomez his notes. He said, to Gomez, "This is crucial. Listen to me. I want to be ready if DMV records don't give us this guy on a spear. So let's not assume anything. The car we're looking for—this old?—it may not be currently registered. Or, if it is—the guy's a killer?—it could be fake. Whatever. So you find Palmer, Cominsky. I want 'em to go through the *Union-Trib* classified. Back a year. I want to know anybody who sold one and who he sold it to. They can check *The Reader,* too."

"*The Auto Trader?*"

"Now you're thinking. And call some places, huh? I dunno. Used car lots? Auctions?" He considered. "There's a national Mercedes club. Is there a local one?"

"You got it."

Camargo was staring.

"Frank, get outa here, willya?" Donahoo told him. "You're standing around, Hudson is gonna make bail. You'll never find him. He's gonna run away to Canada."

"Half a million bail?"

"For First Fidelity Trust? That's birdseed. Now fuck off. Oh, and if you pass a video store, get me *The French Connection,* okay? Buy it, don't rent. It's a present."

Camargo said, "Are we on the same page?"

Donahoo, he was kidding, he said, "Frank, we're not in the same book, we're not in the same library. Fuck off."

Camargo left.

Montrose said, "Jesus, Sarge ..."

Donahoo gave him a look. "Are you still here?"

"Now I'm missing something." Gomez complained. "What are we saying? Hudson may be involved in the killings?"

Donahoo wondered. Was that what they were saying? No. What they were saying, he might be *connected*. Maybe a link, he was going to say, and then the phone rang, on the line set aside specially at the switchboard, and he forgot all about Hudson. So far he'd had three crank calls, and, inconceivably, the real mystery at hand, never to be solved, a wrong number, a lady who wanted a mole removed. But every time it rang his heart jumped.

Montrose turned on the tape machine. Donahoo waited for a second ring. Then he picked up. "Sergeant Donahoo," he said. "How can I help you?"

"You can go to a pay phone," Stryker told him. "Spud Murphy's. I'll call you there. Bah-bye."

Irish Spud Murphy's Boxing Gym was two blocks away, a fighter's gym at Twelfth and Broadway. Gomez drove Donahoo there. "You think he's real?" Gomez wondered.

Donahoo shrugged helplessly. Normally, no. There were so many crackpots out there. The odds were against it. But he had a feeling about this one. He felt—so deeply it was embarrassing—afraid. The caller had sounded like death.

Gomez squealed to a stop. Donahoo pushed out, looking around, trying to figure it. If the guy was for real, he could be watching. There were a hundred places he could call from, probably more. He could be anywhere.

"Let's do the tap," he said. He'd take the chance. He wanted the guy's voice, more of it, all of it, every nuance.

Gomez nodded. There was a pay phone outside the front entrance. They went to it together. Donahoo lifted the receiver while keeping the hook down with his other hand. Gomez quickly taped a tiny microphone to the earpiece cap. The mike was wired to a small recording device the size of a deck of cards. He stuck it to the bottom of the coin box. Donahoo put the receiver back in place.

"Take a look inside," Donahoo said. "There could be another pay phone."

Gomez nodded again and went into the gym. Donahoo crossed to the car and shut the door. He had left it wide open exiting. Too much excitement, he thought. The call had given him a real whack. He could still feel the adrenaline.

Was the guy real?

Maybe, Donahoo thought. Possibly. The call had been like the notes. Total control. No bullshit. In and out. The guy knew what he was doing.

Donahoo glanced around the seedy neighborhood. The police headquarters had been built here, in part, to help restore it, but that hadn't happened yet. It could happen, but it was going to take more time. He was looking at a shabby mix of borderline businesses. Advertising specialties. Plastic molds. Storefronts with living quarters above. Herbal remedies and used appliances. Some battered old hotels sticking up above, facing other streets, checkered with hundreds of windows, each a question mark. He had the stomach-twisting feeling that the killer was hidden at one of them, and that he, Donahoo, was out in the open. The killer was in control.

Gomez came back. "There is one, but it's out of order. There's a sign on it. I also checked. It's dead."

"How long?"

"They say a week."

"Tell Montrose," Donahoo said. "He could be ordering the wrong trace."

"I already did."

"Was he?"

"Yeah. But..." Gomez shrugged. "First choice, inside."

Wrong, Donahoo thought. The first choice was outside. Here, on the sidewalk, where he was out in the open, standing within an easy shot of some fucking maniac.

"The guy said Spud Murphy's," Gomez said, aware of Donahoo's expression. He gestured toward the door. "In there. That's Spud Murphy's."

Donahoo let it go. Spick and Spook. They were always hammering on each other. But if someone else offered the slightest criticism? They came to each other's defense like brothers.

Gomez looked at his watch. "He can still make it."

Donahoo waved it off. He doubted if it really mattered. The killer, in control, wouldn't be on the phone long enough, he thought. He would be fast. Like his notes, in and out. Like the call he'd just made, bang. So he'd be fast and he'd have something going for him. He'd protect himself.

The phone rang. Donahoo picked it up. "Yes."

"This is better," Stryker said. "I'm calling from a car phone, a stolen car phone, a mobile, so I don't imagine you can trace the call, but with this arrangement, it makes me feel more comfortable."

Donahoo had his hand over the speaker. He said, "Car phone."

Gomez threw up his hands. He swore softly.

"I'll make this brief," Stryker said. "I'm very serious. This isn't negotiable."

"Okay," Donahoo said. "I'm not going to try. But I need something from you. Proof you wrote the note."

There was a pause. "You get crank calls?"

"Yeah. The note at the church. What did it say?"

"Talk to me. So talk."

"The note in the park. I need to know you're the same guy."

"I can do it."

"Okay. So talk."

"Listen. I'm going to keep killing until you close the airport. I'm going to keep killing and killing and killing. It's going to be the worst kind of bloodbath. Do you understand?"

Donahoo felt the hair on his neck bristle. "Hey, I hear you, loud and clear. This is something that goes straight to the proper authorities. You can trust me to pass along whatever you want to tell them."

"Fine. Tomorrow, you can let me know, tell me—the proper authorities—their decision. I'll call you."

Donahoo said, "Wait. Just a minute. What have you got against the airport?"

"It annoys me."

"Hey, it annoys a lot of people," Donahoo said. "It pisses me off. But that's not a good enough reason. You've gotta have another reason."

"Oh, you're smart," Stryker told him, not arguing. "I knew that. I've read about you. You're famous. I thought I might get you."

"Get me?"

"That you'd be assigned," Stryker said. "You believe in fate? It's why you're against me. You're the smartest? That's why I get you to outwit and elude." He paused, but only to breathe. "Let's see how smart you really are."

There was a strange tone on the line. Donahoo grabbed Gomez and rolled out into the street with him. The pay phone exploded and took half the wall with it.

Gomez struggled free of Donahoo's grasp. He got to his feet, dazed. He said, "How the fuck did he do that?"

Donahoo, still huddled in the street, was trying to push down the same stomach-twisting fear he had taken to the phone. Oh, Jesus, he was running scared, he thought. The fucking looney had him ... *running*?

CHAPTER TWENTY-ONE

If he had a virtue, it was patience, Valesy thought. He could be very patient. He could stay silently hidden somewhere for long periods. He could wait for hours, days. Once, because he knew he might be that long, he had taken water, provisions, and he had waited a week, a remarkable feat of endurance, in a small space in a factory's air ducts. He had lived on food concentrates and minimal portions of carefully rationed water. He had excreted into Baggies and kept the waste in a garbage bag. He had exercised by stretching like a cat. When, at last, he dropped down for the kill, he had been agile as a monkey.

Valesy smiled. The monkey who infiltrated Pyongyang. The monkey who left three scientists dead and forced a would-be nuclear power to start all over. His most important assignment, considering the stakes, until, of course, the craven revolt against Gorbachev. Boris Yuschev had summoned him. He had shown him two photographs. He had not uttered the names. "Make it look like suicide," he had ordered. Valesy often wondered now. If he had spared them, the revolt, perhaps, would have succeeded. Hard-line Communists would still rule Russia. The USSR would still exist.

Perhaps. Perhaps not. Valesy would never know. The loyalties of that uncertain time seemed to change with the hour. They ushered the strangest consequences. When he reported back to Yuschev, the old general was dead. It looked like suicide.

Valesy was waiting now inside a large hilltop house in Chula Vista. Originally, he had planned to wait outside, in the shrubery in the front yard, but upon checking the house's security system, he had decided to enter. It was a primitive system and easy to override. He was glad he had broken in. It was a fine old house, a comfortable, pleasant place, full of rich furnishings and appealing art. It was stocked with all manner of good food. Caviar. Smoked salmon. Small crackers that resembled goldfish. You couldn't eat just one. A feast in a palace. A thousand times better than waiting in the shrubbery.

He had changed his mind about things several times during the course of the day. At the outset, when to do this, or even if it should be done, that had been in doubt. Then, coming here, he thought Chula Vista, like much of San Diego, was essentially a slum, and that had worried him, the mean, crowded houses, but then he came to this fine neighborhood, the large, expensive homes spread far apart. Lastly, if it got too late, he'd miss the final trolley, that had briefly canceled things, but only momentarily. What did it matter? There were many places he could hide. He would wait until morning, that's all. He was patient.

Not that he had a choice now. At dusk, a Chula Vista police car had arrived, swung up into the circular driveway. A uniformed officer had got out and knocked on the door. He had shouted, several times, "Mr. Hudson?!!"

He had returned to his car and radioed a report. Valesy had heard part of it as the officer drove away. "No. No sign of him." And, "No. There's no cop here."

Valesy had puzzled over the meaning of that. It meant the police, some other jurisdiction, were looking for Hudson, and looking for one of their own—that much he assumed. He also assumed it wasn't very important. If it was important, there would be more officers, they'd probably stay, possibly enter. So, obviously, they were just checking.

Two hours later the same police officer was back and went through the same routine. This time, in his radio report, he mentioned a name, something like Cargo. He said Cargo wasn't around. He said he'd keep checking.

The dispatcher said, "Don't kill yourself."

They were checking. Just checking.

Why? Valesy had picked through the neat-as-a-pin house and found only one clue. It was a note in a cigar box. It read like a housekeeper. It said, *Mr. H. I'm going to take a few days off. Let me know when you're back. Praying for you. Mary.* It wasn't dated.

Well, one thing, Hudson was expected back, so he'd wait, Valesy thought.

He'd wait because he had no choice. If the police were checking on Hudson, it might grow into something more serious, and, possibly, he might be taken into custody. There'd be no killing him then.

A car swung into the driveway. The police again? Valesy moved to the window beside the door. He had opened it a crack for better observation. The new arrival was a late-model Lincoln Town Car. Not Hudson's. Hudson drove a Cadillac Eldorado.

The Lincoln stopped abruptly. The headlights remained on. Hudson exited from the passenger side. He was unsteady on his feet.

"You sure you won't come in for a drink?" Hudson asked, the words slurred.

"No, I've had enough," the driver, a man, told him. "Get some sleep. I'll call you tomorrow."

Hudson looked in at him. "You're sure?"

"Positive. Get some sleep."

Hudson said, "We did have a party."

"Yeah. Now get some sleep."

"Thanks for bailing me out."

"Eric. Get some sleep, willya?"

"What about my car?"

"In the morning."

The driver leaned over and pulled the door shut. Hudson backed off and waved ineffectively. He said, barely audible now, "Thanks."

Valesy was a witness through the crack at the window. The Lincoln drifted back and dipped into the street. Hudson, unsteady on his feet, watched it depart. Then he turned and started for the house. The floodlight came on, triggered by his movement on the path, illuminating him starkly. He reacted as if he hadn't expected it, had somehow forgotten. A big, handsome man with a shock of white hair, almost a mane. The red nose of a serious drinker. His suit was crumpled, the coat unbuttoned. His shirttail was out. No tie.

Bail? What offense? Valesy wondered, but he wasn't going to ask. He eased the window shut and moved over to the door.

Hudson took a long time getting the door unlocked. Valesy didn't mind waiting for him.

"Home again," Hudson said, shoving the door open. He reeked of Scotch.

Valesy put a makeshift knife in his heart. Hudson grunted and fell heavily to the floor.

Camargo was slumped in an unmarked police parked half a block away. The Lincoln Town Car swept past him and disappeared into the night.

"Alone at last," Camargo said. He looked at his watch. Marie was going to kill him. He got out of his car and started up the street toward the big house on the hill. He'd waited all evening for this chance. Five minutes alone with Eric Smith Hudson. The answers to two questions: First, why the hell would you buy property in the glide path to Lindbergh Field? Second, why have we got one track here, two trains coming?

He was going to get answers. He was going to show Donahoo.

Both the entrance to the house and the driveway's half-circle were brightly illuminated. Camargo felt like he had entered some sort of demilitarized zone. A no-man's land where his progress was under careful scrutiny. Hudson was probably watching him approach, he thought. Or maybe he'd be on a television monitor. The place had the bucks for it. This wasn't a house. It was a mansion. Three stories, with bay windows, turrets, a cupola. Try buying it on a cop's salary.

Camargo reached the front door. He looked for a bell but couldn't find one. There was just the big brass knocker. He banged it twice, sharply. The door eased open.

"Hello?" Camargo said.

No answer. Camargo pushed the door open wider. The house was dark. The light behind him sliced inside, an arc moving with the door, revealing a richly embroidered carpet and an elaborate wrought-iron table with a marble slab top.

"Hello?" Camargo repeated. He went inside. "Eric Hudson?"

The moving arc of light followed. It came upon Hudson, sprawled across the carpet, appearing lifeless. Camargo went to him. The stupid fucker, he'd put away enough, he must have passed out, Camargo thought. He started to undo his shirt before realizing that he was dead. He pulled open his jacket and found a stain of puddling blood.

The door slammed shut and it was dark again.

"You came alone?" Valesy asked.

"Yes," Camargo answered, the first thing that came into his mind, spontaneous and driven by surprise and alarm. He instantly wanted to deny it, to say that there were others, more police, on their way, but now he couldn't speak. He was frozen with fear. Death had threatened in the rough voice behind him.

"Then you are stupid," Valesy said.

It was the last thing Camargo heard. An axelike judo chop sliced at the base of his skull. His head exploded with blinding pain.

Valesy rolled him over and found the harness, the gun, the .38 Special. The cop the Chula Vista police had been looking for?

It had to be. He considered briefly. It was never wise to kill a cop. But he didn't know what the cop might know about him. It was possible he possessed information he had yet to submit to his superiors. Better to err on the side of caution. Besides, he didn't want to waste time binding, gagging. He wanted to be long gone from here before any alarm was raised. He wanted all of the night's dwindling hours.

He took the wallet, the keys. He took the Special. Maybe it could like a suicide? He almost laughed aloud at his joke.

114

CHAPTER TWENTY-TWO

"I'm surprised at you, falling for the old pay-telephone trick, Tommy," Saperstein said. He bumped out of the station's parking lot and aimed his new Ford Crown Victoria down Broadway. "The guy says, 'Can't we talk somewhere?' You go rushing over, quick as a virgin. Ka-boom."

"We all make mistakes," Donahoo said. They were already passing Irish Spud Murphy's. The sidewalk was barricaded. The hole in the wall still gaped.

"Not fatal." Saperstein glanced at Lewis. "What's the lab think?"

"Plastic," Lewis told him. "Planted in the coin box. Detonated by a line tone. Kind of sophisticated."

"So now we've got a sophisticate? It gets better."

"And worse."

"Yeah."

Donahoo grimaced. He was tired of listening to their bullshit merry-go-round. He was tired, he was worried, he was frustrated, and, like the gas from a bad meal, the fear still lingered in him. He wanted an answer for the looney. He said, "What do we tell him?"

"All in good time," Lewis counseled.

Saperstein said, "It's why we're going to see the Mayor."

"This is a police matter," Donahoo complained. "It has nothing to do with politics."

Saperstein said, "That's where you're wrong, Tommy."

"I don't think so."

"I do."

Donahoo wouldn't quit. "Give me one good reason."

"It's the same reason that cats bury their shit. If they didn't, people would kill 'em."

Driving with one hand, Saperstein reviewed the report from the investigating officers on the other, more hurtful case of the moment, the slaying of Frank Camargo. This one tore him, and it showed. He hadn't lost an investigator in three years. He was taking it personally.

Donahoo, watching him, wondered what part was sorrow, what part was apprehension. Frank Camargo, he'd be buried in a couple of days, but there'd be an indelible notation somewhere on Saperstein's personnel file, not about to go away. That review board in the sky, someday it was going to ask, "How many men did you put in the earth, Assistant Chief, Detectives?"

Donahoo had yet to deal with his own sorrow. He hadn't believed it when they called them with the news. "You're kidding," that was his first stupid, angry response. It didn't seem possible. It still didn't. Donahoo was waiting to believe it. Then he'd cry.

"Let's reconstruct," Saperstein said. "Hudson makes bail. He is released at four-forty. He leaves with his benefactor, Paul Duffin, senior vice president/operations for First Fidelity Trust. They spend the evening drinking around town. The usual haunts. The Chi Chi Club. Etcetera. Duffin, sworn statement, says he dropped Hudson off at his, Hudson's, house about ten-twenty, in the driveway, nothing untoward. He leaves. Hudson enters the house and is killed by a prowler. It looks like a prowler because he ransacked the house. He stole things, jewelry, a strongbox." Saperstein briefly showed a piece of paper. "Here's a list from the housekeeper. Plus both wallets are missing." He said, "We think it's a prowler because of the knife. It was ground down from angle iron. It's a prison shiv."

Lewis said, a complaint, "Hey," and Saperstein, annoyed, corrected to avoid collision with an oncoming laundry truck. He took advantage of the interruption to make sure he had the full attention of his audience. Lewis up front with him. Donahoo, Gomez, and Montrose wedged in the back, reluctant sardines. They were going to City Hall.

Saperstein said, "Frank Camargo, he's been following them, hoping for a chance to talk to Hudson, and now he's parked outside the house, waiting for Duffin to leave. Duffin does so. Then Camargo goes up to the house to talk to Hudson. And walks in on a murder. And gets himself killed. The prowler stuns him with a blow—a judo chop?—at the base of the skull. Then he shoots him with his own gun. The shot muffled by a sofa cushion." Saperstein looked around again. To Lewis and Donahoo and Gomez and Montrose. "So what do we have here? Is the prowler a wild coincidence? Or did somebody—like maybe Paul Duffin?—want Hudson dead?"

Donahoo had his eyes closed. He was thinking of the fat and warm Marie. This was going to kill her, he thought. She'd be cold forever.

Saperstein said, "Let's reconstruct. Camargo—who knows on this?—apparently saw Hudson and Duffin leave the lockup. Let's, for the moment, assume that. He follows, waiting for them to split up, so he can talk privately to Hudson, and he's prepared to make a night of it. He calls his wife. He says he'll be working late on a case. But he doesn't call in. He doesn't advise his case supervisor. He doesn't request assistance. He's what?—who knows on this?—maybe doing a little grandstanding? Maybe a little glory hogging?"

"I ordered him," Donahoo said.

"To talk to Hudson in jail."

"To talk to Hudson."

"Alone?"

Donahoo gestured. "We'd all put in a full day. We got busy with the bloodbath-killer call. I didn't think it was necessary to double team. It was, you know, a preliminary inquiry, that's all. We could grill Hudson later."

"Out of jail, it would be a two-man job, though?"

"Yes," Donahoo admitted. "Normally." He wondered if he was covering his ass and he couldn't decide if he needed to do so. "Where are you going here?"

"Why wouldn't Camargo ask for help?"

"I told you. It had been a long day."

"He wanted to spare his fellow officers? That's why you couldn't raise him on the radio? That's why he didn't answer his beeper? That's why you've gotta ask the Chula Vista cops to look for him?"

"He's running silent, he must have had a reason, I don't know why." Donahoo looked to Lewis. "What's the problem here?"

Lewis shrugged for answer. He took possession of the report of the investigating officers. He also got the list from the house-keeper. He put them in his tattered file folder.

"Let me ask another question, Tommy," Saperstein said, talking over Lewis's endeavors. "What is Camargo doing there anyway? As I recall, Hudson wasn't Camargo's collar, Tommy. He belonged to these gentlemen." He motioned to Gomez and Montrose. "Why not assign them?"

"How many times do I have to say it? They were busy. More important things. So Frank, excuse me, he was appropriate. In my opinion."

"Okay," Saperstein said. "What we know: Camargo follows them. Duffin, to a degree, confirms this. He says he saw Camargo at Pure Platinum. This was around eight. He doesn't remember seeing him after that. Obviously, though, Camargo tailed them to Chula Vista. He wouldn't go there ahead of them." Saperstein found Gomez. "Would he?"

"That, uh, depends," Gomez said nervously. This was his first car ride with Saperstein in Saperstein's new Crown Victoria. His apprehension showed. "Frank might have decided to go ahead after Duffin spotted him."

"Okay. And another possibility?"

"Frank didn't wait in the street. He went to the house."

"The prowler got Camargo before he got Hudson? Is that what you're saying?"

"It's possible. But what difference does it make?"

"Is that your answer?"

Gomez looked around helplessly. "Yeah. That's my answer."

Saperstein's scowl moved to the rearview mirror and Donahoo. "Tommy?"

"It doesn't make any difference," Donahoo said. "Unless the prowler wasn't a prowler. Unless Frank planned to meet him there. Unless..." He crossed his eyes for Gomez's benefit. "We could do this all day."

Saperstein's face darkened. He was going to answer but they had arrived. He cut off a citizen and turned off Broadway onto Second Avenue. He commandeered the first parking space, which happened to be three slots for motorcycles.

"You guys go ahead," he said then, addressing the backseat. "We'll see you up there. Lewis and I need to get our ducks together."

"What ducks?" Donahoo was still pushing.

"None of your business."

Donahoo shoved out wordlessly, quickly followed by Gomez and Montrose.

"Two things I want," Saperstein said as the door closed. "First, I want Camargo killed in the line of duty. If I can't have that, I want, second, to come out squeaky clean. That means a full and thorough investigation completely independent of Squad 5. That means nobody is spared the utmost scrutiny. Nobody."

Lewis said, "Nobody?"

"Get a hearing aid."

Outside, Montrose was chasing Donahoo. "What the fuck is going on?" Montrose demanded.

"Politics," Donahoo told him. "Just politics." He hoped so. He hoped that's all it was. "This is City Hall."

CHAPTER TWENTY-THREE

Mayor Gordon Fletcher put his slender fingers together, forming a steeple, or perhaps he meant to suggest a house of cards. In any event, it would soon collapse. His hands moved constantly. He kept picking up things, discarding them. Pencils. Notepad. Cigarettes. Ashtray. He was a small, boyish-looking man. He had a baby face, pink, smooth, and large wet blue eyes. His hair was a wispy silk and thinning. He was capable enough, as a line of fallen opponents attested, but he had an image problem. There was a joke going around that he went into McDonald's to order a hamburger and they gave him a picture to color. At the moment he looked like a grumpy child playing at a desk that was too big for him.

He said, his steeple falling, "I don't like this."

"None of us do, Gordon," Police Chief John Helmcken assured him. Helmcken had been waiting when they all filed in, Saperstein, Lewis, Donahoo, Gomez, and Montrose, sorted by rank and tenure, marching in like soldiers, a show of competence and force. "Why such a large a group?" Fletcher had asked, and Saperstein had said, "In case you have questions," and Fletcher had told him, "Okay, the first question is, Why such a large group?"

They still hadn't moved off that dime. Helmcken was saying, "This kind of case—we've all got to know what we're doing."

Why *you* are here, Donahoo thought. You and Saperstein. He felt even more strongly now that the meeting was bullshit. The Mayor wasn't going to be of any help. If they stayed long enough, he'd find a way to be a hindrance.

Fletcher said, "I take it there are … recommendations?"

"That's evolving. It's why we're here."

"Evolving?"

"Yes."

"Now I'm starting to feel lonely," Fletcher said. "Do we have some help coming? Maybe the FBI?"

Saperstein picked it up. "The FBI doesn't investigate murders. We've alerted them, of course, because of the nature of the threat, and if there is some indication of a conspiracy here …" He shuffled some papers. "What we seem to have, at the moment, one crackpot, murders only. We still have jurisdiction."

"Okay. What's the other good news?"

Saperstein picked it up again. He said, "Let's reconstruct. It'll give you a better sense of what we're dealing with. You know about the first murder. The, uh, homosexual in the park."

Helmcken leaned back and out of it. It was typical of him to have come alone, and he would go back alone, too. For the past year he had been distancing himself from the department presence. He was Donahoo's size, a huge gray Scot slab that intimidated without effort, but the fire had gone out. There were rumors of cancer.

"Then the three homeless at First Presbyterian Church," Saperstein said. "The same gun. There also was a second note, 'Talk to me.' Subsequently, an anonymous call was made to the department, responding to a story in the paper. This was a planted item which encouraged such a contact."

Encouraged, huh? Donahoo thought. He was looking around the office and trying not to look at Faye Stuart. The Mayor's executive assistant was a tall, willowy, very attractive blonde who, maybe thirty-five, maybe even forty, could still grace the cover of *Vogue*.

"There was a brief conversation. It was resumed a short time later at an outdoor pay telephone."

Donahoo wondered if there was such a thing as an interior decorator of political offices. It would be a great job, you'd just have to do it once, the rest would never deviate. Big desk, *oversize* desk. U.S. flag, state flag, city flag, all on brown poles capped by brass eagles. Appropriate seal. Picture of the President. Picture of the office holder with the President. Or, if the officer holder wasn't a member of the correct political party, picture of the office holder with the Governor. Or…

"Unfortunately, we do not have a recording of that second conversation."

"Why not?"

"Because the fucking phone blew up," Donahoo said. He finally looked at Faye Stuart. "My apologies."

She glanced at him briefly. Her expression didn't change. It was one of alert but reserved interest. She had come to the meeting with it. Cold fish? Donahoo didn't think so. Ice queen. She was new, on the job six months, not a local, from Sacramento. She was supposed to be helping Fletcher plan a run for Governor. She was supposed to be sleeping with him.

"I have the report here," Saperstein said. He didn't miss a beat. "The conversation."

Fletcher's baby-blue eyes fell on Donahoo. "You're the officer?"

"Yes."

"I know you, don't I? Tommy Donahoo, right?"

"Yes," Donahoo admitted. "But I don't know how right."

"Keep up the good work."

"I'll try."

Saperstein started reading from the report. "This isn't, of course, verbatim."

"Perhaps the officer could tell us in his own words," Faye Stuart suggested. "That might be more…" She looked at Saperstein. "Relevant."

Saperstein set the report aside. "Certainly."

"It's just what's in there," Donahoo said. He was sitting behind Saperstein. He was glad he couldn't see his face. "There was a threat made as follows: The caller said, 'This isn't negotiable.'"

Faye Stuart had picked up the report. She had found the place and she was following along.

Donahoo continued: "He said, 'I'm going to keep killing until you close the airport. I'm going to keep killing and killing and killing. It's going to be the worst kind of bloodbath.' The caller said, 'Do you understand?'"

"You have a good memory," Faye Stuart said, smiling.

"And?" Fletcher asked.

"There was further conversation. I told him I would advise the appropriate authorities. He said he wanted the answer tomorrow, that's today."

"What answer?"

"If the airport is going to be closed."

"Well, for Christ's sake, that's ridiculous, the guy is crazy," Fletcher complained. "He's insane." He looked to Helmcken for confirmation. "We've been struggling with the airport problem for decades. How are we supposed to suddenly close it? Where are the planes supposed to land?"

"They could be diverted," Faye Stuart suggested. "There's Montgomery Field. Or either of the naval air stations."

Fletcher flushed. "That's not an option. I'm not going to let some nut case push this city around. We don't want to give crackpots the idea that blackmail works. The next guy, he'll tell us that we've got to close the harbor, and the next guy, the border. It starts, where does it stop?"

"I was thinking of buying time," she told him.

Here we go, Donahoo thought. All downhill. He couldn't figure Saperstein. The guy was too smart for this shit ride. They shouldn't be here, none of them. Saperstein should have sent over a written report with a written recommendation. He shouldn't be looking for direction. He should be giving it.

"Okay, time," Fletcher said. "If that's what you need, if I can help, sure. But it can't look like we're capitulating. It's got to be accomplished some other way." He again appealed to Helmcken. "How much time do you need?"

Helmcken looked to Saperstein, who looked to Lewis, who pretended he didn't notice, and that left him, Donahoo.

"Oh, hey," Donahoo said, and it wasn't until then, until after it happened, that he tried to dodge being blind-sided. "I'm just decoration here."

Faye Stuart was still holding the report. "You're the officer in charge of the case."

Donahoo waited till he had his anger reined. "Yes, I am," he told her. "I'm afraid I am." He suddenly hated Saperstein. The fucking sonofabitch, he thought. The cocksucker. Saperstein, perfect, unblemished record, gunning for the top job, he didn't want his ass on the line in this no-win beauty. He was passing.

"We're waiting," Faye Stuart prompted.

Donahoo looked at her. Total ice. "What was the question?"

"How much time do you need?"

"Well, as much as we can get, and that's from the killer, not from this meeting," Donahoo said, plunging in.

"I don't want a limit set here. I want it open ended. When I talk to this guy, I want to be able spin it out, go with it. I want to make him think he's winning when he's really losing."

"How do you prove good faith? Are you suggesting that we do divert to Montgomery?"

"No. That's too much, too soon. We don't have to go that far. For the moment, maybe we can offer a smaller carrot. We can tell him closure is in the works. But it's going to take a while to arrange. We can do some things to show our good intentions. Maybe land an airliner at Montgomery. Like it's a trial run or something. Make it public. Leak the landing, in advance, to one of the TV stations, the *Union-Trib*."

Fletcher broke in. "That's capitulation."

"No, it isn't. Nobody knows what it is, it's a mystery. The media is wondering what is going on. They're asking questions, and they're not getting answers. All they know, something's in the wind, and they'll report that, the no comments. That might satisfy him."

"For how long?"

"I don't know," Donahoo admitted. "Two, maybe three days. Maybe two seconds. How do you predict what a looney is going to do? Understand, I don't want to think limit. How this works, the only way it can work, is to make it up as we go along."

"Okay. And what's the down side?"

"Time runs out. He realizes we've been screwing him around. That really sets him off. The bloodbath begins anew. Maybe he starts looking for who's to blame."

Saperstein said, "Let's not get carried away."

"I'm a target, you're a target," Donahoo said. "I almost got blown to ratshit yesterday. And I was being *nice* to him."

Fletcher was back. "What are you suggesting? Retaliation?"

"It's possible."

"Bring in the flack jackets," Fletcher said, for Faye Stuart's benefit. "I'm a thirty-six. That's the chest, not the waist." He said, "I still don't like this."

"Well, there is an alternative, of course," Donahoo said slowly. He waited for Saperstein to stiffen. "We could go the other way."

"What other way?"

"Wait a minute," Saperstein said.

"Let him speak," Fletcher ordered. He looked at Donahoo. "What other way?"

"Excuse me, Miss Stuart," Donahoo said. "My immoderate language. The other way, we tell our crackpot to go fuck himself."

Faye Stuart said, smiling, "Is that your recommendation?"

"I don't think so," Saperstein said finally. He looked to Helmcken. "What do you think, John?"

Helmcken made a vague gesture. He had announced his retirement three months before. A commission was looking for a replacement.

"I'm interested," Faye Stuart said to Donahoo. "Why would you consider that?"

"To push the bastard," Donahoo told her. "To shake him up. He's not going to expect it. Not with four corpses stacked up. So he might do something rash. He might make a mistake." Donahoo was looking at her. "It's a valid alternative. You've just got to reach the right, uh, *political decision* here."

Helmcken complained, "What the hell do you want to do? Provoke the bloodbath?"

"We're going to have one anyway."

"You think so?" Fletcher said faintly. He wasn't up for retirement. He was up for reelection. Or a run for Governor. "I thought…" His voice trailed off. He avoided Faye Stuart's gaze. "It would stop somewhere."

Donahoo shook his head. "It will stop when we stop it."

"Yeah, well, that is probably true, Sergeant," Saperstein said. "Thank you." He tried his best to smile. "I'm sure you're busy. We'll finish up here." He turned to face Donahoo. Read my lips. You fucking grandstander.

Fucking true, Donahoo thought. Guilty as charged. But now it was going to be Saperstein's recommendation and Fletcher's decision. When this thing blew up in their faces, like it was probably going to blow, sky high, they were going to be accountable, not the squad, not him.

"Let me know," Donahoo said. He stood up and excused himself. "Gentlemen. Miss Stuart."

He let himself out. Gomez and Montrose, on signal from Lewis, followed. As the door was closing, Faye Stuart, a trace of amusement in her voice, asked, "Where did you find him?"

"He's Precambrian," Saperstein answered. He didn't sound amused.

Donahoo waited on the sidewalk beside Saperstein's new Ford Crown Victoria. Gomez and Montrose walked the block to Broadway. They were going to catch a cab or hitch back in a passing black-and-white.

Faye Stuart, the ice queen, Donahoo thought. He wondered what it would be like making love to her. Probably like getting into a wet bathing suit. No, he wanted magic, he wanted sparks.

There was a pay phone. He got the book, the Yellow Pages. He found her listed under Psychic Mediums, right after Lala, The World's Most Accurate New Age Clairvoyant. He put in a quarter and punched the number.

"Madam Zola," she said, answering. Her voice was throaty, warm, sensual.

He hung up.

Saperstein and Lewis showed up about ten minutes later.

"Try to buy us some time, Tommy," Saperstein said politely, slipping behind the wheel.

Lewis got in beside him. Saperstein didn't offer Donahoo a ride. Donahoo didn't ask for one.

The Crown Victoria pulled out and away.

CHAPTER TWENTY-FOUR

This is the back room of a commercial photographer's studio in the Cost Cutter Shopping Center in Golden Hill. The room has been arranged to serve as a movie set. It consists of a cheap sofa piled with cheap cushions and a small rattan coffee table with a potted fern. Behind the sofa, hiding the bare-studs wall, a rickety, three-fold Chinese screen, pieces missing from its shell mosaic flame-throwing dragon. On the concrete floor, a cheap, worn oval rug. A radio is playing an old hit, "I just Called to Say I Love You." An entrancing naked girl is giving head.

It was unfortunate there wasn't film in the camera. It had run out, about five minutes before, but the cameraman wasn't going to say anything. He was going to pretend to shoot until the Englishman yelled cut. He'd never seen anything like this before. He might not see it again.

The girl's name was Angela. Or at least that's what she called herself. It could be a professional name. It didn't matter. She was, without doubt, the most beautiful creature the cameraman had ever seen. She had an angel's face. Maybe that's why she had chosen Angela? She had the body of a love goddess. It was perfect, flawless. It was ab-so-lute-ly incredible. She also had the moves of a magical whore.

The Marine, glassy-eyed, moaned softly. "Yeah, yeah …"

She pulled away, smiling crookedly, looking at him with her angel eyes. Her tongue flicked over her rosebud lips. She said, "Now?"

"Please."

She went back down on him, put her mouth around his enormous penis. The Marine came in a flood of ecstasy. The cameraman came, too.

"Okay, cut," Marky Stevens said. He was Marky Stevens now, Marky to all of them, Foley reminded himself. Marky Stevens said in his exaggerated English accent, "That's a take." He helped Angela off the sofa and put a white terry-cloth robe over her shoulders. He said, "That was very nice, darling. Excellent." He said, "You're going to wow 'em at the Pussycat. You're going to be a star."

Angela glanced at the Marine. He was still in repose. He had his eyes closed. He appeared so blissful as to be dead. "He's got a big one."

"Yes," Stevens admitted. He knotted the robe loosely. "If bigger is better, and it usually is, he's going to be a star, too." He gave her a gentle shove. "Take a break, darling." He pronounced it dahling.

Angela smiled at him. She slipped into her sandals and moved away. She gave the cameraman a look as she went by him. He flushed.

The naked Marine still had his eyes closed. "What is this, shall we call med evac?" Stevens asked him.

The Marine smiled and nodded. But he still didn't open his eyes. Stevens thought that he wasn't a bad specimen, really. He had the sharply defined muscles of a dedicated body builder. He had almost no body hair and he was tanned well and evenly. No flaws or scars. No tattoos. And he sure had a winner's cock. Everything a guy could hope for. Except a brain.

The door banged on the toilet at the back. The door with a star on it. Stevens had pasted it there when he arranged for the studio time. One hour for $150. Another $50 for the argument that would be starting pretty soon now.

"Where the hell did you find that?" the cameraman asked, meaning Angela.

Stevens pretended not to hear. It was none of the camera-man's business and he didn't feel like making up a story. He had made up so many stories lately that he could barely remember them all. He sometimes forgot who he was.

The Marine, coming to, opening his eyes, said, "Yeah."

Stevens remained silent. It was none of their business, he thought again. They shouldn't ask questions. But they were both waiting for a reply. They both wanted to know. Finally, he said, "The Yellow Pages."

The Marine grinned. "Yeah. Right."

The cameraman found his cigarettes. He punched one out and lit up. He said, "Whatever."

Stevens wished he could tell them the truth. He had found her at the AmVet Thrift. She was trying to buy a sleeping bag, it cost four dollars, she only had three, and the cashier wasn't budging. He'd put up the extra dollar just to get the hell out of there. He'd been in a hurry—he couldn't remember why now—and then he looked at her. He'd seen what was hiding behind the crooked nose and the bad teeth and the glasses you could start a fire with. He'd seen an angel. To everyone else she was just another street whore. But he knew better. Instinctively, he knew that. He had purchased an angel for a dollar in a thrift store.

The Marine sat up. He looked around. He said, unsurely, ten-tatively, "She's coming back?"

"Not today," the cameraman answered, which was timed perfectly and which was what he was supposed to say. "We've got a wrap."

"What do you mean?" Stevens asked. That also was in the script. The fifty-dollar argument.

"I mean it's over," the cameraman said. "You said I'd have the money today, I don't see the money, do you? I didn't see anybody come in here with it." He took the film pack off the camera. "I'm not running a charity here. I've got bills, okay? These lights cost money. I could be doing something else. I could be in the lab, processing."

"You'll get your money."

"When?"

Stevens made a helpless gesture. "I told you. I got a guy, he's going to take *Blue Balls.*"

"Yeah? What's he gonna do with 'em? Wear 'em around his neck?"

"Hey," Stevens said. "That's a winner there. I'll have my investment back in a week."

The cameraman sneered. "Sure. If you finish it." He kept the film pack. "You get this when I get paid."

The Marine asked, "What's going on?"

"Your clothes," the cameraman said.

Stevens closed the deal at Porkyland. They went there afterward, Stevens, Angela, the Marine. They ordered fish tacos and diet Pepsis and sat out on the sidewalk under a red/green/white umbrella amid the skimpy pigeons and clashing integration that was Barrio Logan. Across the street from the Two Rosas Bar.

Stevens pretended to read *La Voz de Michoacan.* He knew the deal was going to close and he knew it wasn't going to take long. He knew that all he had to do was sit there and let it happen. The hook was in, and it was set in concrete.

"My dad, he used to keep pigeons," Angela said.

"Really?" Stevens said. He was buried in his paper. "From what?"

The Marine, who couldn't stand it any longer, wasn't supposed to, finally took his eyes off Angela long enough to look at Stevens. He said, "What's it take to finish *Blue Balls?*"

"Nothing," Stevens answered. "Not money, anyway." He laughed softly. "Maybe a carload of dynamite. Have you tried this salsa? It's the best." He looked at Angela. "Isn't this the best salsa?"

"It's the best," Angela said. She winked at the Marine. Like it really wasn't the best, she was just going along with Stevens, and she wanted him, the Marine, to know that. She put a taco into her rosebud mouth.

"Absolutely," Stevens said.

Angela, looking at the Marine, laughed and chanted, "*Porky*land, *Porky*land."

The Marine was in love. He said, "That's why you wanted a rocket to blow up the circus bus?"

Stevens nodded. He pretended to think about it, then added, kind of wistfully, "And to get this enterprise back on track."

The Marine said slowly, "Maybe I can get you something."

Stevens was spooning the salsa. He was spreading it along the top of his taco, like it was relish on a hot dog, he didn't want to miss anyplace. He didn't look up. He said, just as slowly, as if he was hardly interested, "Oh, how would you do that?"

"Do it, baby," Angela said excitedly. "We could make a lot of movies. I'll be sucking your big dick forever."

"You know, I got an idea back there, darling," Stevens said. "We ought to call you Miss Brazil." He took a big bite of his taco and the rest was just barely intelligible. "We'll give you this story, how you used to be a Miss Brazil, and you came here, to this country, to escape religious persecution, you were a member of this weird sect, you couldn't help it, your parents forced you, and your sister died." He looked at the Marine. "What do you think, Kirkie?"

Angela put her hand under the table and found the Marine's leg. She giggled. Maybe it just felt like a leg?

CHAPTER TWENTY-FIVE

The Russian name for it, translated into English, was Spigot. The NATO intelligence community had yet to come up with a reason why such a name had been applied to an antitank missile. Possibly, when turned on, or when *enough* were turned on, they swept away the enemy in a flood of destruction, but that was only a guess. Whoever had named the Spigot wasn't available anymore. Or, if he was, he was past admitting it.

"Spigot?" Valesy whispered. His flashlight looked in the dark and airless unit that was part of a huge public storage complex off I-5 in San Diego's Old Town. Its wide beam splashed a windshield. The core probed beyond to a canvas sack that bulged full and somehow ominous. Valesy shut the door behind him. Locked it.

Still here, he thought. There had been an inane fear it might be gone, and he felt, finding it, a surge of relief. It was the same kind of quick peace that came when he knew, for certain, he had escaped clean after killing Hudson and Camargo. Hudson, who was too greedy to live, and the Mex cop who was too stupid, Camargo. He had taken both their wallets and ditched them later. He wanted it to look like a robbery. Quick peace. Accept it, enjoy it, he thought. Who knows when, just as quickly, it will be shattered?

His flashlight moved now to locate a large battery-powered lantern. He pushed the switch and the whole place was bathed in an intense bright light. There was a dusty Wrangler Jeep. A crate the size of a foot locker.

He went first to the Jeep and the Spigot. The launcher had come from the Ukraine, following a devious passage that had taken it through Latvia, to France, to Peru, to Mexico. It had come across the border in a hay truck. He spoke affectionately. "You've waited so long, soon we turn you on, Spigot." Valesy found entertainment in all of the nomenclature and short forms given the antitank systems of NATO and the Warsaw Pact. His favorite was HVAPFSDS, which identified a round of ammunition, and which stood for a high-velocity, armor-piercing, fin-stabilized, discarding sabots round. It could rip through the newest main battle tank. Valesy was also fond of SACLOS, which stood for a semiautomatic, command line-of-sight launch system. It required that the operator merely keep his target in the command system's aiming mark. Electronics did the rest. SACLOS sounded like some sort of robot. Robots were special.

The Spigot, by comparison, was of an earlier generation, using wires to guide its missile, and requiring more of the gunner. It was designated MCLOS for manual control line-of-sight. It fired less powerful rounds. What Valesy needed most in this instance, however, was mobility, not overkill, and the Spigot gave him the option of free-standing tripod or vehicle mounting. He could carry it without assistance. He could point it out of a window or place it atop a building. Alternatively, he could mount it on a vehicle, as he had already done. It was attached by a swivel to the roll bar of the Jeep Wrangler. In the standby mode, as now, it hung behind the front seat, wrapped in its zippered canvas and hidden in part by the Jeep's rag top. To achieve the ready mode, he merely had to pull away the top, which was already unfastened, unzip the canvas bag and swing the launcher on its swivel. It came up over the roll bar and locked into place. He had clocked the operation a dozen times after setting it up several months before. Always under ten seconds. To achieve fire mode required three more seconds.

For his purposes, that was an eternity, Valesy thought. Three seconds? What he could accomplish in that gift of time! He could imagine it happening. The Jeep is parked at the chosen intersection in the glide path. It's in ready mode, the launcher locked in place, pointed in the proper direction. It appears, to the casual observer, to be a movie camera with a special lens. Now: The faint, distant roar of the approaching airliner. Now: Load the round, sight on the plane, fire.

Three seconds. Impossible to miss.

In the other scenario, stationing in advance, he would remove the Spigot from the Jeep, positioning it in an apartment or a house, or perhaps on a rooftop. The circumstances would differ but the result would be the same. He'd lie in wait. He'd fire.

Valesy hadn't decided which. He liked the Jeep, it's mobility, it had a cowboy quality. To fire from cover like a sniper also appealed. He'd make up his mind closer to the date. What he also liked was options.

The choice of round had already been made. Through his old contacts in the Russian military he could have obtained HEAP (high explosive, armor piercing), HEAT (high explosive, anti-tank), or HESH (high explosive, squash head). HEAT had been his first pick. A low-velocity missile, it employed a shaped charge of explosive which detonated offset from the armor surface, and, acting like a rocket motor in reverse, blasted a super-heated jet stream at 20,000 m/s through the metal and into the tank's interior. It would do the job. But, on second thought, penetration wasn't the prime objective. Rather, it was destruction. So he had decided on HESH. Another low-velocity system, it had a high explosive squash head which, upon impact, crumpled, making a large contact area before exploding. A tailor-made weapon for destroying an airliner lumbering in for landing like a gooney bird. There would be no escape. It would just crash. And everybody on board would perish. They were DAMNED, he mused, which, when translated, meant death assured by massive nullifying with explosive device.

Valesy pulled on surgical gloves and uncrated it lovingly. This would be a first for him. In the past, he had killed, at most, five people at once, and he couldn't be absolutely sure of that. He hadn't stayed around to count the pieces. He'd had to rely on uncertain press reports. This time, though, it would be mass murder, that was guaranteed, and he got to pick the plane. He could choose any one he wanted. He could select the biggest in the sky. It was up to him. His choice.

The crate was stamped CONTENTS: FIRE EXTINGISHERS. 12 TYPE ABC. DRY CHEMICLA. THIS SIDE UP. HANDLE WITH CARE. The misspellings were intentional. They were meant to bring a smile to a border-crossing inspector if he happened to chance upon it. Dumb fucking Mexicans, he would think, but if he had to stamp a crate in Spanish, he'd proably make similar errors. Valesy got the top off, revealing a dozen square compartments, much like the slots for wine bottles, only these swarmed with small pressure gauges atop fire-engine red steel cylinders. He chose one in particular and removed it purposefully. He turned it over and used a small penknife to scrape off the thick red paint around the rim. With the paint removed, a fine hairline appeared, revealing the false bottom's cap. Next, again using his penknife, he scraped away a small embossed number, 26, at the center of the cap. It came away easily, and so did the soft material below it. He quickly punched out a small square hole. For the last step, he used a hex wrench, which locked into the hole like a precision instrument. He applied as much pressure as he dared and the seal broke and the cap unscrewed. He put it aside and reached into the supposed extinguisher. He came out with a deadly-looking rocket—a high-explosive, squash head HESH.

"Spigot, a present for you, something to stick inside you," Valesy said, laughing. "Does it turn you on?"

Valesy practiced the Jeep scenario one more time. Top off, bag unzipped, launcher up and locked. Eight and a half seconds. Load, aim, fire. Three seconds. He couldn't want better than that. To get caught, he'd have to encounter, the faintest chance, a passing police patrol. And, in that eventuality, he had other rounds. If they could destroy a battle tank ... what harm would they do a car?

No. He wouldn't get caught. Either scenario, when the smoke cleared, he'd be in Mexico. And they'd be seeking someone else. Valesy got the small kit with the fingerprints he had lifted at the office of Joseph R. Foley, Realtor. He transferred them to strategic points on the Spigot. There's your criminal.

He turned off the lantern and sat in the dark for a while, laughing softly.

CHAPTER TWENTY-SIX

Donahoo drove over to Balboa Park, the scene of the first murder, the fag, Garrett. He looked around for a while and found the lone witness, Shortie. He took him downtown to the main branch public library.

He found some old car books in Reference. He found a good photo of a '72 280SE 4.5 in a book titled *Classic Mercedes*. He found photos of two other cars that were dissimilar, but were, at least to his mind, classy, a DeSota sedan from the fifties, an older Plymouth, undated. He showed them, reverse order, to Shortie. Shortie picked the 280SE.

"How did you know?" Shortie asked. "This is it. See these round lights? The parking lights? They're like oranges. Distinctive. I remember them. I was thinking I could eat 'em." He said, "You got some shoes you don't want?"

Donahoo looked at him. He thought, boy, would he slosh. He said, "You want to sleep in 'em, huh?"

He gave him five dollars. Shortie said he'd walk.

The library had six books on the subject of flies. Four of them were in the Juvenile Section. Donahoo sat in a small chair, flipping through a few. *Flies,* and *Discovering Flies,* and *The Story of Flies.* There was no mention of fireflies.

He went back to Reference. He found a book, *American Insects.* He discovered, something he hadn't known, that the firefly was actually a beetle, not a fly.

Fireflies, also called lightning bugs, are much in evidence on warm summer nights [he was reading this]. A search through forest litter on such nights will reveal the glowing larvae of some of these species, and often the female flashing her light to attract a male of the same species. Sometimes a hungry female of certain species will flash the pattern of yet another species and is soon feasting on one of the latter's amorous, but hapless, males.

Camargo, you dumb fuck, it's not going to work, Donahoo thought. The fly is a beetle, and the killer is a broad. It's not going to wash. He kept reading, though.

Some adults are predacious [he was reading this]. The larvae are also predacious.

Predacious, huh? Donahoo thought. A predator. One who plunders or abuses others for his own profit.

"Okay, Frank," Donahoo said softly. He was looking at, and talking to, the ceiling. "I'm going to give you this one. You got it. The Balboa Firefly."

CHAPTER TWENTY-SEVEN

The Sickos, Crackpots, Underwear & Mad Bombers squad room had been hastily expanded to take up all of the storage room from whence it first came. It was the only space available for an expanded operation apart from dismantling and moving some existing office. The police headquarters, although relatively new, was already overcrowded. This was the only option. Folding tables served as desks. Folding chairs substituted for the usual swivels. Malibu pot lamps had been strung together like Chinese lanterns for overhead lighting. Wide strips of white butcher paper had been unrolled as makeshift carpeting over the slippery concrete floor. It would have looked laughable, except for the banks of new telephones, the just-out-of-carton computers, and the grim, coatless, gun-in-holster cops working them.

Donahoo surveyed the scene with a degree of satisfaction. He had gained his first requirement, everybody together, one place, so they could instantly communicate, constantly interact. There wasn't anybody on the case who wasn't here, or who didn't work out of here. The undermanning had been addressed, too.

Gomez had the people he needed for a thorough combing of the glide path. They were making phone calls and they were going door-to-door. They weren't just asking questions. They were conducting interviews. Have you seen anybody suspicious? Have you heard anybody complain about the planes? Did he sound serious? Did he act crazy? When was this? What exactly did he say? Can you describe him? Was he in a car? What kind?

Montrose had another crew following up on the property-owner-ship leads. Purvis, the D.A.'s financial whiz, had given them a crash course. They were looking for a pattern in the maze of corporate, partnership, and fictitious names filings, the dba's, "doing business as." They were trying to establish significant multiple property holdings in Balboa Park by a single person or entity.

It had all come together in hours and was a small miracle. Donahoo still wondered how it had been accomplished. Normally, this would have taken days, a week. Normally, it wouldn't have happened at all. It wouldn't have happened now except that Saperstein wanted to be one hundred percent certain he had a one hundred percent run at being top cop. Timing was everything.

A small miracle, and now, let's have another one, get the effort to pay off, he thought. It didn't mean squat unless it paid off and they still had no leads on The Balboa Firefly.

Gomez hadn't located anyone who could recall someone threatening bloody mayhem against Lindbergh. There were all kinds of people who didn't like the noise, who hated the noise, who even feared the low-flying airliners. But they didn't look or act the type who would kill to express their displeasure.

Montrose had bombed out at the offices of three investment firms. They had merely confirmed what Purvis had already told him. It was impossible to trace most offshore connections. He'd need an indictment to get any information. Defeated, he had returned with a plaintive question, "If you could trace offshore, why go offshore?" He was now reading two books, *TAX HAVENS—How to Bank, Invest and Do Business—Offshore and Tax Free,* and *OFFSHORE HAVEN BANKS, TRUSTS & COMPANIES: The Business of Crime in the Euromarket.*

Donahoo had flipped through *TAX HAVENS* and gotten an Excedrin headache. There were thirty-two major tax havens plus more than a dozen marginal ones. Anguilla to Western Samoa.

He hadn't even heard of some of the places. Nevis. Vanuata. Who the hell had heard of them? So, for the moment, forget offshore. Try, instead, to navigate the twists and turns, the layers, here in the good old USA. One corporation owned by another corporation which in turn is owned by yet another corporation. Telephones no longer in service. Offices vacated. So far, a fax/modem bill that would choke a whore, they knew one suspicious corporate figure, Eric Hudson. They knew that and they knew nothing.

The hunt for the Mercedes wasn't going any better. Twenty-two possibles, 280SE's and 280SEL's, '71 and '72, registered in San Diego County. They'd all been tracked down in a blitz by four undercover cops borrowed from the Special Investigations Unit. None of the owners even faintly resembled a guy who'd blow away a blow job. So the Mercedes, if it existed, wasn't registered. It probably had stolen plates. The only way to find it was to get inventive. The SIU guys were sifting through about a zillion parking tickets. Maybe there'd be a needle in that haystack. The only way to find it was to get lucky.

Once more, once again, it boiled down to luck, Donahoo thought. He could hear Ben Jelley. A shuffle of the cards. Luck, fate. It governed most of the world's give and take. Whether you got Einstein's brains. Or were born with, who needs them, four feet. Luck.

He leaned back and closed his mind to the hectic activity all around him. He wondered if there was a chance he'd get lucky and be able to buy some time from The Balboa Firefly. Maybe a day? Two days? How would the fucker react when asked for a little mercy here? One thing, though, for sure, no pay phones.

He'd kept his promise. In honor of Frank Camargo, a final, first tribute, he had tagged the case The Balboa Firefly. It was what Camargo wanted. Maybe his last wish. The last one Donahoo knew about, anyway. He hadn't informed anybody, hadn't asked permission, he figured he didn't have to, there wasn't any rule or regulation covering it, not as far he knew. It had never come up. So all he had to do, drift into the press room, slip the word to Pete Calvelli, the police reporter for the *Union-Trib*.

"You know," Calvelli had said, "I always thought, The Stardust Donut Shop Murder Case, that was you at your lifetime peak, impossible to surpass, numero uno. Not anymore." He seemed to like it.

The Balboa Firefly, and the guy was going to call again, Donahoo thought. No luck required at this juncture. He had said he would call and he would call. Killers, once they called, they always called again. Now that was a rule. Killers either called or they didn't call. Either they liked to share or they didn't like to share. Once they started to share, it was like the murder itself, a compulsive act.

Donahoo knew that like he knew the dawn's early light. All he had to do was wait. His new red phone was going to ring. And it was going to be—little nod of the forelock to Frank Camargo— The Balboa Firefly.

Lewis came in, looking distressed, reluctant, looking every place else but at him. Donahoo had a premonition as soon he saw the how-do-we-tell-the-widow? expression. Oh, whoa, why me? he thought.

The beefy Captain, Detectives did the tour before coming over to Donahoo's desk. He stood there for a long moment. Donahoo wasn't about to ask.

"You're getting Chip Lyons," Lewis said then. He said, "Chipper, he's gonna be your replacement for Frank Camargo, okay?"

"No."

"Yeah, well, I guess I shouldn't have asked that question," Lewis said. "Others have answered before you. It is okay."

"Whose idea?"

"The brass."

Donahoo looked at Lewis doubtfully. Bullshit, he was going to say, but it was possible, it could have been a joint decision,

Saperstein and Helmcken. Lyons was a no-doubt-about-it hot-shot. He got results. He'd been dead right several times. The Chief liked him.

"You could use the help," Lewis said.

Donahoo motioned to the expanded squad room and its fresh bodies. "I've got help."

"Take it," Lewis said.

Cominsky called softly from across the room. "Sarge! I'm transferring a call to your red phone!"

The reaction was electric. Every cop in the place got up.

Donahoo took a deep breath. No need to scramble around this time. Everything was automated. The trace was already starting. The conversation would be recorded. It also would be computer translated into print, appearing, almost instantly, on the big monitor overhead. Yelker, the department's resident electronics genius, had rigged it for what he termed call viewing.

The red phone rang. A red light blinked. Donahoo's mouth was dry. He ran his tongue behind his lips. He braced himself.

"You gonna get that?" Lewis asked. The other cops were quietly leaving their positions and moving in to watch the monitor.

Donahoo picked up the phone. "This is Sergeant Donahoo."

There was laughter in the voice. "Hi! Remember me? The Mayor's bimbo?" Donahoo was already looking around for Cominsky. He was going to kill him. "Of course. Miss Stuart."

"You can call me Faye, Tommy."

"Faye." Donahoo could feel his neck turning red. The whole conversation, both sides, was going to the monitor, large letters, moving along like a billboard message. "How can I help you?"

"I was going to suggest dinner."

"Uh, no. I'm, uh, kinda busy here."

"Then how about a drink?"

"I'm sorry. It's, uh, kinda hectic."

Now she was teasing. "Oh, are you seeing someone else?"

Jesus, lemme up, Donahoo thought. He had a dozen cops hanging on every billboard word.

She was teasing him. "You're not afraid of the Mayor?"

"No," he said. He actually said that, he thought.

"Good. I'll look for you at Mr. A's. Five-fifteen. Don't disappoint me."

Donahoo hung up and the last of the transcript ran out on the monitor. The room was silent. The cops went back to their own desks. They weren't looking at each other. The first one to laugh was Palmer. He started laughing and he sat down on the floor. He didn't want to fall down.

"You want to take a walk?" Lewis asked.

Donahoo shook his head. "No, I want to find Cominsky."

Lewis took him into the hall and shut the squad room door. It suddenly sounded in there like the House of Mirrors at the Fun Palace.

"I don't want any problems here," Lewis said. "Personalities getting in the way of getting the job done. I don't want any of that." He said, watching for Donahoo's reaction, "Tell me, can you, yes or no, live with Chip Lyons?"

Donahoo was still listening to the bedlam. "I gotta live with him?"

"He's your partner."

Donahoo gave him a look. "Why?"

"Because you need him. Take the help, Tommy."

"Help," Donahoo said angrily. "You're giving me a fucking maniac. He's not a cop, he's the judge and jury. He's Death Row. He's killed three people and he brags about it." Donahoo stopped only to get his breath. "The guy's had too many rides on the Twirling Teacup. You oughta get him off the street before he throws up on somebody."

"That's how you feel?"

"Some of it. I just got started."

The laughter had ceased abruptly in the squad room. Gomez pulled open the door. "Sarge! You gotta another call."

Donahoo didn't want to take it. He felt drained. He went back in. There again was a semicircle of men near his desk. But their expressions were different this time.

He picked up the red phone. "Sergeant Donahoo."

Stryker, the guttural voice, said, "I missed, huh?"

Donahoo felt a chill. Cominsky's stupid prank was forgotten. Chip Lyons didn't matter anymore. The only thing in the room, in the world, was this familiar voice, and the murderous message it brought.

"Yeah, close, though," Donahoo said. He sat down. "Why would you try? You kill me—how can we talk?"

"That's one way of talking."

"Killing?"

"Yes. If it makes an impression."

Donahoo hesitated. He didn't want to give that any validity.

"Has it?" The briefest pause. "Are you going to close the airport, or not?"

"Yes, we are," Donahoo said quickly. "That's what I've been waiting to tell you. We're going to do what you want. We're going to close it. But we need time."

"No. No time. Time has run out."

"Give us a few days," Donahoo said. "There's a lot to be done. We've got to get approval for an alternative field. There's federal bureaucracy. All the logistics. Changing schedules..."

"No."

"Three days, okay? Just three days."

"No."

"Two days."

"No."

"We can't do it in less than two days."

"No," Stryker said. "You've got one day. Tomorrow, that's your last day." He said, "Watch tonight. Tonight you'll see what happens if you're lying to me, if you don't close, Sergeant. Tonight, a lesson. Tomorrow, a day to obey. After that, remember, the worst kind of bloodbath. And you can't catch me."

The line went dead. Donahoo hung up. Somebody said, "Portable phone." Gomez said, softly, "Holy fuck."

Donahoo closed his eyes.

"There's nothing more you can do here, Tommy," Lewis said. "Everything that can be done is being done. You gotta take a break, change of scene, get some rest. You're gonna go nuts if you don't get outta here. Walk on the beach. See a movie. You gotta girl? You must have a girl. How about the Mayor's bimbo?" He considered for a moment. "Have you paid your respects to Frank Camargo's widow?"

"Gimme a pencil," Donahoo said, reaching back. His eyes were still closed. It was the first time he had smiled all day. "I better make a list."

CHAPTER TWENTY-EIGHT

Stryker put the stolen portable phone aside. Briefly, he became Mark Stevens, and then he realized that wasn't necessary at the moment, and so he went back to being Joseph R. Foley, Realtor. He wondered if he was crazy.

It was a good question, he thought. Some of his earliest memories were of being so accused. His father shouting, "You crazy little bugger," and the dead kitten on the floor, strangled with a silk tie. He had run sobbing to his mother, "I was just dressing it up, Maw," and she had believed that, or had wanted to, but his father hadn't. His father had torn him from the sweet folds of her skirt and had beaten him mercilessly. Foley sometimes thought he could still feel the strap's fierce lash. From that beating and a hundred others. A thousand? Foley had long ago lost track. It didn't matter, he thought. The beatings, they hadn't worked. He grew up with everyone around him saying the same thing. "That crazy Joe Foley."

At first, he had set out to prove them wrong. When he left home, the hated streets of despised Omaha, sixteen dollars in his pocket, one for every year of his tormented life, his intent was to show them. His plan, carefully formulated, reviewed every night, was to become rich and famous. He was going to start some sort of business that made a lot of money and attracted a lot of attention. The people he knew about who were rich and famous were the people who were in business for themselves. Starvin Marvin, the furniture man, for instance. He was starvin because he undersold everybody else. He was famous because he had his picture in a big ad in the paper. He was rich because (this was from personal observation) he had an office with a big window where he could sit and watch everybody on the floor work.

Foley smiled at that memory. His hero, Starvin Marvin. Only an abused boy could reach out for such a champion. Rich is behind a glass wall spying on your employees? He had been so naive, Foley thought, but that would change, if slowly. What he hadn't known, hadn't even begun to comprehend, was that he was immensely more powerful than most men, however wealthy. He knew he exercised the power of life and death. He knew it was a power that everyone held. But he hadn't yet come to realize that only special people had the boldness of spirit to use it.

The kitten had been just the start. There had been other animals, smaller, bigger. There had been frogs, mice, cats, dogs. There had been birds. Sparrows on the wing and pigeons in the nest. He held dominion. He acted on it.

Foley smiled. When he arrived in California, in San Diego, he had two dollars left, the clothes on his back, a satchel of dirty laundry. He was as poor as any wretch who ever walked the earth. He also was about to learn the greatest lesson of his life— that he could kill for profit as well as pleasure. Two great lessons, actually. He also learned to be secretive. He was starting over. And nobody was going to call him Crazy Joe. He was to keep that secret. Nobody had to know but him. Nothing had changed. Except, in future, he would be careful not to share.

The boy's name was Jerry. He met him, the first day, at the bus station. Jerry was friendly and helpful and got him a place to stay. Room and board for doing chores. The first Sunday, Jerry took him to the beach, lied about swimming all the way to Catalina.

They became pals. They shared things. Lies and secrets. Jerry was the water boy at Lohman's French Gardens. He watered the plants and polished the furniture and dusted the merchandise. He made deliveries to customers and he took deposits to the bank. Foley remembered how easy it was. He lured the sucker into an alley, toward a high window. "You wanta see a naked girl?" He killed him and took the deposit money. He took it back to Sid Lohman. He said he'd found it in a gutter.

The cops couldn't figure it. One was kind of suspicious. But the other said no. There was no way a kid could kill that viciously. No way at all.

Foley smiled. He got a reward. He got Jerry's job. The rest, like they said, was history, and he especially enjoyed the part where, a few years later, he killed Sid Lohman. That was perfect. No one suspected. No one. He was in the will, and no one suspected. They all said, "Joe, he was like a son."

Yes, and, now, Stryker, he was like a brother. Stryker, he took to it, didn't he? Like a fish to water. Like a bird to sky. First time out, no problem, a breeze. He could do it all. He was worthy.

Foley found the morphine. He wasn't smiling now. He was coming to what he called the bad part. All the years he had spent investing and selling and reinvesting and then selling again. All the single-minded time and effort he had devoted to ferreting out the few true opportunities in the mountain of real-estate false-hoods heaped like bullshit across the face of San Diego County. All the machinations in the painstakingly slow and volatile process that had brought him to the juncture where he could focus his resources and make his final play in Balboa Park.

It hadn't been a mistake, Foley reminded himself. It was a good, smart, solid move. He had done his part. It was the politicians who hadn't kept their word. The pols, the fucking pols, if they had kept their word, this wouldn't be necessary. None of it. If they had moved Lindbergh. Like they *promised.*

Foley sat waiting with the morphine. He took a deep breath, waited. Everything else was ready. The catapult. The fireworks. The belt with the pack of dynamite. The detonator. The little model airplane with its noisy motor. All he had to do was wait for the appointed time. When it came, he'd shoot up, and he'd wait just a bit longer, and then the pain he always felt would subside.

He would stand up and he would walk out of here and...no.
Stryker. Stryker, he would walk out of here, Foley thought. He
made that correction.

Stryker, moving quickly.

Stryker didn't limp.

CHAPTER TWENTY-NINE

Donahoo went to get his fortune told. He'd had it told once as a child. He'd had an aunt, Alice, his mother's sister, who read tea leaves. She wasn't a professional. She just had the "gift," or at least that's what she claimed. She read for the neighbors. Donahoo wasn't too clear on how it worked. The best he could recall, you drank your tea, letting the leaves settle randomly, and the pattern they assumed on the bottom and side of the cup determined—for someone with the "gift"—your fortune.

Something like that. The pattern, and also the size and shape of the leaves themselves. He could remember, as a child, he was perhaps six or seven, being fascinated by the idea, and he also could remember his fortune being told, but he couldn't remember what his fortune was. He could just remember his mother being very angry and saying it wasn't the kind of fortune you told a little boy.

Donahoo hadn't heard of a tea-leaves reader for a while. There were some palm readers around. Some crystal-ball gazers. But he couldn't recall noticing a tea-leaves reader. Maybe they'd been put out of business by the tea bag? Maybe not.

MADAM ZOLA was OPEN. Donahoo went by and around the corner. He still wasn't sure he was going to do this. He might change his mind. So he allowed ample space for maneuver in the walk back up. He could just do a little twirl. Walk back to the Chevy. Get the hell out of here. No harm done.

He parked and sat there for a while. More time to change his mind. He wondered if, as he suspected, as he *hoped,* that the tall, dark beauty in the clinging skirt and sandals would turn out to be Madam Zola. He had no solid reason for equating one with the other. Just that she lived upstairs. Or appeared to live upstairs. She could have been visiting when he saw her. Anything was possible. So he didn't even have that. What he had, only, was that she looked, in his mind, what a Madam Zola ought to look like.

Donahoo sat in his car for a while. Maybe he should just go, he thought. The key was still in the ignition. Then a plane came over, very low, very close, jets screaming. Four seconds of bedlam. He remembered her smiling and waving. He remembered thinking, there's a woman, nothing bothers her. His kind of woman. He pulled the key and got out of the car and walked back up the hill.

The door was wooden and weathered. Most of the varnish had scaled off. The curved brass handle was a mottled green. It suggested something had failed behind it. As if, perhaps, it harbored bad fortunes.

Donahoo hesitated. He glanced again at the curtained display window. MADAM ZOLA, and, below that, something he hadn't noticed before, a line of much smaller print. The Future Predicted. The Unknown Explained. By Appointment Only.

Yet another reason to turn back. He stood at the door for a long moment. He didn't know what was wrong with him. Doors didn't bother him usually. He had kicked some down. But he couldn't open this one.

He backed off. Screw it, he thought, this was crazy, he was crazy, and then the door opened and an older woman emerged, her face younger than her hands. It was the first thing he noticed about her as she quickly adjusted the brim of her hat. He also saw a brittle smile and very stylish clothes too warm for the day.

"Next" was all she said, and she hurried away, up the hill, toward a black Rolls kneed into the curb.

Donahoo, reflex, grabbed the door before it could close. He went inside.

It was like a small antique store, dimly lit, smelling of incense. There was a kind of anteroom with a glass display counter topped by an old brass cash register. A narrow passage next to the counter permitted access to a larger room lined with shelves piled with supposed occult merchandise. A round wooden table and two plain wooden chairs were in the middle of the room. A large crystal ball was positioned in the center of the table. Beyond, to the rear, hidden by a bead curtain, some other room or rooms.

Donahoo waited. The door hadn't signaled his entry. There was no bell on the counter. He waited and no one came through the multicolored beads. He said, loudly, "I don't have an appointment!"

Madam Zola appeared then. The beads parted for her like slithering snakes. They caressed her body and released her reluctantly. She brought a radiant, electric presence into the room, and a new, powerful scent.

Donahoo stared, shocked. He said, "Well, it's you."

"You know Madam Zola?" she asked.

He shook his head. No, he didn't. He knew the woman who lived upstairs. A few things about her, all physical. Nothing, really, but also enough. He could spot her in a lineup. That was his litmus test.

"Then how do you know it's me?"

"I was driving by the other morning," Donahoo told her. He had so wanted the woman on the stairs to be Madam Zola. That's why he had come here, fragile hope in hand. That's what he had wanted for his fortune. That's what he'd gotten. But now he didn't want Madam Zola to be the woman on the stairs. There was too much purple eyeshadow and too many bangles and beads. Too much perfume. "You were walking down Kalmia. You went up the stairs—the apartment outside?—and a plane came over. Air Alaska. You waved. You smiled and you waved."

"At you?"

"No. At the plane."

"Oh," she said, smiling again, the same smile. It suggested that she had been teasing him. "Yes. I always do that. Sometimes I think, the plane's so close to the houses, the passengers might be afraid they're going to crash. So I like to let them know that's not going to happen. If they see me waving and smiling they'll know it's okay. They won't be afraid."

Donahoo found the notion wonderful as well as absurd. He laughed. "For a few seconds? They'll be safe on the ground in a few more seconds."

"Every moment is precious."

Yes, Donahoo thought. He'd heard that somewhere. He looked around. It was part head shop, part occult bin, part gypsy fortune stall. One of those mixed bags that Saperstein found so distressful. No real focus.

"What else did you want to know?" Madam Zola asked. She moved to the table, her long black gypsy shawl spinning counter to her long black gypsy skirt. "Perhaps your future told? The unknown explained?"

Donahoo looked at her. He thought her eyes were like dark pools. If you fell in, you'd never, ever make it back to shore.

He really ought to get out of here, he thought. He said, "I'd like my fortune told."

Madam Zola beckoned. "You came to the right place. The crystal ball tells all."

"No," Donahoo said. He knew where he was going finally. "Actually, I want my tea leaves read."

She looked at him, disappointed. "I don't do tea leaves."

"Oh?" he said. He glanced around to locate the door. "I'm sorry. I thought, you know …" He paused. "I thought you did."

"I read palms."

"No."

"Cards."

"No."

"Okay, hold it," she said. "I'll put some tea on. How do you like it?"

"In a cup."

Madam Zola went back through the beads. Donahoo checked out the merchandise while he waited. He'd better watch out, he thought, smiling. Gypsy women, they had the stuff. Amulets. Charms. The Abyssinian Wish Box. Lotions and potions. Feathers. Boy, if she got fired up, there'd be no resisting. A Wanga doll, more powerful than voodoo. Samahad's mystical powers. Medicine bone. Gris-gris. She could raise all kinds of hell.

Madam Zola peeked through the beads a couple times, to make sure he was still there, or maybe to see if he was stealing something. The third time she came out with the tea. She had a cracked pot and two mismatched cups on a black lacquered Chinese tray.

Donahoo sat down at the table. She joined him and poured before letting it steep. It spilled into his cup like spoiled water. The leaves were there, though. They swirled and slowly settled.

"Let's see what you've got," she said, peering in.

"I think I'm supposed to drink it first."

"Yeah, I know that," she said, very close. "Go ahead and drink it. But just don't disturb the leaves. You've got some great leaves there. They … are … great."

"Really?" Donahoo wondered how he was supposed to drink the tea without disturbing the leaves. Her perfume was almost overpowering. He couldn't figure out what it was. It was really strange. Eucalyptus? He took a sip. He said, "Maybe you can read it now?"

She nodded and took the cup away. She stared into it deeply. A plane went over and the droopy faux crystal chandelier started dancing.

"I'm getting vibrations," she said.

Yeah, well, who the fuck isn't, Donahoo wondered. He wanted the tea leaves read. He had expected a phony. They were all phony. But *this* phony?

"Vibrations. Definite vibrations." She appeared to be going into a trance. "Please be quiet."

"I thought you saw something," Donahoo prompted.

"I said you had great leaves."

Oh, Donahoo thought. He sat waiting. The initial shock was over. He was feeling a little better. He reminded himself that the perfume, the makeup, the bangles and beads, all the gypsy shit, that could be just a pose. Part of the game. It was like a cocktail waitress. They were supposed to bump up their tits. So Madam Zola wouldn't go to bed wearing eucalyptus. No more than a circus clown would wear his red nose.

"You are going to meet a strange woman," Madam Zola intoned. She was staring into Donahoo's teacup. Looking at the meaningless scramble of tea leaves on the bottom. "She is tall, slim, very beautiful. Striking. She has dark, flashing eyes. A full, sensuous mouth. She has flawless olive skin and long black silky hair. She is compassionate and caring and a total romantic."

Donahoo looked at her. Now what the fuck was going on? He said, "Is she looking for a relationship? Dinner and dancing? The movies? Holding hands and walking in the moonlight?"

"Yeah. She is five star settle down hot."

Sure, Donahoo thought. He said, "From the description, that could be you."

"It could be anybody," Madam Zola told him. "That will be twenty dollars."

CHAPTER THIRTY

NBWJT GBSSPX. The jumble translated to Mavis Farrow. It appeared that way on the slip of white cardboard in the narrow brass nameplate, specially typeset for the sole purpose, and looking strangely out of place. All the other names were handprinted. Many of them were scratched out and written over. They were in different colored inks. One was in pencil.

Rich Sechrist, one said. Simon Cardew, another. Jane Hampton. Mendlesohnn, that's all. Marvel Montagne. And J. Fisher Brown. There was a mix. Balboa Park irregulars, gathered here in this once-fine old apartment building, this descending old pile, The Ramparts.

Valesy pushed the buzzer under the name Mavis Farrow. The intercom clacked on almost instantly. "Who is it?"

He answered in a singsong. He had practiced it a lot. He had it down perfect. "Pharmacy!"

There was a loud buzz and he opened the door and slipped inside and started up the long, narrow, musty-smelling stairway. There also was a dog smell. Biscuit and Bertie.

Mavis Farrow appeared at the top. She was an old lady, a small stick woman, pale complexioned but with heavily rouged cheeks and bright black eyes. She was in a burnt-orange bathrobe and yellow flipflop slippers. Her blue-rinse hair was in pink curlers. She was a little flat box of watercolors.

"You're not David," she said accusingly. Biscuit and Bertie arrived with the accusation. They stood at her feet, one on each side, barking fiercely.

Valesy smiled for her. He held up a stapled brown paper bag. "No," he shouted over the manic Chihuahuas. "I'm Nick."

"Where's David?"

"He's sick."

"*Sick?* What's wrong?"

"I dunno. I think a cold."

"Oh." She looked at him with her black bird eyes. "I'll get rid of the dogs." She pointed, screamed. "Biscuit! Bertie!"

Actually, he's dead, Valesy thought. Poor David, he's in a dumpster, and he won't be coming here no more, no more. Never gonna sing, "Pharmacy!" Valesy waited as the dogs, still barking, retreated to a room somewhere, had the door slammed on them. Then he went up the remaining stairs. He went through her door, which she had left ajar. He closed it behind him. The latch clicked.

Mavis Farrow came back. He handed her the stapled brown paper bag.

"Thank you." She took it eagerly and tore it open and looked inside, sorting through all the smaller stapled white bags, the identifying slips attached, making certain everything was there. She confirmed that. She visibly relaxed. "It's all here." She looked at him. "Wait a minute."

Valesy waited, looking around, listening. He didn't expect her to have visitors. David, eyes filled with pain, eager to tell everything, eager to tell all, David had told him that, that he'd never seen her with visitors. But there was always the chance, of course. He stood listening.

There was just the one conversation. Mavis and a bird. "Bad bird," she said. "*Bad* bird." One-way conversation. The bird didn't say anything. Biscuit and Bertie were barking faintly.

Valesy looked around. The apartment, it was like a museum, he thought. Old furniture, old rugs, old pictures. Old paint. It hadn't been painted for years. There was nothing new here. Only the past.

Mavis returned with a small black leather change purse. She opened it and took out a quarter. She handed it to him. "Thank you." She hesitated and then got another quarter. "Will you be seeing David?"

No, I don't think so, Valesy thought. He shook his head.

"If you were, I thought you could give him this," she said, holding the coin out.

He shook his head.

"Very well," Mavis said. She put it back in her purse. "David, he's a nice boy. I knew him when he was ..." Her voice trailed off wistfully. "We used to say: knee high to a grasshopper. Now that's a dumb expression, isn't it? How can anybody be knee high to a grasshopper."

"Yes, the world, it's full of lies," Valesy told her. He grabbed the phone and ripped the line from the wall. "And people believe them."

She looked at him in horror. "What are you doing?"

Valesy took hold of her throat. "We used to say: That's for me to know ... and you to find out."

"Let me go!" she cried in a strangled voice.

"Do you know what farrow means? It's to give birth to pigs."

"Please! *Let me go!*"

Valesy tore open her bathrobe. First he'd fuck her. Then he'd kill her. She was a stubborn old lady who refused to sell the property she owned in Balboa Park. Perhaps her estate would be more reasonable.

"*Bad* bird!" The bird finally said it.

Biscuit and Bertie were barking faintly.

CHAPTER THIRTY-ONE

Faye Stuart was waiting in the bar at Mr. A's. She saw him before Donahoo spotted her. Donahoo knew that by her waiting-to-be-discovered smile. It was kind of artificial, but it was still a nice smile, Donahoo had to admit. Very nice. He went over.

"Hello, Sergeant," she said. She had a Scotch, it looked like a double, which she lifted in greeting. She also smiled again. Her butter-blond hair was up and back in a tight bun. She was wearing a severe dark blue wool business suit with a loosely knotted tie. Her glasses were on a string around her neck. Still, she looked very feminine. She had that quality.

He said, "Why don't you call me Tommy, Faye?"

"Okay. Tommy Faye."

He was going to take a stool, but she slipped off hers and gave him a slight push. "Let's get a table."

Donahoo hesitated. It was supposed to be drinks, not dinner. He looked at his watch. He had a lot of things to do. The place was filling up. "I don't think we can get a table just for drinks."

"Don't worry," she said, grinning. "I know the Maitre d'. I also know the owner." She brushed by him, smelling of jasmine. "Come on."

Donahoo followed her to the best table in the restaurant. The best table and the best view. A Balboa Park landmark, Mr. A's occupied the top floor of the Fifth Avenue Financial Center, on the north perimeter of the Lindbergh Field glide path. To the south, on the other side of the glide path, the downtown's business towers loomed dramatically. To the west, the harbor, Lindbergh Field, Point Loma and the Pacific.

The waiter was especially obsequious. Donahoo told him, "Old Crow, no ice, chilled glass, please." Then he said, this to Faye Stuart, "You come here often?"

"Yes." She smiled. "You don't?"

"No," Donahoo admitted. "The last time I was here, they wouldn't sell me a drink, I wasn't going to stay for dinner. They had the bar reserved for people who were having dinner."

"Well, it's a small bar."

"Yeah, I guess it's a kind of a dinner bar, huh?"

Faye Stuart smiled again. "It's also who you know."

Donahoo wished he still smoked. It was times like this, the awkward times, waiting for the first Old Crow, that he missed it most. He could blow a couple minutes, lighting up, the whole business, waiting for the Old Crow.

"Tough day?"

"It wasn't easy."

Faye Stuart twirled her Scotch. "The killer … he gave you a deadline, huh? Two days?"

Donahoo looked at her. Under the circumstances, the Mayor's aide had a right to know that, of course, but the idea still made him uneasy. He felt more secure in the normal scheme of things. Until they made an arrest, laid a charge, police business was police business. He liked that way best. No civilians.

"I'm glad you could make it," she told him. "You'll forgive me for being so forward?" There was a hint of apology in her smile. "I'm afraid I'm fascinated. I can't imagine what it's like being you."

"Oh? Why is that?"

"All that responsibility." She was staring back at him. "What are you going to do?"

He shrugged, trying to think of a suitable, noncommittal answer. The Old Crow came and saved him. "Catch my breath."

"Gordon, the Mayor," Faye Stuart said, running the slip and the correction together just a little too fast, "he's still dead set against closing Lindbergh. He's recommending against it. Fighting against it. He ..." Her Scotch did another little twirl. "He says it's blackmail and he doesn't want to give in to blackmail." She leaned closer. "You know there's a meeting tomorrow? Everybody involved? Port Authority, FBI. It looks like we're going to get the FBI. In some capacity."

Donahoo sampled his drink. No, he hadn't heard. It also was the first time he'd heard that he wasn't involved.

She must have seen something. "I'm sorry."

"Saperstein will cover for me. I'm expecting a full report."

She laughed and he wondered what the hell he was doing here. He had a lot of reasons, but he wasn't sure any of them were valid. He wanted this bird's-eye view of the planes landing at Lindbergh. He wanted to have a drink with a woman who belonged on the cover of *Vogue*. He wanted to hold hands with someone this close to the Mayor. He wanted her to somehow be of some help to him—to give him, from her ample sieve, some little shred of information that he didn't yet have, but should have, to get lucky again. Madam Zola had given him the brush.

"So, you got a girl?"

He was glad he had the Old Crow. She was fast. "No. You got a guy?"

"No."

"I thought you were sleeping with the Mayor."

"No. We just make it look that way. That's enough to satisfy him."

"Oh."

"What I heard," she said, smiling, "from Saperstein, you're Precambrian. Are you?"

Donahoo had to think. Precambrian. Probable origin of the earth from solar dust cloud. Oldest dated rocks. Jellyfish, flagellates, amoebas, worms, sponges. That's life. The only life.

"Are you?"

"Fuck him." He didn't like this. She was too sure of herself. "Tell him a worm said, 'Fuck you.'"

"You interest me," Faye Stuart said.

"You don't know me."

"Oh? Let's see. You're considered the very best at what you do. No officer in the department has more citations and commendations. No one has solved tougher cases." She was looking at him. "You are, however, a loner, not a team player. You're a poor administrator. You've refused advancement in rank in order to stay on the street. You head the department's most elite squad as a Sergeant because there isn't a Lieutenant half as good. Your superiors gladly let you take the worst cases and assignments. But they watch you warily. You're unpredictable." She smiled winningly. "Have I missed anything?"

"Yeah. I'm lucky."

"Maybe not this time," she said. "There's something you should know. I'm taking a chance here, but I like you. I like what I see here. So I'm going to take the risk. You watch your ass on this one, Tommy. Don't trust anybody. No one."

"Why not?"

"Camargo's killing? That set something off. Saperstein is wondering if there's something more there. He hasn't got anything, but he's worried. He's watching you. Saperstein, you know where he's coming from, he wants to be Chief, he's paranoid. This is the big one. If you fuck up, if you *seem* to fuck up, he fucks up. It's that kind of powder keg where bad things happen to good people."

Donahoo looked at her. She didn't know anything he didn't know. He'd seen Saperstein at work in Lewis's sheepish expression when Lewis brought in Chip Lyons to replace Frank Camargo. Lyons, the cop. Lyons, the judge. Lyons, who probably had a direct line to Internal Affairs.

"I thought you ought to know."

Donahoo wondered what the town was coming to. The Mayor's office was a sieve. The police department was a sieve. He sighed. He'd come looking for help, he was getting this bullshit.

"Maybe I can protect you."

He shook his head. Protect him? No, but she could harm him, he thought. Women looking for vicarious thrills were always dangerous. To see what would happen, they could push you too close to the fire.

"We could make it fun. See each other."

No, Donahoo thought. He was sorry he hadn't finished his drink. He said, "Do I have to sleep with you? Or is it okay if it just looks like it?"

The waiter was at his elbow. "Will you be staying for dinner?"

"No," Faye Stuart said.

CHAPTER THIRTY-TWO

Stryker could see him and he could imagine what was happening. Paul Aldrich sitting in his car, alternately staring at his note, the one he'd made when he got the directions, and at this destination which didn't make sense. Stryker could imagine Aldrich thinking, hey?!! He'd taken the information down correctly. South on I-5. Exit at Convention Center. First right. Another right. But where the hell's the building on the northwest corner?

Stryker laughed. He could imagine Aldrich talking to himself. Forty bucks, down the tube. Forty bucks he needed. He'd already spent it. Or the wifey—what was her name, Arlene?—hadn't been out to dinner in over a month, she'd spent it.

Well, enough. Time to put him out of his misery, Stryker thought. He moved the Mercedes from behind a vacant house and into the open. He bumped across a cracked weed-strewn parking lot and pulled up alongside Aldrich's woebegone Cadillac. He drove the whole way with his left hand. His right was in his pocket.

Stryker, smiling, stuck his head out the window, shouted the question, "You Mr. Aldrich?"

Aldrich showed a wave of relief. He yelled back. "I sure am!" He yelled, "I thought I messed up!"

"You're a little early, aren't you?"

"I didn't want to be late."

"Well, get in, let's go."

"I thought the meeting was around here."

"It was. But it's been changed. Let's go."

Aldrich got out of his Cadillac, locked it, got in the Mercedes, pulled the door shut. He did it fast. He sure wants to participate in this survey, Stryker thought. Forty bucks.

"You like old cars?" Stryker asked, looking at him, and also at the Caddie. It was ready for the dump.

"I don't have much choice."

Stryker pulled away. He studied Aldrich. He'd be seventy, seventy-five, older than Stryker had expected, and, despite his agility, frail. His face was weathered, gathered like snakeskin, and his hair was shock white, set atop his head like a fresh mop. He hoped the old guy wasn't going to shit himself.

Aldrich was looking around. He noticed the long, narrow green box on the backseat. The kind used for packing long-stemmed roses.

Aldrich asked, making conversation. "Who're they for?"

"You."

"Me?" Aldrich grinned, uncertainly.

Stryker pulled his right hand out of his coat pocket. He showed a hand grenade to Aldrich. Then he offered it to him.

"Here's something else for you."

Aldrich stared at it fearfully. "What do you mean?"

"Take it," Stryker said. "Carefully." He smiled. "You want to make sure you keep the lever down. I've already pulled the pin. I've already made the count. There's no time to throw it away. You let go and it goes off. *Take it!*"

Aldrich took it clumsily, "Oh, God."

"Now, listen to me," Stryker said. "You're fucked, okay? You can't get away. You run, something will happen, you'll stumble, drop it, something. You ask for help and the person will be just as afraid as you. They'll run. Or, if they try to help, which is very doubtful, you'll both get blown to ratshit. You're dealing with a hair trigger there. Understand?"

Aldrich nodded bleakly.

"All right. Now, you put it in your pocket, you keep it there, and no matter where we go, who we meet, I don't want you shaking hands."

Aldrich put the hand grenade in his pocket. He held it there.

Stryker moved the Mercedes down the street. He smelled something. He hoped it wasn't shit.

CHAPTER THIRTY-THREE

Donahoo found himself again at Madam Zola's. It was dusk, almost seven, but she hadn't closed, a light showed in the window, turning the curtain a pale yellow. There also was the sign, OPEN. He drifted past and parked, as before, around the corner, where he could change his mind. He sat there for a while.

His police radio was chattering. Man down. Purse snatched. Auto stolen. Officer in trouble...

They come out after dark, Donahoo thought. They can strike anytime, but they wait until dark, most of them. They like the dark. They can hide in it. They like the shadows. They can move in and out. And, sometimes, all anybody sees is a brief dance of light, the death dance of The Balboa Firefly.

Donahoo thought that maybe he was working the wrong shift. He was looking in the right places but maybe it was at the wrong time of day. The fag in the park. The homeless on the steps of the First Presbyterian Church. Eric Hudson. All after dark.

He looked at the turning sky. The darkness was coming, and they were coming, too. He wondered if, among them, there would be a light, and if... whoa. Jesus Christ, give yourself a break, Donahooie.

A fire alarm clanged across the street at San Diego Engine Company No. 3. The door raised and a ladder truck exited, engine chugging, siren wailing. An Amtrack commuter train blasted a warning for the Hawthorne crossing. Overhead, impossibly low, an airliner bumped it jets, ensuring it wouldn't be short of Lindbergh. It roared across the turmoil of the freeway. A car alarm went off somewhere.

What was he doing here? Donahoo thought, and then he remembered. He wanted a woman. He snapped off the police radio and pushed out of the Chevy. He walked back up the hill. He was going to get her. His kind of woman. She could put up with anything.

Madam Zola was just leaving. She turned the sign to SORRY, WE'RE CLOSED. She locked the door. Only it wasn't Madam Zola. Donahoo stopped a few steps away. It was the woman he had first seen walking down Kalmia. The gypsy stuff was gone. Only a hint of makeup and no bangles and beads. He didn't know what kind of perfume, but it was subtle, transient. Just enough to set the lure. She looked radiant. The woman he had first seen. She was wearing another clinging dress. It embraced her body like a lover.

"You again," she said.

Donahoo stood staring at her. He couldn't help staring. He could feel the electricity. It had been that way with Monica. So alive, in a way that could never happen with a cold, ambitious string-puller, never mind the cover of *Vogue*.

"I'm sorry, I'm closed," she said. She gave him a quick, cursory look. "I've got to go."

"Listen," Donahoo said. "It's dark. Maybe I could walk you home?"

"I live upstairs."

"I know."

"Oh, good. Get out of here, will you? Go away."

Donahoo felt a kind of desperation. He had this one chance, here, now. He was losing her. He said, the desperation talking, "Do you ever have fantasies?"

"Yes. And in my favorite, you're leaving. Get the hell out of here, okay? Or do I have to call a cop?"

She spun away and headed for her stairway.

"I *am* a cop."

He was holding up his badge when she turned around.

"You're a cop?" she said, puzzled. "What is this? What the hell is with you?" She was angry. "Are you *investigating* me?"

"No."

"Then what?"

Donahoo didn't know what to answer. He said, "You know what I think?"

"No. I don't know what you think. I'm a fortune teller, not a mind reader."

Donahoo was lost.

"I'm outta here," she told him. "If you want to arrest me, arrest me." She went for the stairway again. "Otherwise, beat it."

Donahoo watched her go up. The ass that was designed in a wind tunnel. She didn't look back. She unlocked her door, went in, slammed it. He stood on the sidewalk. The landing was like a balcony. He wondered if he should get a guitar.

The door opened and she came out and looked down at him. "You're a cop?"

"Yeah."

"You're an asshole." She went back inside. The door slammed.

Donahoo headed for the Chevy. He was almost to the corner when she yelled.

"Hey! What do you want?"

She gave him a Jim Beam. Close enough. He thanked her and went to the window that looked west over the engine company and the freeway. Her apartment had what the classified ads called a "peek" view of the water. He could see a glint of it, fast fading. A small boat, the running lights.

"Presh, huh?" he said. "Where would you get a name like that?"

"It's short for precious. My dad called me that. Only I couldn't pronounce it."

Presh Carling. Donahoo liked the name. It had a little more going than Madam Zola. He said, "How long you been a fortune teller?"

"Since college, university. It's how I worked my way through. Then I got my degree and I couldn't get a job."

He turned from the window. "What kind of degree?"

"A master's in philosophy."

"They don't need philosophers?"

"They don't need to pay 'em. How long you been a cop?"

"Forever."

"There was a cop here this morning," she said, getting her own drink, a glass of red wine. She moved to the sofa and indicated that he could take the easy chair. "Palmer. You know him? He asked a lot of questions. He was looking for somebody but he didn't know who."

Yeah, well, Palmer, Donahoo thought. Palmer didn't know shit. He sipped his Beam. He liked this lady. There was a nice directness about her. She was open.

"Some guy who doesn't like the planes."

He grinned. "I can see that happening."

"I don't mind them," she said. "They're a tradeoff. The rent I pay here? It would get me something in a barrio. I'd be in Encanto. National City. I don't want to be there. They're too tough for me." She raised her glass in toast. "This world. It's tough. How did it get so tough?"

Donahoo didn't know. It was tough, though, he thought. Out there, they'd tear your heart out. They'd let their dog fuck it. But he didn't know how they got that way. He just had theories he never shared. Humanity, like the bottle opener, replaced by the twist cap. It was obsolete.

"Where do you live?"

"Uptown, but I want to live in Coronado."

"My best wishes for that."

"Yeah."

"Tell me about the cop," she said. "The only cops I've known, they were at the other end of speeding tickets. You're my first cop."

Donahoo made a gesture. Where to start? He didn't know. He had no idea. He could tell her about The Purple Admiral Case. But that wouldn't tell her anything about him, the cop. It wouldn't explain anything. He said, "It's a disease. There's no cure. You get it, there's no cure. You're in for the whole run."

"And you've got it?"

"Oh, yeah."

She wanted details. He told her about The Stardust Donut Shop Murder Case.

"That's why you can't quit?" she asked when he had finished.

"No," he told her. "You can't quit on account of the perks. I mean, you know, in this tough world, how many people get to say, 'Stop ... or I'll shoot.'"

"Make one move. I'll blow your fucking head off?"

"Yeah.

She was having fun with it. "Okay, cocksucker. Freeze?"

"That, too."

They both laughed. She was looking at him differently. She said, "Well, I take it you're looking?"

"Yeah. I guess you could say that."

"You ever been married?"

"Once."

"What happened?"

"Tight lids," Donahoo said. He'd never told anybody this before, but she was looking at him differently. "Monica, she was kinda small, her wrists weren't very strong, and she was always accusing me of putting the lids on too tight, the ketchup, the mustard, the peanut butter, that kind of stuff, on purpose to annoy her. I really wasn't. I kept swearing to her. It's normal tight. She wouldn't believe me. So, one day, I'm standing there with the mayonnaise, and it occurs to me, what I should do is put this lid on so tight she couldn't get it off with a hammer. So I'm doing that and she walks in and catches me and all the trust goes out of the marriage."

"Well," Presh Carling said. "I guess that's enough for one night." She didn't offer him another drink.

So soon? Donahoo didn't want to leave yet. He wanted to tell her about The Balboa Firefly. He wanted to warn her about the planes that kept her safe. One might kill her. Any moment, it could come crashing, consume her in hellfire.

He wanted to tell her but he couldn't. Sapterstein was right. You couldn't let that word out. Spread panic in the neighborhood. It had enough troubles already.

"It was nice meeting you," Donahoo said. "I mean that with all my heart."

Presh Carling said, smiling, "Donahooie."

Kismet, Donahoo thought.

CHAPTER THIRTY-FOUR

Stryker arrived at One Harbor Drive. Twin residential towers that thrust up like black rifle barrels challenging the approaching night sky. They were dark, silent. They stood by themselves in a kind of enclave across from the San Diego Convention Center, Harbor Drive, and the trolley line between. The first tower had one resident. The other none. There'd been a story in the *Union-Tribune*. The resident and one doorman. What a joke—what an opportunity.

He parked in the curved driveway in front, directly opposite the palatial, glass-walled lobby and its huge glass doors. Quick getaway, he thought. He could see the doorman. The guy was putting a newspaper aside. He was frowning.

"Now, you let me do the talking," Stryker told Aldrich. "Don't volunteer anything, and if he asks you a question, don't answer. You think you can do that?"

Aldrich nodded tightly.

"Okay, here we go," Stryker said, pushing back the first tug of fear. The doorman was a lot bigger than his passenger. A lot younger. He felt for his gun, got out of the Mercedes. He motioned to the doorman.

The doorman opened the glass door. He was a raw, tall man in a dark mauve doorman's uniform, the peaked cap, the long coat with the epaulets. He was holding white gloves. He said, "I'm sorry. The sales office is closed."

Stryker gestured, come here. He opened the Mercedes's trunk. He stood waiting. Aldrich, unbidden, got out. He was shaking.

The doorman lumbered over. He had a fighter's hard face. He frowned. He said, impatient now, "The sales office ..."

"I need some help with this stuff," Stryker said. He pulled out his gun and then the silencer. He put them together. He had his courage back. The doorman watched in dumb fascination. "Maybe you could get the whiz bangs, the belt with the dynamite? I've got the detonator. Oh, and let's not forget the roses."

The doorman, ashen, pocketed his white gloves, then silently, carefully, removed a carpenter's tool belt from the trunk. It was fitted with eight sticks of dynamite. He held it one hand and then reached in for a brown box marked FIREWORKS.

Stryker had the Mercedes's rear door open. He slid out the long green box. With an effort, the gun in one hand, he fitted it into the crotch of his left arm. He frowned with the weight of it. He motioned with the gun. "Let's go."

The doorman took them into the black tower's dazzling lobby. Stryker used the muzzle of the silencer to push an elevator button. When the door slid open, Stryker went inside first, stood with his back to the wall of the car, motioned the others inside. They entered. He motioned again, saying turn around, face away. They did so.

"Top floor, please," Stryker said.

They rode up in silence. The elevator was fast, but it seemed to take a long time. Finally, it came to a stop. The door opened.

Stryker pushed the silencer's muzzle against the doorman's skull. "Would you like to die with your gloves on?"

The doorman didn't reply. But he did reach into his pocket, get them out, pull them on raggedly. He was hurrying.

Stryker fired and the doorman pitched forward just in time to block the elevator door from closing. It rammed against his fallen body.

Aldrich cried out and fell to the floor, a huddled, small trembling ball.

"Now what?" Stryker was waiting, for the rush, the release.

Aldrich's answer was a scream. "*I let it go!*"

"And it didn't go off?" Stryker said, waiting. "What do you expect? It was made in Yugoslavia." He used the side of his shoe to kick Aldrich in the ribs. Now, here, the rush. "Get up, old man. We'll find you something more reliable."

CHAPTER THIRTY-FIVE

Donahoo paid his respects to the widow. Marie, she wasn't doing the black thing, which he expected, maybe would have preferred. Disconcertingly, she was in a red, green, and white sack dress, the colors of Mexico, a big bow at the neck, like a drawstring. She was in the kitchen and she was baking sugar cookies. The women with her, two, maybe three of them, were escaping by the back door as he entered. He saw them as fleeting shadows. They'd wait in the yard until he left. Some of Frank's relatives from Tijuana. They were shy.

"I thought we'd get a head start," Marie told him, setting a cookie sheet to cool on the countertop. "You want one?"

Donahoo looked. They were covered with sprinkles, the same colors as her dress. No, he thought, they looked festive, inappropriate, but he took one anyway. He took a small bite.

"We're coming back here after the funeral," Marie said. Her fat brown eyes were swollen from crying, but there were no tears now. If anything, she looked resigned, that's all. "The reception. I'll be fucked if I'll call it a wake."

Donahoo nodded, reminded that Marie was Italian, not Mexican. She looked Mexican, but she was Italian. So the colors on her dress, they could be either, Mexican or Italian. Either or both. Camargo had met her while praying to Our Lady of Perpetual Help. Camargo, he never had a chance, Donahoo thought. He was already on his knees. He thought she was Mexican. He was engaged to her, he thought she was Mexican. She was fat, she had brown eyes, and dyed her hair red. She was a Catholic. It sort of piled up. Donahoo said, "The Irish have wakes."

"What do Mexicans have?"

He didn't know. He didn't want to guess. He wanted, just for a moment, the picture he had painted, the two innocents kneeling before Our Lady, *Their* Lady. Whom they both truly believed to represent the mother of God. He shrugged helplessly. Bad luck?

"I oughta know," Marie said. "I've been to enough of them. I just never heard the term. Maybe the whole process just gets jammed together, you think? The vigil, the service, the burial, the tears, the fall-down, pick-a-fight drunk. Let's not get choosy here. It's a fucking funeral."

Donahoo shrugged again. He hadn't thought about it. He didn't know. He knew a lot of cops, but he didn't know a lot of cops' wives. The cops he knew, they'd have a few drinks at a sports bar, or they'd go have Chinese. Maybe, once in awhile, they'd go to Jack Murphy, watch the Padres lose. They'd part, at night, around their cars, suggesting safe journeys, and then they'd go their separate ways. No wives. Camargo had been different. It was like he had an end-of-shift recording. He'd say, Marie is waiting. Well, shit, then let's not disappoint her, Donahoo had said finally. That's how Donahoo had come to meet, and possibly know, the fat, warm Marie.

"There's gonna be five million people in here," she said. "Mexicans, they're like the Jews, you know? There's either one of them or too many. You ever notice that? You can't just have two?"

Donahoo nibbled at his sugar cookie. That sounded like an oversimplification, but it was something else he hadn't given much thought to, so maybe she was right. You can have one. But two, they multiply. He said, "You okay?"

"No."

Dumb question, Donahoo decided, and he wondered if maybe he shouldn't have come, or at least not alone. Maybe he should have asked Lewis. It would be nice, Lewis to have come, Camargo's captain, make that special trip, not just show up at the service. He said, "Me, either."

She looked at him. She didn't say anything.

Donahoo could remember his first time here, that was a party, Frank and Marie had just bought the house, a two-bedroom, one-bath cottage, the smallest place in Kensington. There were five million people then, too. They were out in the street. They were down the block. They were fixing their cars.

"We're gonna have a closed casket," Marie said, her voice changing. "I guess you know. They took most of his head?"

Yeah, Donahoo thought. This was a mistake. There was no way he was going to give comfort tonight.

"With his own gun?"

"These things..." Donahoo started.

"I'm thankful," Marie said. She put another batch of cookies in the oven. "You know what I'm saying? The time we had together?" The door banged shut. She looked at Donahoo. "You think I'm so dumb I didn't know he was dumb?"

Donahoo didn't know what to say.

"Frank, he was dumb," Marie said, the tears finally starting. "He was a dumb cop." She was looking at Donahoo. "Cops' wives, they watch their husbands leave, they wonder if they're coming back. Me? I *know* he's not coming back. He's so fucking dumb, one day, he's gonna get wasted, *with his own gun!*"

Oh, fuck, Donahoo thought. He was holding half a cookie. He couldn't eat it. He didn't know where to put it.

"So that's why I'm thankful, Tommy," Marie said. "The time we had together, it was longer than expected, okay? It went on for fucking ever, beyond my wildest dreams, and that's why, you're my witness, I thank God, He took so fucking long, this extensive search He conducted, to find some prick to blow my dumb Frank's head off."

"Marie, Jesus," Donahoo said.

She grabbed the tray from the counter and flung it across the kitchen. The cookies went flying everywhere.

"Jesus."

"Naw, it's okay," Marie said. "I get these spells. Don't worry about it. In a minute, the Mariachi Sisters are gonna be in here, they'll clean up." She found a handkerchief. She blew her nose. She looked at Donahoo. "Frank, he really liked you, you know that, Tommy? He wasn't sucking up. He admired you. He thought you were the best cop in the department. He always wanted to work with you. He said you were the best." She was looking at him. "Did you let him down?"

"Maybe," Donahoo admitted. Here, now, this way, it was hard, but he had to admit that. "I'm not sure. But I'll try to make it up to him, Marie."

She wasn't buying that.

"Later, this is over, we can talk," Donahoo said, plunging ahead. "Frank, you know, maybe he had something, he hadn't got around to telling me. Sometimes, he was a slow release, you know? He didn't want to be wrong. Maybe he said something to you. I dunno. Something to somebody."

She shook her head.

"Well," Donahoo said. "Either way. I'll make it up to him."

Marie, sniffing, said, "Yeah, I'll read about it in the paper, Tommy. You'll be in the paper. Frank'll be in his grave."

CHAPTER THIRTY-SIX

The San Diego Convention Center opened its doors and a large group of people spilled out onto Harbor Drive. Some hurried toward the long line of waiting taxis. Others set out for the trolley stop across the street.

There was a flash of light followed by a loud bang. Everyone stopped and looked up to the sunset-tinged sky and the death throes of a skyrocket.

A man—it looked like a man, but perhaps it was a dummy—came hurtling from the top story of the west tower of the twin black skyscrapers located across the street from the Convention Center. The body traveled some fifty feet horizontally, as if shot from a cannon, or perhaps catapulted, and then it tumbled and dropped and exploded. It blew apart in the sky. Bits and pieces rained down on the trolley tracks below.

A woman in the crowd screamed.

High overhead, apparently from the tower, a small model airplane suddenly appeared, circling where the body had been blown apart. The plane kept circling, slowly losing altitude, its tiny gas motor making a racket. Around and around. Down, down, down. It was almost at ground level before anyone reacted. Then a man left the crowd and ran into the street and grabbed it out of the air. He yanked a wire and the racket stopped.

There was writing across the wings. The man held the plane so he could read the message.

THOSE WHO FORGET THE PAST ARE CONDEMNED TO RELIVE IT.

CHAPTER THIRTY-SEVEN

"Who the hell said that?" Saperstein demanded. He slammed the report on his desk. "What are we supposed to do now? Look up familiar quotations?"

"George Santayana," Gomez told him, unable to keep the pride from his voice. "He was a Spanish philosopher and writer in English." Gomez had looked this part up. "In the U.S., England, and Italy."

Saperstein did a very brief double take. "Do you know what it means?"

Gomez hesitated. "You gotta profit from your mistakes?"

"Very good," Saperstein had to admit. He looked around for a better victim. "You, Tommy, if you were to profit from your mistakes, you'd be a rich man by now. You'd be a fucking millionaire." He found another report in the pile scattered in front of him. "You go get your fortune told and a little old lady is fucked to death. You go see Frank Camargo's widow and a guy's thrown off the town's tallest building with a stick of dynamite up his ass. What the fuck are you doing? Let me tell you something, from now on, you don't do widows."

Lewis said, "I told him he should take the day off."

"It's the second tallest," Donahoo said. He drank his coffee. He had been up all night. He had a headache that wouldn't go away. He barely had the will to defend himself. He'd gone home happy in the knowledge that he had a shot with Madam Zola. Then Mavis Farrow's body was found. And then, in the middle of that, Paul Aldrich had taken his unscheduled flight.

"Mavis Farrow," Saperstein said, shuffling his reports. "A little old lady. What is she? Ninety? And it's the worst rape I ever heard of. Every body orifice. God in heaven, what kind of a monster? Why pick on her?"

Lewis said, "She was a mattress millionaire."

Saperstein looked at him.

"She kept money there, cash," Lewis said. "We've been talking to a niece. The niece says she would keep, two, three hundred thousand there."

"In her mattress?"

"Yeah."

Saperstein was looking at him. "I didn't know people still did that."

"Well, it's safer than banks."

Lyons said, "You gotta get out more, Chief."

Saperstein looked at him but let it go. "The money's gone, I suppose?"

"Our guys didn't find any. But they did find impressions."

"Impressions?"

"Indentations. Places between two mattresses where money packets could have been hidden."

"You're saying she's a two-mattress millionaire?"

"Was."

"Right." Saperstein put the report down. He had only the initial findings of the first investigators on the scene. He was filling in the gaps as he went along. "So what you're saying, this pharmacy delivery guy, nobody can find him, he's already on a plane to the Riviera?"

"Maybe."

"Maybe not," Montrose said. He had his list of property owners in the Balboa Park glide path. He held it up as a show-and-tell for Saperstein. "The deceased owned eight pieces of property, Chief. They're just houses and they're scattered around, no one big holding, but that is substantial."

"Six?"

"Yeah."

"And you think there's a connection?"

Montrose shifted uncomfortably. "Well, yeah."

"So do I," Saperstein said. He thought for a moment. "Listen, I want that fucking list out of your pocket and up on the wall, okay? I want a big blowup. I want every individual parcel outlined. I want the name of the owner on it, the person, the dba, the corporation, whatever. I want you to do that now."

"Now?"

"Gomez has interpreted Santayana. Were you planning to outdo that?"

"No."

"Well, then, yeah, I'd like it done now, Montrose. Any other questions?"

Montrose took his coffee and left. Donahoo thought that was what Saperstein was going to do. He was going to dismiss them, one at a time, and then he'd be alone, at last, with the one he wanted to destroy.

"If there's a connection..." Saperstein was talking to himself. He turned to Gomez. "If there *is* a connection, the link is Mavis Farrow to Eric Hudson. It's not..." He looked at Donahoo. "What was the name in the *Union-Trib*?"

"The Balboa Firefly."

"Not The Balboa Firefly," Saperstein saild, looking at Donahoo. He looked at him for a long moment. "The Balboa Firefly, when he kills, he leaves a note. The Balboa Firefly, when he kills, he doesn't rape."

Donahoo's headache wouldn't go away. Six aspirin and it wouldn't go away. "Well, now, wait a minute. He did get his cock sucked."

"Once," Lyons said. "That's not a pattern. It's just a good time."

"The Ramparts, this is an apartment block," Saperstein told Lewis. "There's a lot of people living there? Why don't we have any witnesses?"

"They've got separate entrances." Lewis went through his stuff. "There's one old guy. He saw somebody go in. He doesn't know if it was the delivery guy or not. He can't remember."

"There's a lot of that," Gomez said. "My grandmother, she can remember eighty years ago, every precise detail, her sister was mean to her, but ask her who was that on the phone?"

"The pharmacy delivery guy," Saperstein said to Gomez. "Find him. He's stuffed in a toilet somewhere. A sewer pipe. Find him."

Gomez nodded.

"Now."

Donahoo watched Gomez leave. You want a pattern? This was it, Donahoo thought. Saperstein was thinning them out, one at a time, and Lyons, that wiseguy, he ought to watch his mouth, he was in as much shit as anybody. How could he not be in shit?

"Okay," Saperstein said. "Let's talk about Aldrich. His wife says…" He got the preliminary report. "His wife says he was taking part in some sort of survey. Somebody phones him, a cold call, asks him if he'd like to participate in a survey, forty dollars for a couple hours work, he says yes, they mail him a form. He fills out the form—the usual crap, education, likes, dislikes—mails it back, what he doesn't know, into a vacuum, there's no such PO box. They still call him up, though, say he's been accepted. All he has to do is come to their office. Group meeting."

Saperstein glanced up. He wanted everybody's attention. "After dinner. Aldrich goes there, at least as far as the parking lot. There's no office, it doesn't exist. So, this is conjecture, but we've got Aldrich's car, it's pretty solid, the killer intercepts him in the parking lot and says the meeting has been changed to another location. The killer takes Aldrich to One Harbor Drive. There's nobody there but the doorman and one condo owner in the whole fucking building. How does the killer know that? There was a big feature story about it in the paper a couple weeks ago. A guy buys a condo and nobody else buys a condo, but the developer has to live up to the homeowners' agreement and the agreement calls for a doorman." Saperstein shook his head. "Anyway, skipping along here, the killer bumps the doorman…" He looked to Lewis.

"It looks like the same gun," Lewis said.

"The same gun," Saperstein repeated, looking now at Donahoo. "Which makes him The Balboa Firefly. Would you say that, Tommy?"

"Yeah. The Balboa Firefly."

"Thank you. The Balboa Firefly. He bumps the doorman and he bumps Aldrich. This is in the elevator. We got the holes all over. Then, the killer, The Balboa Firefly, with the doorman's keys, gains entrance to a vacant penthouse condo, where, in the rooftop garden, he places Aldrich on an ingenious, lightweight, quickly assembled—what term shall we use?—body launcher?"

Lewis nodded. "The whole thing, including the spring, apparently fits in a box for long-stemmed roses. We found the box. We didn't find the roses." He hesitated. "The lab gets through, we'll break it down, see if it fits in the box."

"I await the results breathlessly," Saperstein said. He looked again at Donahoo. "The Balboa Firefly, in an act beyond my comprehension, catapults Aldrich out of the penthouse garden, belted with a pack of dynamite. Aldrich explodes, midair, over several hundred horrified delegates to a comic book convention, just now exiting the San Diego Convention Center. A model airplane comes circling down. It bears a message, quote: 'Those who forget the past are condemned to relive it.'" Saperstein looked around. "Now. What is different about this case?"

"It's not random," Lyons said.

"Wait a minute," Donahoo said softly. His headache was killing him. "Paul Aldrich. What's his middle initial?"

Saperstein frowned but checked his report. "Samuel. S."

"PSA," Donahoo said. "Pacific Southwest Airlines."

They were all silent for a long moment.

"Oh, good," Saperstein said then. He leaned back in his chair. He was visibly shaken. "The sonofabitch, what he's saying, an airliner is next, Tommy."

No one else spoke.

"An airliner," Saperstein repeated. "Holy fuck. In the glide path, they're flying so low, you could hit 'em with an automatic weapon, a bazooka or something."

"You could throw rocks at 'em," Donahoo said. His headache was worse. He didn't think that was possible.

CHAPTER THIRTY-EIGHT

Angela, softly, a whisper, barely audible, the faintest of sounds. Three little words. "He's got it."

Mark Stevens, it took him a moment to become Mark Stevens, to become Marky, said, falling into the accent, "Now?"

"Yes."

"Where?"

"Here."

Now, Stevens thought. His heart was suddenly racing. He said, whispering to himself now, ever so softly, "Keep him there, darling."

It was Foley who hung up the phone. He thought he ought to send Stryker.

Angela lived in a small house on Texas Street in North Park. There were three houses on the one property. Hers was at the back on the lane, a very small house, tiny, actually. A living room, bedroom, kitchen, and bath were fitted into what would be one room in a normal house. Her doll house, Angela called it, and she was happy, because she could remember when she didn't have *any* place to live.

The Marine said, "Do you wanta fool around?"

Angela said, "You need to rehearse, do you?"

"Practice makes perfect."

"Maybe later."

The Marine accepted that. He checked out the house. This was his first time here. He'd been surprised, almost shocked, by how small it was, but he was getting used to it. He thought she had done a really good job. He liked the furniture, it was old, but it was nice. He liked all the movie posters.

"We could play a tile game," Angela suggested.

The Marine shook his head. He wasn't very good at games. He always lost and that made him feel stupid. He said, "You've got a nice place."

"Thank you."

"I like the posters. Where did you get 'em?"

"The thrifts."

"You shop the thrifts?"

"All the time," Angela told him. "It's like a treasure hunt. Everything you see, I got it at a thrift, I mean everything."

He looked around. "Wow."

"Let me show you something," Angela said. "You're not gonna believe this. Yesterday, at AmVets, I got a Brooks Brothers suit, it was made for me, for $12.95. I don't think it's been worn. Brooks Brothers."

He pretended to be interested. "Oh? Let's see."

"No. I'll wear it for you."

There was a rumble in the lane. An old Mercedes that needed a valve job.

Angela said, "When you come back, I'll be wearing it for you, okay?"

"Sure," the Marine said. He wanted her clothes off, not on, but what the hell, if it made her happy. He wanted her happy. Maybe, he thought, next time he came, he'd bring her something from a thrift. Maybe a movie poster. He'd seen one he liked, James Dean in a railway station, slumped on a bench, smoking.

Angela kissed him on the cheek and went into her bedroom to get the Brooks Brothers suit.

Stevens turned off the Mercedes. So, this it, huh? he thought, staring at the Marine's van, an old Ford Econo parked in a narrow slot off the lane. It had been repainted, badly, in camouflage colors. Stevens thought that maybe Stryker should have come. He'd appreciate it more.

The Marine came out of the tiny house. He stood on the miniature back stoop, looking pleased with himself. He was wearing his off-base uniform. The khaki Marine T-shirt that showed off his Marine muscles. The baggy pants with the baggy pockets stuck low on the legs.

Stevens pushed out of the Mercedes. "You got it, huh?"

"Yeah," the Marine said. He came down into the parking stall. "It was easy. Pendleton, it's so big, there's hundreds of guys driving off base all at the same time. They just wave you through. Spot check." He grinned. "They didn't check."

"You took a chance."

"Yeah, well, I figure it's worth it."

Me, too, Stevens thought. He changed hands with the leather jacket he was holding like a bundle. He peered into the van, across the front seats, into the back, which was stripped for cargo. He couldn't see anything. It was piled with junk. "The Breaker, huh?"

"Yeah."

"It's loaded, I trust?"

"I brought you two rounds."

"Good man. You going to show me how to use it?"

"Better than that. I brought you a manual."

"Manuals are good," Stevens said. He said, "Well, let's go for a ride, huh?" He said, "Let's take the van."

The Marine said, "Let's do it."

Stevens waited for the Marine to move the van out of the parking slot. Then he put the Mercedes in its place. He thought of going in, saying hello to Angela. Then he decided no. That would be a lie. He'd be saying goodbye.

"Where we going?" the Marine asked.

Stevens got in beside him. "Straight to hell."

The Marine laughed.

CHAPTER THIRTY-NINE

Donahoo was taking Chip Lyons on a guided tour of the Balboa Park glide path. He was telling him what he knew, which was very little, and what he suspected, which could go on forever. He was telling him, from time to time, in a variety of ways, that he didn't much like him. He thought that should be made clear, up front.

Chip Lyons was half listening and not caring at all. He could have been someplace else for all he seemed to care. He was dressed in gray sweats, the tight pants, the loose shirt, the hundred-dollar Adidas trainers. He'd come on shift that way, a bright blue poplin jacket in one hand, a 44-ounce BIG GULP full of coffee in the other. He was wearing his harness like a pirate. His Dan Wesson 744V .44 magnum with the 10-inch barrel was stuck in it like a cannon.

Donahoo looked into the one eye. He said, he was talking about the Dan Wesson, "How much does that thing weigh, Chippie?"

"It's Chipper."

"Excuse me. How much does it weigh? Chipper?"

"I dunno. I never weighed it."

"It weighs sixty-three ounces. That's four fucking pounds."

"You weighed it?"

"No. I read that somewhere."

Donahoo turned a corner and stopped the Chevy. They were on Juniper, where it dropped sharply from Front Street. They had the big view, unobstructed. The Bay, Point Loma, the Pacific. The

Bay was hustling. Windy day, lots of sailors out. The sails were a hundred white handkerchiefs waving at them.

Donahoo was looking at Coronado. He said it to himself, but it was audible. "You don't know a fucking thing about that gun, do you?"

Chip Lyons smiled. He said, "I know what it can do."

Donahoo let it go, and the Chevy, too. He reminded himself that he was looking for The Balboa Firefly. He ought to concentrate on that. Try, as part of this exercise, bringing Chippie up to speed, to figure where he might be hiding.

When he saw him, he'd know him, Donahoo thought. He had this picture of him in his mind. The sonofabitch, he hurt, and that would show on his face. That was why he wanted to hurt others. So the first thing to watch for was the hurt. The pain. But he'd also look superior. He killed so easily, so readily. He must think of himself as almighty. He had the power to snuff existence. He could turn life into dust. Dirt. So look for that. The next thing, also important, furtive. He was afraid of being caught, so he'd look that way, furtive, nervous, maybe a little scared? He didn't want to get caught. Not yet. Afterward, maybe. He might want to get caught then. But not now.

"Why are you so pumped up on the offshore theory?" Chip Lyons asked.

"There's no profit otherwise," Donahoo told him. "If he closes down Lindbergh, the only way he collects is to own a lot of land here, to be able to sell it, and the only way he can sell it and not be identified is offshore."

"I dunno. He can't hide forever."

"Maybe not. But it doesn't matter. He could go someplace it's tough to extradite. He could sit there forever and have agents here sell off for him. Even if he was identified, that doesn't convict him, just because he owns and sells land at enormous profit, benefiting from what could be somebody else's crime. He could say he just got lucky. A shuffle of the cards. It appears very suspicious. But does it warrant an indictment? I don't think so."

Chip Lyons looked doubtful. "You're giving an awful lot of credit to a whacko."

"Then how to explain all the sales activity around here? For the past two years somebody has been buying up this whole goddamn place."

"Maybe somebody. Maybe a lot of people. You don't know that yet. Maybe a lot of people decided they don't need you to know their business, huh? Maybe it just happened that way, the law of averages fucked up. You know the law of averages?"

"Sure. It's what prevents every woman in the world from picking today to get a yeast infection. Now tell me something I don't know."

"You're giving a lot of credit to a whacko."

"The flaw," Donahoo admitted. The possibly fatal flaw. Because they were dealing with a whacko. No doubt about it.

"Me?" Chip Lyons said. "What I think, fuck offshore. That's gonna take too long. All those layers of corporations? No, what we've got to do, concentrate on the Mercedes. We could get lucky with the Mercedes. Not with offshore. Takes too long. The dirty deed'll be done and you're still wondering who really owns Fortune Holdings. You know what I mean?"

Yeah, Donahoo thought. Okay, okay. He pushed the Chevy along. Time was running out. They needed to do something spectacular. Today's meeting of the powers-that-be, the one he wasn't attending, might provide that. They could come out kicking ass. They could call in the National Guard. They could demand entry at every door in the glide path. If The Balboa Firefly was here, if a device that could bring down an airliner was here, they ought to be able to find him, locate it. *If* he was here. *If* it was here.

Would they do that?

Probably not, but they could, if they pushed it, Donahoo thought. He knew that one by heart. The Fourth Amendment does not prohibit police officers from making warrantless entries and searches in response to emergency situations. So they could do it, if that was the way they decided to go, declare an emergency. Maybe it wouldn't stand up later. But later wouldn't matter if they averted a disaster.

Donahoo could imagine them agonizing over the concept. To get a search warrant, to get a thousand search warrants, they needed probable cause, and there was no lock on arguing that successfully. All they had was a few corpses and a few notes. All they had was a whacko pulling their tits. He might be going after an airliner. He might have the means to do that. Maybe.

But The Balboa Firefly was here, damn it, Donahoo thought. He most surely was here. Donahoo was positive of that. He was somewhere close, somewhere in the glide path, and he was getting ready to do it, and time wouldn't stand still.

Valesy stopped the Jeep Wrangler at the corner of Ivy and Albatross. He didn't remove the ragtop. He didn't want to take that risk and he didn't need to. He had practiced this over and over in the storage unit. All he had to do now, in place, ready, was rehearse it in his mind at the actual site, here where it was going to happen, at Ivy and Albatross.

The Jeep Wrangler was positioned. He went through the motions in his mind. Pull off the top. Unzip the canvas bag. Swing the Spigot on its swivel. He timed it. Eight seconds. Perfect. He could do it. Now, load the round. Sight on the plane. Fire.

The sky rumbled. Jet coming. Valesy watched for it. A huge airliner crossed very low half a block south.

It was like a duck, Valesy thought. He'd lead it.

A short distance away, on Curlew, near Juniper, Foley would soon be crouched at his attic window, preparing a nest for the TOW that Marky had arranged for and that Stryker would bring.

Foley might also think that the plane was like a duck. But he intended to fire head-on.

Donahoo, cruising, back and forth, up and down, thought he knew what his quarry looked like. He was watching for the hurt, the pain. Someone who appeared superior and at the same time furtive. Maybe a little scared? But also determined. Someone hard to stop.

A Jeep Wrangler was approaching. The man at the wheel was very plain and ordinary. He had a face without distinction. He had nothing to set him apart.

Nothing like that, Donahoo thought. The Wrangler passed him in a rush. It went down the block and turned the corner and disappeared.

Donahoo watched in his rearview mirror. Nothing like that. But he could be wrong. He'd been wrong before. That was the problem. It could be anybody and you couldn't check everybody. You had to get lucky. A shuffle of the...

There was a rattletrap Ford at the corner, hood up. There was an Auto Club tow truck giving it a jump start.

"Did anybody check the Auto Club?" Donahoo asked. He was talking to himself.

Chip Lyons looked at him with that one eye. Donahoo jammed the Chevy.

CHAPTER FORTY

The backyard had the right smell about it. A hundred crank-
cases emptied here, and most of it spilled on the ground,
Donahoo thought. The soft earth reeked with used oil. Old car
parts were scattered around. A back seat, busted headlights, a
generator. Starters, carburetors, radiators. Parts tossed everywhere. A backyard junk yard.

Chip Lyons showed two fingers. Two minutes, and then, he,
Donahoo, should kick in the garage's side door. Chip Lyons was
going around to the lane access. He got a new grip on his Dan
Wesson 744. Two hands for four pounds. He'd been holding it
that way since they got out of the Chevy.

Donahoo nodded and looked at his watch. He didn't know
why he was suddenly taking orders. He should be giving them,
but he didn't want to speak, argue. They were very close. They'd
heard metal clang. A man complain, "Fuck."

He tried again to find a peephole in the whitewash covering
the glass inset in the flimsy plywood side door. There wasn't a
speck uncovered. He looked at his watch. Waited.

They had already checked the house. It was a two-story yellow clapboard at Fourth and Maple on the edge of the glide path.
The shared residence, according to the four mail slots, of Charles
Schmidt, L. B. Loza, G. Shaw, and Chance Kruger. They were
interested in Chance Kruger. Two weeks previous he had called
the Auto Club and requested a tow. From the Sports Center swap
meet to S & R Motors. Request denied. Membership expired. But
the Auto Club had a record of the call and the membership files

had Kruger's name, address, age, occupation, etc., etc. He was an open book and he was in trouble. The disabled car was a black '72 Mercedes 280SEL. California license 8GHI620. DMV said it wasn't currently registered. The plates traced—last registration five years ago—to a Colin Reinhart in Santa Cruz.

Donahoo looked at his watch. Fifty-two seconds. They'd been through the clapboard. The front door wasn't locked. They'd been in Chance Kruger's room. It had been locked, but it wasn't anymore. A rumpled bachelor's room. Unmade bed, clothes strewn. Minestrone soup turned to a hard crust in the dented aluminum pot on the single-burner hotplate. He was a kid. Twenty-two.

Thirty seconds. Big kid, Donahoo thought. There'd been a photo in a dime-store frame. Chance Kruger lounging against an old Studebaker Hawk. Big kid in blackened mechanic's overalls. Bad haircut. Big smile. Scrawled on it, "Take a chance with Chance." The Balboa Firefly?

Hardly, Donahoo thought. But you never know. You never, ever know. Twelve seconds. He got out his Colt Model Python. He counted them off. He kicked in the flimsy door.

Chip Lyons had his Dan Wesson in Chance Kruger's face. He said, very softly, "Drop the wrench. Drop it or I'll kill you."

Donahoo aimed his Python. The garage's alley door was fully raised overhead. Chip Lyons had Chance Kruger backed up against the 280SEL. The backlight from the alley silhouetted an about-to-take-place murder. The kid wasn't going to drop the wrench. He was frozen with fear.

"Shoot him, I'll shoot you, Chippie," Donahoo said. "I mean it."

Chip Lyons hesitated.

"I'm a virgin, remember?" Donahoo said. "We're having a shootout with a wrench? I could get nervous. I could try for him and get you. It could happen."

Chip Lyons took the wrench. He tossed it to the ground. He shouldered the Dan Wesson. He looked at the 280SEL.

"You Chance Kruger?" Donahoo asked.

The kid nodded.

"This your car?"

Another nod.

"How come it's not registered?"

No response.

"You know," Chip Lyons said. He was looking at the car. There was no motor. No transmission. "What it takes to register a car that's not on the street? It costs five bucks." He turned with the one eye. "Five bucks. Five fucking bucks."

"That's what this is about?" the kid asked. "Five dollars?"

Donahoo put his Python away. In a way, yeah, he thought. It was an overstructured society. Every day, more rules, more ways to break them, more opportunity for error. More chance of a rule keeper losing it with a rule bender. One of these days, the way things were going, you could get killed for the quarter you didn't put in a meter.

CHAPTER FORTY-ONE

Angela called Farthest Star Productions. There was no answer. Always, before, the phone was answered. Either by Marky or by the machine. But now, nothing. It just rang and rang. She had tried the number several times. They'd been gone for hours. She'd go over there, but she didn't have the address, didn't have any idea of where it was, or even if it was for real. Farthest Star wasn't listed.

They weren't coming back, she thought. Not now, or ever. It was over. She knew that. Marky, he had warned her, this could happen, and now it was happening. He told her if it happened, just forget it, dahling. Pretend it was just a dream. Especially if a cop asks. And never, ever share this phone number, dahling. You never had it, never called it. Throw it away.

Yeah. Just a crazy dream, and now it was over. Someone would come in the night to get the Mercedes. They wouldn't come in. She'd hear it go, that's all. She'd go back to sleep. It was over. That saddened her. Marky was a nice man. Nice, and strange, too. He wasn't English. Once, when he was excited, when she smiled for him after the dentist, showed him her new caps, he forgot the accent. He also was a liar. He was going to make her a star? That was so silly. But it was fun playing the game, pretending. He treated her well. He never asked for anything. Never once. And he had given her the gift of beauty. That was a special gift for which she would be eternally grateful.

They weren't coming back. So now what? she wondered. Angela sat before her cracked mirror in her Brooks Brothers suit. Such a pretty lady, she thought.

The former Miss Brazil.

CHAPTER FORTY-TWO

Donahoo went home thinking about Chance Kruger staring into that one eye and the blow hole of a four-pound Dan Wesson 744V. Oh, whoa, Donahoo thought. That must have been perfect hell. The kid's whole life, going past. Going into the toilet.

"Pussy," Donahoo said. "Where are you?" He was thinking of the cat, how maybe he'd be nicer to it. He was thinking of the Old Crow. He was wondering how he'd react with a gun at his head. Two seconds away from life's final indignity. What was that like?

Donahoo hurried. He could hear Cody. Cody saying, "Tommy?" He didn't want to see Cody right now. He got the door unlocked. He went in, almost closed it. He stood looking around. There was something wrong. The balcony slider was open wider than the usual pussy width.

A pistol was jammed at the base of his skull.

"Hello and goodbye," Valesy said.

Donahoo froze. He said, very softly, "Think about it."

Cody was at the door. "Tommy?"

The pistol pressed harder. "Who's that?"

"My neighbor."

"Tell him to go away."

"Tommy?"

"Cody, fuck off," Donahoo said. "I'm having a bad day."

"Tommy?"

"Fuck off."

Cody, grinning, pushed open the door, stood there grinning like he was having a bad day, too, only you didn't need to be shitty about it.

Valesy moved the pistol to shoot Cody. Donahoo grabbed the barrel with his left hand. His right grabbed Valesy by the testicles. Valesy screamed and fired at the ceiling. Cody hit the floor. Donahoo had the pistol and Valesy's testicles. Valesy was screaming. Donahoo was like a bulldozer. He pushed back, across the room, through the glass slider, smashing it to bits, across the narrow balcony, through the railing, wood splintering.

Valesy twisted free in the fall. Donahoo dropped sixteen feet and landed on his back. Instinctively, he rolled away. He wedged against a rock. He looked up at a knotted rope dangling from a pike hook lodged in the balcony's deck. He heard someone crashing madly through the underbrush toward the freeway. He tried to move. He couldn't. Not for a while. He hurt too much. It was difficult to breathe.

Cody came tentatively to the busted balcony rail. "Tommy?"

Cody, Donahoo thought. You never listen.

Valesy reached the freeway. He thought that he'd pass on UPNNZ EPOBIPP, and on KPIO MBTTJUFS, too. All this killing for what? He'd just do the big job, he decided. He'd bring down the airliner. He'd go home.

CHAPTER FORTY-THREE

The Marine had taught Stevens everything he needed to know about The Breaker. Stevens was very sure he could pass that knowledge along to Stryker. Actually, for a modern, sophisticated weapon, it was fairly simple to operate, he thought. It was about as simple as rock. It just crushed more skulls.

They drove now to Marilou Park. It was an area, not a park. Federal Boulevard ran through it, along a canyon. There wasn't much traffic. California 94, nearby, siphoned it off. Stevens said the circus bus was in Marilou Park. Now he gave instructions to pull over, stop. They were on Federal Boulevard. They were on the canyon's edge.

The Marine didn't understand what was going on. There was no other road. Just a steep path.

Stevens got out the morphine.

"What the hell?" the Marine said.

"Diabetic," Stevens explained. He shot up.

The Marine stared at him. "Fuck."

Stevens waited. The pain he always felt, *they* always felt, began to ease.

"What's going on?"

"Let's check it out," Stevens said, meaning the circus bus, which didn't exist, here or any other place. He pushed out of the van.

The Marine got out on his side and looked around. "There's no bus here."

"Come on, I'll show you," Stevens said. He started down the steep path leading into the canyon. "I don't want to go in the front way. The caretaker might get nosy. Let's see if we can haul it through here."

The Marine slid down after him. "I don't think so."

Stevens kept going.

"How come you're not limping?" the Marine asked.

Stevens turned. He unfolded his leather jacket to reveal the gun with the silencer. He said, "Stryker doesn't limp."

He was Stryker now. Not Stevens, not Foley. Stryker. He emptied the gun into the Marine. Thud, thud, thud. Every round. He dragged the body down the rest of the slope and kicked it over a ledge. It crashed down and disappeared in the tangle of brush far below.

CHAPTER FORTY-FOUR

Donahoo called on Presh Carling, cap in hand, so to speak. He was wearing it when he knocked on the door. He took it off before she answered, and held it with the small bouquet of mismatched flowers he had picked up at Vons. He didn't want to look dumb with a cap on. He didn't know why he'd worn it anyway. Probably because he was nervous, he thought. He'd been nervous when he phoned, when she answered, when they talked. He'd been nervous when he asked her out and he'd been nervous when she said okay. He didn't know why. It wasn't complicated. All he wanted was to be with her. That's all he wanted to start. To start, he repeated that, and he wondered whether he should be holding the cap, or whether he should be wearing it. He was holding it when she opened the door.

"Hi," she said, smiling. "Is that for me?", and she took it, the cap, not the flowers. She stuffed it in an umbrella stand like he was never going to see it again. "Don't just stand there. Come on in."

He followed her. She was dressed in black. Black and white. A long black skirt, black stockings, low black pumps. The plain blouse, like a shirt, it was white. The jacket was black. It was waiting on the back of the sofa. Her long black hair was down.

"There's a story behind that cap," he said.

"You can tell me later."

Kismet, Donahoo thought again. Very definitely Kismet.

He'd been here the once, when he walked her home, from downstairs, but it was changed now. There was some new art on the wall. Three pictures, one quite large, it dominated the room. It was of a figure of a man, done very starkly, in bold, almost harsh colors. The way the man was dressed, in a kind of surrealistic armor, made him look like someone in the future, but the armor spoke of the past, too. The shield across his chest was patterned on the latest bulletproof vest. The smaller pictures were by the same artist. They were of faces. One was of a clown. The other was of a druggist. Or maybe a dentist. He had the high collar.

"You know who invented the high collar?" Donahoo said, giving her the flowers. "Saperstein. He got the buttons from here." He showed her where, the middle of his chest. "So he could put his hand in here." He showed her where Napoleon did it.

"Saperstein?"

"I never told you about Saperstein?"

"You can tell me later."

She put the flowers in a small vase that already had water in it. Donahoo wondered if all the men she knew brought her flowers, she expected to get them. He wondered how many men she knew. He wondered what kind of flowers.

"So?" He was already down one, he thought. "Who's the artist?"

"A friend."

"Oh."

She went to the small bar. She had everything ready. The Old Crow. Her martini in the shaker. The waiting glasses. They were going to have a couple drinks and then they were going to dinner. The Old Crow, it was a nice touch, Donahoo thought. The last time, when he asked, all she had was Jim Beam, so she had remembered the Old Crow. He felt better.

"Chuck Bladen," Presh said, meaning the artist. "I got them in trade," meaning the paintings. "He used to have a studio here. There's a loft over the coin laundry. He was always wanting me to tell his fortune. He didn't have any money. I'd tell his fortune and tell him he could pay me when he was successful. He showed up yesterday and hung 'em."

"What was his fortune?"

"He was gonna be successful. I've got the gift, remember?"

Donahoo smiled. He hadn't seen that coming. He'd been too busy looking at her. She was a very beautiful woman. He was afraid he'd been staring.

She brought him the Old Crow. He started for the easy chair. She gave him a little tug. She was smiling. He joined her on the sofa. She touched her martini glass to his tumbler.

She said, "How the hell are you?"

He was okay now. He said, "I'm fine."

"Good."

Donahoo took a sip of his drink. Not exactly the first of the day. He'd had a couple before leaving his apartment. He'd also had a couple when he got there, or at least shortly thereafter, come to think of it. He and Cody. Doubles. The fouled-up raid had really rattled him. Chip Lyons preparing to blow the kid away. Then the brush with the mystery prowler. That had scared the crap out of him.

He thought there was an off chance it had something to do with The Balboa Firefly. But he couldn't figure what. The voice was totally different. All he knew, he was lucky.

He said, "You want to tell me about yourself?"

She gave him a two-minute biog. Raised in Portland. Reed College and Berkeley. A mother, Lillian, and a brother, Rick. Rick looked after mother, but he could be a pain in the ass. Once he bought her a freezer and then got mad because she didn't put anything in it. He found a *Pennysaver* advertising chickens for fifty cents. She could still hear him yelling, "Why isn't that freezer full of fifty-cent chickens?" She had told him, "I don't know," and she had moved to San Diego.

That reminded Donahoo. He said, "You got a place you'd like to eat?"

She shook her head. "Let's go someplace you go."

Donahoo almost choked on the Old Crow. "I go to The Waterfront."

"Then let's go there."

"It's a dive."

"So?"

"Well, wait," Donahoo said, embarrassed. "I didn't mean to suggest it. You can eat for two bucks. About the only thing on the menu is hamburgers and fries."

"Are they good?"

"They're okay."

"Then let's go there."

Donahoo looked at her.

"I'd like to go where you go," Presh told him. "I want to see your hangouts. I want to meet your friends. That's how you get to know somebody."

Donahoo wondered. What was she saying? That he couldn't fake it at The Waterfront?

He said, "Yeah, well, that works both ways. I want to get to know you."

"Okay. But one beanery at a time."

The Waterfront was practically empty. There were four guys in a corner, arguing football, and a lady of the evening at the juke box, complaining that they didn't have "Ebb Tide." In the pool room, which was also the dining room, a guy, unseen, was telling another guy, also unseen, that if a woman was ever going to look at him, he'd have to stuff a sock in it, meaning the crotch of his pants.

This was a mistake, Donahoo thought. He picked the first table by the door, his reserved table when he could get it, the one that offered the fastest exit, and, now, a clear view of his Olds Toronado. He hadn't put on The Club.

Ginny came around from behind the bar. Usually, you had to go to her, but she wanted a closer look at Presh Carling. She said to the woman at the juke box, " 'Try Boulevard of Broken Dreams,' dearie." She said to Donahoo, looking at Presh, "This is your answer?"

Jesus, a real mistake, Donahoo thought. He said, "Huh?"

"To your want ad?"

"Oh," Donahoo said. "Give me a break, willya?" He made the introduction. "Presh Carling, Ginny Watson. Ginny will be your server tonight." He said, rushing right along, "A martini, straight up, for the lady. My usual."

"Shall I bring the bottle?"

"No. Just my usual glass."

Ginny got out her pad. "Will you be eating for a change?"

Presh was already enjoying herself. "What do you recommend?"

"The hamburger and the fries."

"Okay. I'll have them."

"The big hamburger or the small hamburger?"

"How big is the big hamburger?"

"Half a pound."

"That's the biggest?"

"Yeah."

"Give me two of them."

Ginny looked at her. "You want 'em cooked?"

A mistake, Donahoo kept thinking. A major mistake. He said, "My usual." He didn't have a usual.

Ginny went away. Donahoo said, "Listen, I'm not complaining, but can you eat a pound of hamburger?"

Presh was examining the menu. "Take it home to your cat. Have you seen these prices? It's cheaper than pet food."

Actually, it would have been okay, Donahoo thought. It would have been fine, except that some cop came in, he didn't even know the cop's name, Burden, maybe Barden. The cop had come in just as they were leaving, and he had said, he was a little drunk, he was laughing, "Hey, hotshot, I hear you blew a big one today?" and he had said, "I hear they're gonna call you guys the SCUMB bags."

Donahoo, if he had it to do over again, he'd do something different, he'd come off his stool kind of awkwardly, like it was only an accident, and he'd stepped on the cop's instep really hard. The guy had screamed and jumped around a lot.

Ginny had said, "You can be a real idiot, Donahoo," and he had said, "When he stops jumping around, tell him the bright side, he doesn't have to walk his beat."

Presh had wanted to know what that was all about. He hadn't told her.

Now, in the Olds, driving back to her apartment, she asked the other question he'd been dreading, "What kind of cop are you?"

"Sickos, Crackpots, Underwear and Mad Bombers," he told her flat, the whole thing.

"Why didn't you tell me that before?" she said, which wasn't at all what he had expected.

"I dunno," he said. "First date, I guess." He had expected her to ask for details. He thought she was pretty smart to leave it alone like that. Now that she knew, she knew she didn't have to know any more, and that she didn't have to ask any more questions. "I didn't want to show up, say, 'Listen, what I do, I work in the terlet, where do you wanta eat?'"

"I just ate."

He grinned and shook his head.

"Yeah, I guess I understand," she said, becoming serious, or at least trying. "It's not something you'd want to come to me with straight out." She put a hand on his arm. "I understand, okay?"

"Thanks."

"You're welcome. Now can I borrow your Liquid Plumber?"

"It's not all crap, there are some good moments, the rising spirit of man stuff," Donahoo said, blowing a little smoke, that had been a lot easier than he had expected. "It can be interesting. I figure, I retire, I'll maybe write my memoirs or something." He waited, but she didn't pick up on it. "But, you know, you go into a library, all those books. You know who you're competing with? Tolstoy and Hemingway? Shakespeare? There's all those books in the library. *The Wind in the Willows*. People can read 'em for free. Why would they want to pay money to read me? I don't know what I'm thinking about, going up against Truman Capote, I'm bleeding already."

"Oh, yeah, you've got it cut out, all right. When you think the most oft-quoted line in the world's greatest literature is, 'Romeo, Romeo, where art thou, Romeo?' I don't know how you're gonna top that, Officer," she said, smiling.

Donahoo didn't know what part of her he liked the best. Probably her ass. But he liked her long black hair, too. The way it sparked. He liked her deep brown eyes, the fun that was in them, a bonus. He liked all of her.

He said, "Sunday, I thought I'd drive up to Desert Hot Springs, you want to come?"

She said, "Okay."

CHAPTER FORTY-FIVE

Foley, he was Foley now, Joseph R. Foley, Realtor, put the TOW, The Breaker, in the attic of his plain little Craftsman house in the glide path to Lindbergh Field. It took him a long time, no help, Marky wasn't there, nor Stryker, but he got the job done. He had the nest prepared for it at the narrow window stuck under the front peak of the roof. From the window he could see, at an angle, the gabled roof of a big rococo rooming house three blocks up the hill, toward the park. He opened the window.

Stryker had shown him how to do it. He loaded a missile into the launcher. He positioned himself behind it. He aimed. He wasn't going to wait, he thought. He'd given them ample warning. Six months. He'd given them all the time they deserved.

He felt good. He felt safe. Nothing could happen to him now. He'd been careless with the Mercedes. But even if it was found they couldn't connect it to him. It was hidden six blocks away in the garage of an empty house that was somebody else's sales listing. A long, difficult walk for him, but not for Stryker.

A plane was coming. He could hear it. In a few seconds, it would appear, flashing over the rococo house. He would fire at that moment. As it came over the rococo house.

But not now. He closed the window. He wanted to consult his airline schedules. He wanted to pick a really big plane. The biggest plane in the sky.

Yes, he had the time for that, he thought. The rocket in place, everything accomplished, the police no wiser, he could afford to take his time. He could taunt them some more. Drag it out for Donahoo. Today, tomorrow.

You can't catch me, but he could catch a plane, he thought, smiling. The biggest plane in the sky. He could do that.

Valesy already had his target picked. Trans World Flight 723, originating from London's Gatwick Airport, the same flight that had brought him to San Diego. It was one of the last planes to land every night, at 12:29 A.M., the scheduled cutoff time for landings at Lindbergh. If it was on time, it would cross the Balboa Park glide path at 12:28. He'd be waiting then. Actually, he'd be there earlier, of course, and he'd be prepared to stay later, too. He'd risk being in the open a few minutes either way. He'd have the cover of darkness and there'd be almost negligible street traffic. He wanted Trans World 723. On time, early, or late, it wasn't going to make Lindbergh. It was coming down.

If the MD 80 sold out, there would be 175 dead, counting crew, plus whatever on the ground, Valesy thought. Worse than the PSA crash. Maybe, if it went down in a big apartment building, the worst crash in U.S. aviation history. He needed another 100 on the ground to equal the worst, the May 25, 1979, American Airlines DC-10 crash on takeoff at O'Hare, in which 275 died. He'd love to go after a jumbo, but they couldn't land them at Lindbergh, the airport couldn't handle them, so the MD 80 was about as big as he was going to get. If he got lucky, he could do it, though, he thought. Maybe a new record. Something for the books.

There was another reason he'd picked Trans World 723, had chosen Sunday night, or more correctly, Monday morning. The stewardess, Gloria, her last name was Clark, he'd found that out. Stewardess Gloria Clark. Who was going to be aboard. And who, very shortly now, just a couple more days, could, in her last waitress function, drop dead.

Valesy was waiting, as before, at the abandoned house across from JOSEPH R. FOLEY, REALTOR. He was waiting for Foley to return in the Mercedes. Foley's fingerprints on the Spigot were compelling enough evidence of Foley's guilt. But he intended more than that. Foley's photo, doctored, put with another, showing him in Mexico, posing with an arms dealer, Primitivo. He had subjected the doctored photo to intense heat, to almost flashpoint, a KGB trick. Now it would be very difficult to prove the photo was a fake. Also, the Personal Organizer. The garbled hit list. DHQB GTCRNM. NBWJT GBSSPX. KPIO MBTTJUFS. UPNNZ EPOBIPP. A smart cop could decipher it. He had engraved Foley's initials on the back, JRF. Altogether, three pieces of evidence, but he couldn't leave them together, they might appear planted. They should be in different places. The fingerprints on the Spigot in the Jeep Wrangler. The photo swept into a corner in the storage unit. And, now, the Personal Organizer in the Mercedes' glove compartment. That would be more natural. There was always a lot of different stuff in a glove compartment. He had never seen a glove in a glove compartment, but, always, a lot of other things. A Personal Organizer would not seem out of place.

But where was the Mercedes? Earlier in the day, he had passed the house twice, driving the Jeep Wrangler. It wasn't there either time. He had been waiting now for more than two hours. Still no sign.

It occurred to him that Foley no longer had the car. It was old, it billowed smoke, it needed a valve job. Perhaps it had broken down on him. It could be with a mechanic. Or he might have abandoned it. He might have another car now. The curb was full of cars, pickups, vans. There was a new van tonight. Ford Econo camouflage job. Or, another possibility, Foley, despite the limp, might be on foot, Valesy admitted. He could have gone some short distance and gone on foot. He, Valesy, was on foot. People still walked here. Even at night they walked. It was stupid of them, but they did.

There were no lights showing at JOSEPH R. FOLEY, REALTOR. Valesy decided to hide the Personal Organizer in the house. When they came for Foley, and they were going to come for him, they'd take the house apart like a muffin. They'd examine every crumb. They'd find the device there just as readily as in the Mercedes. It didn't matter where he put it. What mattered was that it be found.

Valesy crossed the street. He used his pick again and was inside in a moment. He checked all the rooms. No one.

He fingered, in his pocket, the Personal Organizer. Where would Foley put such a thing? He went to the office that looked like a command center. The huge maps on the wall and the three telephones with the three answering machines with the recorded greetings by three supposedly different people. But there was only the one phone and the one machine. He noticed that.

Too much for him to handle? Valesy mused, smiling. He pulled open a drawer. It was full of junk. Paper clips, scissors, a comb, coins. Newspaper clippings.

Valesy took out the newspaper clippings. The fag in the park. The homeless on the steps of First Presbyterian Church. The man who had exploded in the sky above the San Diego Convention Center. The stories were about The Balboa Firefly.

He wondered. Why would Foley cut them out this way, keep them? Like he was going to make a scrapbook? What purpose?

He stood stricken. Oh, fuck, he thought. He was frozen with a fear he had never felt before. Here, in this room, this place, he had found his competition, he realized. It was *Foley*!

Foley and his threats weren't empty. He was killing. *Foley,* and, if he wanted, the crazy fool could go for a plane! Oh, fuck. Valesy looked at the phone. He had to tell Grenier. They were on collision course. They'd all crash. Fuck, *fuck!!*

There was a creaking sound behind him. He spun around.

A flimsy folding stairway fell out of the ceiling. Foley's feet appeared. He descended the stairs awkwardly.

Valesy was waiting when Foley's head came out of the dark hole that was the attic. Valesy's pistol was pointed at his heart.

Foley looked dumbstruck. "Who are you?"

Valesy's finger tightened on the trigger. He almost pulled it. But then he realized that would be a stupid thing to do. Foley had to stay alive to take the blame. He couldn't shoot down an airliner if he was dead. No. Dead, he couldn't be blamed.

"Excuse me," Valesy said. He circled around the stairway, around Foley. He bolted from the room. He ran out of the house.

Foley stared after him in shock and disbelief. Then a strange calm came over him. He eased out of the stairway and limped to his desk and got his morphine.

The chase ended six blocks away on the First Avenue overpass crossing Interstate 5.

Valesy, winded, stopped there, hung on the railing, trying to get his breath. He wasn't afraid of Foley catching him, not with that limp. He ran from other dangers. The whole scheme falling apart. Of being implicated. Suddenly, he thought, everything was madness, and he didn't know how to escape. All he could manage was to run. Run, and hope.

Stryker, he was Stryker now, not Foley, caught up to him there, caught him by surprise.

Valesy, on the railing, staring down at the surging traffic, its noise blocking out anyone's approach, this time turned around too late.

Foley was walking toward him. He had a gun with a silencer. He was going to fire.

"No," Valesy said, in surprise and shock. He held up a hand, as if that could stop a bullet. "Please, *don't!*"

Stryker's finger closed on the trigger.

"Please. I have money. It's in my belt. You can have it all. You can have anything."

There was no reply. Just the burning eyes of a dedicated executioner.

Valesy eased up on the low railing. Now, death so close, he was calmer, ready to deal with it, and also to take any chance. He thought he might have the courage to flip over backward. If he was lucky, he'd land on the signage girders that were behind him, below him, straddling the eastbound traffic lanes. He might be able to dodge across the girders to the other side. It was an insane gamble but there was no other escape possible. He had made a mistake, he thought. He'd been afraid of that, right from the start, and now he'd made it, and it was his last.

Valesy looked at Foley. You don't limp, he was going to say that, an accusation, and an excuse for his mistake, but there wasn't time for more talk. He thought merely, briefly, of Larisa Krasnitskaya, effective woman, then flipped over backward onto the girders. He struggled to his feet and started away. He took two bullets to the head. He spun away and down. He landed on a speeding car and bounced to another and then onto the roadway. The cars kept coming. He was crushed and shredded.

CHAPTER FORTY-SIX

Donahoo took the case. The slugs in the head were the right caliber. It had happened on the periphery of the glide path. So there was a pretty good chance it was another killing by The Balboa Firefly. He hadn't left a note this time, but that could be explained. It might have got stuck on a car or something. It could be in Los Angeles by now.

Palmer was working on the most interesting item. Somehow it had survived intact. A small electronic reminder called a Personal Organizer. It had been shaken up, though. None of the entries made any sense. DQHB GTCRNM. NBWJT GBSSPX.

Palmer thought it was a code. He was working on it.

Sure, Donahoo thought. But he let Palmer do it. You never know, Donahoo thought. You never, ever know.

Gomez and Cominski were making telephone calls. They were calling the dispatchers at taxicab companies, airport shuttles, the all-night food-to-go places. They were trying to find anybody whose route might have taken them across the First Avenue overpass.

It was a long shot, but they had to start somewhere. Donahoo felt about them the way he felt about Palmer. You never know. Himself, he was going to the morgue. He wanted to see the deceased. There wasn't much to see. He still wanted to see what was left. It might tell him something.

Saperstein and Lewis came into the squad room. They were puffy-eyed and unshaven. It was five in the morning.

"I never sleep anymore," Saperstein said. "We've got to get this guy. He's killing me." He picked up the report lying on Donahoo's desk. "Now what?"

"It's all there," Donahoo said. It wasn't, it never was, but he'd had less sleep. Two, maybe three hours. They'd called him at one-thirty. Sarge, you said to call.

Saperstein skipped through the report and handed it to Lewis. He said, talking to himself, "The deceased is wearing old clothes. He's got two hundred grand in a money belt."

"Maybe it's drugs," Chip Lyons said. He'd also left a wakeup call. He wasn't going to miss a thing.

"What's the lab say?" Saperstein asked Donahoo.

"To be patient. The ballistics guy has to come in from Escondido."

"We've just got one ballistics guy?"

"No. The other ballistics guy won't answer his phone."

Saperstein scowled. "So send over a car."

"We did. The reason he won't answer his phone is he isn't home."

"The middle of the night?"

"He's balling somebody somewhere."

"Fuck, the sex act," Saperstein said. He took the report back from Lewis. "This guy is killing me. I can't get any sleep, you know? I'm awake, thinking. What fucking next? What...fucking...next?"

Lewis said, "Still no ID?"

Donahoo shook his head. "No wallet. No papers. Just the money. Oh, and this." He borrowed the Personal Organizer from Palmer. "There are initials engraved on the back. JRF."

Saperstein squinted. "For recovery if it's stolen? He'd do that for a twenty-dollar item?"

"No. For what's inside. It's hard to remember DQHB."

"What?"

Donahoo gave the Personal Organizer back to Palmer. "It's fucked. It got scrambled."

"Cominski," Saperstein yelled. "JRF. Put that in the computer. See if there are any killers with the initials JRF."

"We put it in an hour ago, sir," Cominski told him. "No luck."

"And the gun?" Lewis prompted, reading the report. "This is the deceased's gun?"

"Yeah, the Browning. It's in the bag."

Lewis looked, picked it up, stared a moment, put it down. "The numbers are filed. It looks like a dead end."

"What isn't?"

"I say it's drugs," Chip Lyons said.

"Who carries no ID?" Sapperstein wondered. "Everybody carries ID. Fake ID, maybe. But they carry ID. What kind of a deceased is this? Mr. Nobody?"

"Yeah, that's what Quigley says," Donahoo told him, talking about a morgue attendant. "The body is a pulp. It got shredded pretty good. But the head is surprisingly whole. What Quigley says, we've got a very plain, ordinary guy."

"You seen him yet?"

"No. I'm waiting for the sketch artist. I thought we'd give his picture to the paper, ask if they'll run it on the front page. Do you know this man?"

"Where's the sketch artist?"

Donahoo shrugged.

"Maybe he's balling somebody somewhere," Chip Lyons said. "Is anybody listening to me? It's drugs."

Sapperstein responded with a look. He obviously didn't think so. He said, "Never mind the sketch. Give 'em a photograph of the head."

"They don't want it. They don't want to run a full head shot of a corpse."

"You gotta be kidding."

"It's a family newspaper."

"Hey, Sarge," Palmer said excitedly. "I think I've got something here. Come and look. Come here."

Donahoo moved over to Palmer's desk. "You broke the code?"

"I think so." Palmer handed him a sheet of paper. There was a line of gibberish, DQHB GTCRNM. And, below it, another line, ERIC HUDSON. "How about that?"

Yeah, how about it? Donahoo thought. He said, "How did you do this, Palmer?"

"Easy. I just added one letter of the alphabet for each character. D becomes E. Q is R."

Saperstein grabbed the paper. "What code?"

Donahoo said, "How do you know about codes, Palmer?"

"I got a brother-in-law in the Navy."

Saperstein was yelling. "What code?"

"Take it easy," Donahoo said. "Palmer here just got started." He said, "Palmer, you're a genius, we're gonna make you a Corporal, give us some more of this D is E."

"Okay."

They all crowded around Palmer.

"Somebody better tell me," Saperstein muttered.

"It's the electronic reminder found on the deceased," Donahoo explained. "We turned it on, it was all jumbled letters. I thought it had got shook up. Palmer didn't think so. He gets all the credit here. Palmer and his brother-in-law."

"Will you shut up?" Saperstein asked. He said to Palmer, "And the first entry comes up Eric Hudson?"

"There it is."

"Very interesting."

Lewis said, "Keep going."

"Okay, here we go," Palmer said. Now that he had it, he was flying. "Next entry." He printed it carefully on his sheet of paper. NBWJT GBSSPX. Under that he wrote, MAVIS FARROW.

Saperstein said softly, "We've got a hit list. People who own property in the glide path. Keep going, Palmer. Next entry?"

Palmer printed KPIO MBTTJUFS. Then, JOHN LASSITER.

"You're sure?" Lewis said. "That name hasn't come up before."

"I'm sure."

Montrose came out of the computer room. He hadn't had any sleep at all. He'd been up all night, tracing back through all the dbas, the corporations, trying to find the real owners. He was pulling a tail of computer paper. He was black, but he looked white. He was trying to say something. He couldn't find the words.

"Keep going," Saperstein ordered Palmer. He said to Donahoo, "Every John Lassiter in the county. I want a guard on him."

Donahoo was signaling to Cominski. "It's already happening."

"The killer is dead," Palmer said.

"Don't think. Decode."

Palmer printed UPNNZ EPOBIPP. Then, TOMMY DONAHOO.

There was a long silence.

"Don't fuck me, Palmer," Donahoo said then. "I'm a lousy lay." He said, "Come on, we're in a hurry."

Palmer, stricken, said, "This is you, Sarge."

"I'm on the hit list?"

"Yeah."

Saperstein took the sheet of paper. He went through the letter changes. He studied it awhile, then handed the paper, wordlessly, to Lewis. Lewis just stared at it blankly.

"You were wondering about your mystery prowler? Why he wanted to kill you?" Saperstein asked Donahoo. "Maybe now you know?" He asked Palmer, "Are there any other entries?"

"No."

"Well," Saperstein said. "When we locate John Lassiter..." He looked at Donahoo. "You think he'll own property in the glide path?"

Donahoo felt like he was going into shock. "Yeah. I'd put a couple bucks on that."

"Do you own property in the glide path?"

"No. I don't."

"Yes, you do, Sarge," Montrose announced. "I'm sorry. But you do." He held up the computer paper. "You own a couple houses right in the middle."

"I don't," Donahoo said again. He turned to Saperstein. "I don't, okay? Why the hell would I buy there, I want to live in Coronado?" He said, "I'm being framed here, Saperstein. Give me some room. We'll sort this out."

"I know," Saperstein said. "We will." He flicked a look at Lewis. No objection there. He said, "You're off this, Tommy."

"Off it? What the fuck do you mean, *off it?*"

"I mean, you're not on it anymore," Saperstein said. "I want to see you in my office. Lewis, you go with him" He pointed a finger at Chip Lyons. "You've got it, mister. It's all yours. But I gotta say something to you. I don't think it's drugs."

"You're making a mistake," Donahoo said.

Chip Lyons said, "That's what they all say." He was holding the plastic bag with the Browning.

Donahoo took it from him. "Model 1935, high power. 9 mm Parabellum. Semiautomatic, 13-shot clip. Imported from Belgium ..." He hefted it, changed his mind. "Alloy frame. It was made in Canada." He looked closely to confirm that. "There's no FN trademark." He handed back the bag and walked out.

CHAPTER FORTY-SEVEN

Donahoo went to the morgue. Quigley, the nightside attendant, was leaving as he entered, bundled into a miniature
Navy peacoat, a merchant seaman's blue stocking cap. He
worked in the cold and that made him always cold. He shivered
now as he stopped for Donahoo. He blew on his tiny hands. He
had a cold job that wouldn't let him get warm. The cold was
inside.

"Stay awhile, Quig," Donahoo said. "I want to see the body."

"You want to see the head," Quigley said, blowing. He looked
up from three and a half feet. "There ain't no body." He said, "No
body here but us chickens."

Morgue attendants, Donahoo thought. Cops and morgue
attendants. He followed Quigley into the chiller. The stories about
the twisted dwarf were legion. Or, as Frank Camargo used to say,
used to like to say, American Legion. When the Legion closed,
that's when Quigley came to work. He'd come in, all beered up.
He'd raise all kinds of hell.

Quigley, he ought to be dead, a long time ago, Donahoo
thought. He ought to be in one of these chiller drawers. Once,
Quigley had snuck into the Good Earth Cafe, had conspired to
put a severed finger in Saperstein's all organic LT, hold the B.
Saperstein had not been amused. Quigley couldn't understand
that. Hey, it wasn't like it was pork.

"Tell me, how is Saperstein?" Quigley asked. He always asked
that.

"Tough as ever," Donahoo said.

In his office, Lewis the only other one present, Saperstein had made it short and sweet.

"I don't know what's going on," Saperstein had said. "All I know, I want you take a vacation, Tommy. For your own protection. For your own protection and maybe mine. I want to tell you, frankly, this has me worried, and you should be worried, too. Until this is resolved, I don't want you anywhere around here, I don't want you working on the case, I don't want you offering advice, or opinions. You are out of here until this is over. Comprende?"

He, Donahoo, he had said, "I don't want a vacation."

"Take the vacation."

"Is it paid?"

Lewis had told him, "Take it easy, Tommy." Lewis had said, "You want some advice? If I were you, I'd rent a bus, the kind that are converted, you can live in 'em. I'd drive it down to Mexico, park it by the beach, by a whorehouse. I'd fish, fuck, and forget it."

Quigley pulled open a chiller drawer. He took back a sheet. "The deceased in question."

Donahoo looked at the head. It was like a miracle. There were a lot of abrasions. But it was intact. The body wasn't. It was in pieces. It was squash.

"Seen enough?"

"No," Donahoo said. He'd seen the head before. The face. He'd seen it ... where? "Gimme a minute."

"Alone?"

"Gimme a minute."

"Okay."

Donahoo stood looking at the head. It was a very plain, ordinary head. He stood staring at it for a long time and then it came to him. He'd seen it the day before at the wheel of a Jeep Wrangler.

"Are we finished here?"

"Yes."

Donahoo drove home. He got out the Old Crow. He thought about it for a while. He phoned Saperstein.

"Listen," he said, barging in, no preliminary. "I was over to the morgue."

"Mother of God," Saperstein exploded. "What does it take? You're not supposed to go to the morgue." There was a nanosecond pause. "Unless you're dead, of course. That would be all right."

"It's about the case."

"Then phone Chip Lyons," Saperstein said, hanging up. "Chip Lyons has the case."

Donahoo put the phone down. This was all new to him. He'd never run into anything like this before. He didn't know what to do. He finally phoned Chip Lyons.

"Chip, listen," he said. "I was over to the morgue. I took a look at the deceased. It's a guy I saw yesterday when we were cruising the glide path. He was driving a Jeep Wrangler. He was in the glide path, Chip."

"That's very interesting."

"I think so."

"The Wrangler. What year?"

"Pretty new. Maybe this year. Did you see him?"

"No. What color?"

"Red."

"You get the plate?"

"No."

"Any of it?"

"No. I wasn't looking for one. The guy just went by us."

"California?"

"I dunno. You don't remember a Wrangler?"

"No. You're sure he's the deceased?"

"Positive."

"Okay, thanks," Chip Lyons said. "If you remember something else, call me."

Donahoo was holding a dead line. Well, fuck you, too, he thought. Fuck you all.

The cat came over.

"Pussy," Donahoo said. "They got me. My luck ran out."

The cat gave him that cat look. So what?

CHAPTER FORTY-EIGHT

Grayson Grenier waited for Valesy's telephone call. It was past the appointed time. The phone hadn't rung. Valesy was five minutes overdue. He had never been late before. He was punctual to a fault. So why didn't he call?

Well, he'd wait another five minutes, Grenier thought, pacing. Another five minutes. Give him that much. Some leeway.

He waited two minutes. Then, a kind of panic overtook him. He felt threatened, lost. Something had gone wrong. If he was free, if he was alive, Valesy would have called, Grenier thought. There were only two possibilities. He'd made a mistake, he'd been caught. Or, the lesser, he was dead.

Grenier went to the pay phone. He put in a quarter and dialed a Yonkers number and told the woman who answered that he wanted to speak to Rosetta.

"I want to move things up," Grenier said when, breathless, Rosetta came on the line. "I want to announce Pilgrim Restores America tomorrow in San Diego."

"Monday?" Rosetta stammered. "This is the weekend. I can't arrange it that fast."

"You can if you want to keep your job," Grenier told him. The rest was like a snarl. "Move your ass, Rosetta."

He hung up, then this time made a collect call, to Fairmont Boat Yards in Miami, to a man called Cappy. The Hatteras MY, *Endless Summer,* was lying there. Cappy had brought it around several months before. It was ready to go.

"Cappy, we're going to sea," Grayson announced. "Stores for ten days, okay? I'll come aboard Monday afternoon. And I'll want to sail as soon as I'm stowed."

"Aye," Cappy said.

"Do you want to know where we're going?"

"Does it matter?"

Grenier smiled. "No."

He rang off and thought that it was these two kinds of men who had gotten him into trouble. Rosetta, who was so typical of his executives at the Pilgrim Tobacco Company, they only knew what they couldn't do, and Cappy, who had absolutely no idea that there might be some limit. He'd left his affairs to the first, and he'd run off, dumb but happy, with a star-chaser. Now he was back to pay the piper on behalf of both.

Grenier waited by the pay phone for another half hour. Valesy didn't call.

The Colonel, he's made a mistake, he's dead, Grenier thought. He went to the phone and placed another call, this time to United Airlines, making a reservation for San Diego. Flight 73, departing La Guardia at four o'clock, arriving Lindbergh at 5:20. He'd be there for dinner. Perhaps he could have it with the Mayor. Or, what would be really pleasant, the Mayor's aide, Faye Stuart. He got out his calling card. He'd see what he could arrange.

Grenier punched in his card number. He had always killed from a distance, remote, removed. He saw none of it. He never watched his victims in their howling cancer deaths. He never saw the survivors mourn.

He wondered if he could take the quantum leap required to shoot down an airliner.

He'd find out soon enough.

"Hello," he said. It struck him that he had forgotten to call Ruby. She'd need time to pack. "Remember me?"

Faye Stuart said, "You're that awfully dignified Mr. Grenier, aren't you?"

CHAPTER FORTY-NINE

Donahoo picked up Presh Carling for the run to Desert Hot Springs. She came out in a flimsy damask blouse and half-length white cotton shorts. She was carrying a baggy cardigan sweater that she wouldn't have to wear until she got back and maybe not then and only if they went for a walk along the beach in the cool of the evening or something. Donahoo was getting way ahead of himself. He hadn't seen her in anything but long sleeves and long dresses. He thought she looked good in the revealing blouse. He also thought she had nice legs. They were long and lithe. She'd be a knockout in a swimsuit, he thought.

He got the door open for her. "Hi."

She smiled at him and slipped into the car. She was wearing her hair up in a loose, silky pile. It was the first time he had seen her neck fully revealed. It was long and graceful. It had the deep indentation at the base of the skull that he liked. He wondered if he ought to ask her to drive. He wasn't sure he could stay on the road.

He said instead that he liked her damask blouse. He got behind the wheel and they set off. It was natural and comfortable. He felt good right away. He had made himself a promise, he wasn't going to think about Chip Lyons, he wasn't going to worry about The Balboa Firefly. He wasn't going to let them dehumanize him. He was going to devote himself to this wonderful woman. He was going to reveal what he must of himself. He was going to ask the privilege of knowing her, too. She didn't ask who they were going to see. He didn't tell her.

"Desert Hot Springs, it's going to be hot, isn't it?" was all she said.

He said, "Oh, yeah."

Desert Hot Springs was a two-hour-plus drive to the northeast, a small, sun-weathered, second-class resort city near Palm Springs. Donahoo left I-15 at Temecula, taking the back way, Winchester Road, through French Valley. They were on two-lane blacktop now, snaking through the gentle, rolling land. Past the hayfields, past the cows. Past the houses on the hilltops. Past the "For Sale" signs. Zoned industrial, zoned commercial. Put a plastic extruder there, Donahoo thought. Put a K mart over here, over there a Wal-Mart. Get rid of those cows. Trade them for a zillion crackerbox houses.

"How come she left?" Presh asked, meaning Monica.

"Oh, I dunno," Donahoo said, which wasn't really true. He said, "That's not really true. She left because she didn't like being married to a cop. She liked it at first, she liked the drama, she liked the gun, but then she didn't like it. She didn't like the weird hours and the uncertainty. She didn't like the poor pay."

"What did she want you to do?"

"It never got that far," Donahoo said. "I'll always be a cop."

They got on I-10 at Beaumont and then took a break at a truck stop, Wheel Inn, in "Friendly Cabazon." They got out and into a blast furnace. August in the desert. They looked at each other. Mostly, Presh was looking at Donahoo. She said, "Why are you doing this to me?"

He glanced at the thermometer over by the dinosaurs. 114.

"You get used to it."

"Sure."

They had unknowingly become part of a Wheel Inn tableaux. They were looking now at a cute kid with his baseball cap on sideways. The kid, he'd be five, maybe six, was staring at the huge concrete dinosaurs, staring at the tourists halfway up the stairs leading into the belly of one of the dinosaurs. The tourists were staring at the woman who was supposed to be taking their picture but who wasn't ready. A couple of truckers had stopped to watch. Nobody moved for a while. All frozen for that moment. No one quite sure what was going on. Muddle America.

"You come here often?" Presh asked.

"All the time."

They went in, easing by a smiling trucker carrying a metal peacock with a clock in its stomach.

Donahoo hadn't seen one before. "Hey, nice."

"The wife."

Presh gave Donahoo a look. He didn't have any apologies. He liked the Wheel Inn, and he liked the dinosaurs, too. He liked the Wheel Inn best. It was more prehistoric. Play the Neo Geo "King of the Monsters." Check your sex power. Deposit quarter, place finger on sensor. Over 100, cold shower, quick. Homemade biscuits and country sausage gravy. Why we die on the road.

"You come here often?" Presh asked. She wanted an answer.

He bought Cokes that were mostly ice.

Father Charlie Donahoo was standing on the sidewalk in front of St. Paul's Mission for Men on Belardo Street in downtown Desert Hot Springs. Once he had looked a lot like Donahoo. He had the same big Irish head and big Irish face. He had the height, and the large hands, the large feet. The resemblance, now, was vague, uncertain. He was old and wasted. The head was a prune turning to pit. The body was sticks. He had more than thirty years on Donahoo. In two years, he'd be, God willing, eighty.

He was the only human being to be seen for blocks in any direction. Belardo looked like a street in some ghost town. Desert Hot Springs's citizens were barricaded inside against the day's blistering heat. It was 116. It was going to hit 120. The air was deadly still. The wind that usually came had left.

The Olds Toronado came down the lifeless street and pulled into the curb. Father Charlie found his pocket watch. He opened it, checked the time, smiled.

Donahoo was out first. He said, "For Christ's sake, get inside, you're gonna fry your brains here, Charlie."

Father Charlie ignored him. He was looking at Presh.

"Hi," she said, smiling.

He said, "My, my, my."

Donahoo did the introductions. He suggested that they all get off the sidewalk and into St. Paul's Mission for Men.

"Oh, yeah, it's hot," Father Charlie said. "I called up *The Sentinel*. I says, send a photographer over here, will ya, I'm gonna fry an egg on the sidewalk. So they send over this kid and I fry the egg, and he says, 'Wow,' and he eats it."

"Is that true?" Presh said.

Father Charlie and Donahoo said no at the same time. They took her into the mission.

It had been a church before it became a mission. It had a high, domed ceiling, difficult to air-condition, and then only at great expense. Swamp coolers had been substituted. The air was moist and uncomfortable.

There were no rooms, just beds, cots. They were in rows, like in a barracks, or as in an armory turned into a shelter. The cots were all neatly made up. No one was around.

"They're on a bus trip," Father Charlie explained. "The Monsignor, he thought they ought to go up Yucaipa, see that old drive-in theater screen where Our Lady appeared, in living color, to some Mexicans. It was in the paper."

Donahoo said, "We could have come some other time, wouldn't you wanta see that?"

Father Charlie, looking at Presh, an Irish twinkle in his eyes, he said, "No, you see one miracle, you've seen them all."

They had lunch in the kitchen. Meat loaf, gravy, canned peas, bread. Dessert was some sort of custard. Tea. There wasn't any coffee.

Father Charlie told Presh about his work at the mission and the good work that the mission performed. That reminded Donahoo. He got out the envelope with the two hundred dollars. Father Charlie took it and thanked him. He said, "Thank you, my son." He said, "Incidentally, last time you bought Hoyt a guitar. He's around here somewhere, he doesn't like Yucaipa, maybe he'll play you a tune."

"I did, huh?" Donahoo said, pleased. "I'd hate to see you spend it on more of that custard. How is old Hoyt?"

"He's singing his heart out."

They set off on a tour.

Later, leaving, they did find Hoyt. He was on his cot, cross-legged, cradling an old, badly tuned guitar. He wasn't a man. He was a boy in his midteens. He was skinny, pale. He had corn-yellow straight hair that swept like a broom across his smudged eyes.

Presh reached out to briefly touch him when they were introduced. She didn't say anything. Hoyt, at Father Charlie's urging, agreed to sing a song for her, his own composition, "Never Gonna Pass You." He accompanied himself on the guitar.

Hoyt sang,

" 'I can pass the potatoes,
"I can pass the gravy, too.
"But on this narrow, twisty road,
"Ain't never gonna pass you.' "

Presh smiled her appreciation. Father Charlie explained that Hoyt, in the song, was stuck behind a pickup truck driven by an old man who refused to speed up or pull over, and that you often ran into that kind of situation in life.

They said goodbye. Father Charlie walked them to the door. They said goodbye again. They could hear Hoyt faintly singing.

" 'I won't miss the ten minutes

"I'm wasting here behind.

"I've lost so many years

"Ain't never gonna find.' "

In the car, Presh said, "How long have known he was your father?"

"I was sixteen," Donahoo told her. "Hoyt's age. Kathleen, my mother, she was going to die, she was dying of cancer, and Mike, my stepdad, he already was dead. So Kathleen told me. Her first husband, he was in the Army, he got killed, Normandy. Father Charlie, he, uh, started calling on her, consoling the young widow, and it just got outta hand there, they both lifted their skirts." Donahoo was looking at the mission. He said, "Mike and Kathleen, dead practically at the same time. The doctor says, 'Boy, it's just something you've got to live with.' Actually, I lived with the neighbors." He said, "I finally went up to see him. I'd be nineteen, twenty. He was on the faculty at Loyola Marymount. I went up to see him and he was coaching the girls' baseball team. I thought, Jes-us, and I changed my name to Donahoo."

"You're not bitter?"

"Oh, no, I'm just so fucking sorry. His whole life, he's in a cage, he can't get out. He gets out once, to give me life, and then he has to go back. I'm out here, free. And he's inside."

"He chooses to be."

"No, I don't think so," Donahoo said. "I think it's more complicated than that."

CHAPTER FIFTY

Chip Lyons left the Police Administrative Headquarters. Usually he tried to put a little extra oomph in his walk, let them know he was still full of piss and vinegar, the end of a long shift. He liked to do that, there always was the chance somebody was looking, watching hell-for-leather Chip Lyons, but today he couldn't manage it, didn't care.

He was beat, exhausted. He'd put in almost three straight shifts. He'd gotten a few hours sleep on a cot, that's all. Dumb trick, actually. He knew he wasn't at his best when he was beat. But he had walked into all that unfolding drama, the lynching of Tommy Donahoo, the ascension of Chip Lyons. That was a rush. Wooosh. And there were all the things he had to do, take over the squad, show them he could do it, they were in good hands with Chip Lyons. He had to do that. But now he was limp, fucking tired. He was going home. He wasn't going to eat. He was just going to hit the pillow.

He'd feel better Monday, he thought. He'd come in refreshed and thinking straight. He'd review and he'd set some priorities. He'd beef up the hunt for the old Mercedes. The old Mercedes was key. He had always figured that. They were giving up too easily. It had to be out there somewhere. Even if it wasn't registered, even if it had false registration, it still had to be out there. Old Mercedeses didn't disappear, he thought, pleased with the idea. They just got parted.

He crossed E Street to his car, a new, supercharged Pontiac GTO, all the whips and jingles. Early Saturday, predawn, the street had been clear of cars, so he had taken a parking place that usually went first, in a driveway that was chained off. It was a free spot. No parking meter.

He got in the Pontiac and started the motor. He let it warm up a minute. He was thinking about making it home and hitting the pillow. Then he noticed the parking ticket. He thought, What the fuck?

He shifted to neutral and got out and pulled the ticket off his windshield. He read the citation in disbelief. Obstructing driveway.

Fuck, he thought again. Obstructing? The driveway, it was fucking chained, for Christ's sake. The fucking lock was fucking rusted. It was fucking Sunday.

He tried to relax. He was all pumped up again. The adrenaline was doing loop-the-loop. He didn't want this, any of this, he wanted to go to bed, that's all. Let him go to bed, okay? Just let him go to bed.

He crumpled up the ticket and threw it into the street. He'd talk to the asshole later. He'd tell him/her, drop it. He'd tell 'em stuff it up his/her ass.

He got back into the car. You work two days, he thought. Triple fucking shift. He sat staring at the fucking rusted lock on the fucking rusted chain.

"Maybe it's an omen?" Chip Lyons wondered. He was talking to himself, suddenly calm and rational, very happy about what he was thinking. The SIU guys, they'd gone through the parking tickets, they'd done all that, but what if they missed something? They were undercover guys. They caught rapists on the beach. Drug dealers. What did they know about computers and traffic tickets. They could have fucked up. They must have. Everybody got a parking ticket. The Mercedes got one. It had to. San Diego financed itself with its fucking parking tickets.

Chip Lyons slammed the Pontiac out onto E Street. He left burning rubber and headed across town to the Traffic Division on Aero Drive.

CHAPTER FIFTY-ONE

Donahoo and Presh Carling were returning to San Diego. An eventful day, Donahoo thought. Presh had his Python, she was holding it in her hand, hidden in the folds of her cardigan. She'd been holding it like that for two hours. She was holding it like, Jesus, I dunno, Donahoo thought. But he did know. She was holding it like she had hold of him.

Flashback. They were leaving Desert Hot Springs. Presh said, "What do you mean, Monica *liked* the gun?"

Donahoo answered, "She just liked it, that's all. She liked the way it looked, the way it felt. She liked to pick it up. She liked to hold it."

"Did she ever fire it?"

"Monica? No."

"Why not?"

"Monica? Not the type."

"She wouldn't shoot anybody?"

"Not with a gun."

They'd gotten about a block, they were on Palm Drive, leaving DHS, headed for I-10.

"Teach me how to shoot," Presh said.

"Sure. Name a time."

"Now."

Donahoo took Varner Road and went several miles out of the way to a makeshift outdoor target range set into a low mountain back of Thousand Palms. He'd shot there before. It was a quasi-legal community range. Nobody bothered you as long as you didn't kill somebody.

He had his service revolver wrapped in oilcloth in the trunk of the Olds. He took it out, showed it to her, the Colt Model Python, .357 magnum.

"First, you listen," he said. He explained it to her, the double action, the six-shot swing-out cylinder, the simultaneous ejector. The sights—blade front, adjustable rear for windage and elevation. The barrel's ventilated rib and nonglare Coltguard finish. Why he preferred the six-inch barrel, not the two and a half, three, and four, not the eight. He told her how much it weighed. Forty-two ounces. Over two and a half pounds. Then he gave it to her.

She hefted it. Pointed it toward the mountainside's disarranged targets. Picked out a lone wine bottle that had somehow survived intact. Said, "When do I shoot?"

He gave her six bullets. He watched as she slowly, carefully, loaded. He explained, while she half-listened, about rimless and belted cartridges, primer and powder, firing pin and flash hole. Burn rates and chamber pressure. Bullet weights, styles, and jackets. Flat base and bobtail. Spitzer, hollow point, flat nose, and round nose. He told her she would be shooting a Nosier Bullet Company bobtail with a Nosler Ballistic Tip. Hercules 2400 magnum handgun powder.

She said, "When do I shoot?"

He had never shown a woman how before. He had to move in behind her, take hold of her shoulders, change her stance, shift her body. He had to raise her right arm, stiffen it. He had to move her left hand to a supporting position. He had to show her how to sight. He had to put his face next to hers. He had to brush against the stray tendrils of her hair.

They were very close to each other all that time. It was very hot. He could smell her. Not just her perfume. He could smell *her*.

He said, "Okay, now you can shoot," and, a very lucky first shot, she blew the wine bottle apart. "Bulls-eye!" she screamed, and she turned to him, dark eyes sparkling. "Now you're in trouble."

They left an hour and three boxes of reloads later. Expensive date.

Now Donahoo was in kind of a daze. He didn't know what to do. He didn't know what to suggest. He thought, maybe, the best thing, he'd just take her home. He could regroup and start over tomorrow. He could hit the Murphy and lie awake and wonder how the hell he could have got kicked off the most important case in his career. He could lie awake and wonder about the shuffle of the cards. How, sometimes, when they took something away, they gave something back. Maybe. He wasn't sure yet. He was changing lanes now to get onto 52 West and over to 5. They'd drive by the sunset. Say good night.

"No," Presh Carling said. "Keep going."

"Where?"

"To your place."

CHAPTER FIFTY-TWO

The monitor scrolled. Parking ticket, parking ticket, parking ticket. Hundreds of them. Thousands.

"Look at 'em all," Chip Lyons said, amazed. "Thirty bucks a pop. Forty more if you don't pay on time." He shook his head. "How the fuck can we have a budget problem? This could finance health-care reform."

Marilyn Perkins, the traffic clerk running the search for him, said, not really that interested, just trying to keep him reasonably subdued, she said, "What's this all about, anyway?"

He told her, "Shut up and keep scrolling."

They were looking for a Mercedes, any Mercedes. Any Merz [the computer contraction] that had been given a parking ticket in the Balboa Park glide path since the first of the year. They were looking for an SIU screwup.

He had listed the glide path's streets and avenues in large block letters on a cardboard sheet propped up next to the monitor. Kalmia, Juniper, Ivy, Grape. Albatross, Fir, Elm, Front. First through Sixth. He had them all listed as an easy reminder and reference.

"Here's one," Marilyn said, pausing. She looked something like her namesake, a soft, attractive blonde, but she had spent too much time in a computer chair, her hourglass figure was settling. "Merz. California 4JOP221. Ticketed 1/13 in the 400 block Fourth Avenue."

Chip Lyons squinted at his list. The SIU had checked it out. It came up as an '82 500SL. It belonged to a Granville Hastings. He owned Hastings Electronics. He was not considered a suspect. He got around in a wheelchair. He was seventy.

"Keep scrolling."

Marilyn nodded. They were working backward from the most recent entries and they were nearing the end. "Here's one."

Chip Lyons looked. Merz. California 8SUN290. Ticketed 1/08 at the foot of Hawthorne. Very close to the worst of the glide path's howling madness. It had possibilities. He reviewed his list. '72 280SE registered to a Diana Rockford of Snow Creek. Repeated efforts to contact. Blind messages left on answering machine. No response. Riverside County sheriff visited property two occasions, no one home, but neighbors reported seeing subject on property every day during period under investigation. Not considered suspect. Woman living alone two hours from San Diego.

Possibilities? He picked up the phone, dialed information, asked for the number. He got it and made the call and got lucky.

"Hello? Diana Rockford?"

"Yes?"

"I'm calling about your Mercedes."

"You're a little late, mister. It's almost all gone. I've got the hood, the front bumper. The transmission and four wheels. I've got the shell."

"You're parting it?"

"Yeah. Parting is such sweet sorrow."

"How long?"

"Three months. What's left, I can make you a deal."

Possibilities? Not likely. He said thanks but no thanks and hung up. He made a motion. Keep scrolling.

A couple paragraphs disappeared into the top of the screen. Then the text locked.

"End of the line," Marilyn said.

Chip Lyons stared at the unrelenting monitor. He was suddenly tired again. He didn't think he could move. Fuck, he thought. He'd been so sure this was his way out of the maze. The way to break it. Find a SIU screwup. "That's all?"

"Yeah. The past year. Unless you want to look at the tickets that haven't been processed yet."

He looked at her. He could kill her. "There are tickets that aren't in the computer?"

"Yeah. Right there." She pointed to another desk and an in-basket the size of a trash can. "You said computer."

Chip Lyons grabbed the in-basket and dumped it on her desk. He divided the scrambled mess of tickets in half. He shoved one pile at her.

"Do it," he ordered, staring her down. He started through his pile. He checked four or five and then it was in his hand. "Never mind."

"What have you got?"

He didn't answer. He was reading it again. Merz. California 2MRX007. Ticketed four days before. The 2400 block Curlew. Parking, partially, on a neighbor's lawn.

"What?"

He looked at the city map blowup on the wall behind the computer. He leaned in, expectant, joyous. The 2400 block Curlew. Dead center—absolute dead center—of the Lindbergh Field glide path.

"Oh, I like this one," he said softly. He showed her the ticket, the license plate number. "How do we get the registered owner?"

She turned to a smaller computer and punched in the query. The response came back in a few seconds. AUTOMOBILE. Year, 77. Make, CHEV. Vehicle ID Number, 1H57U7D496771. Body Type Model, SD. Plate Number 2MRX007. Registration Expiration Date, 03/24/92. Registered Owner(s), FLANAGAN JEROME P 412 JANE BARSTOW CA

"What do you think we've got here?"

"I guess somebody took some plates off an old Chevy and put 'em on an old Mercedes."

"Do you think Flanagan did it?"

"Let's find out."

She punched in the query. The response formed like a million little stars coming together to write a message in the monitor's sky. FLANAGAN JEROME P was moving up in life. He had dumped the Chevy. He was living in Santa Barbara and driving a Jaguar.

"You want to know more?"

He waved that off. He was looking at the ticket again. The issuing officer. Mendosa. He showed the name to her. "Do you know this guy?"

"It's a her."

"Whatever," he said. He was feeling good. He said, "Get her."

"She's been off sick."

"Even better. Get her."

Marilyn got her list, found the number, made the call, asked for Minny, waited for her to come to the phone, handed it, wordlessly, to Chip Lyons.

"Hello, Minny," he said. "This is Investigator Lyons. I have a couple urgent questions for you. Okay?"

There was a sniffle at the other end. "What's wrong?"

He said, "You ticketed a Mercedes four days ago. It was on the neighbor's lawn. Partially on the neighbor's lawn. The 2400 block Curlew. Balboa Park."

"They're fighting that?"

"Minny, listen," he said. "This is very important. What kind of Mercedes? Do you remember that?"

"Sure. It was a black '72 280SE 4.5. Four-door saloon. I remember because I was feeling like hell and it made my quota." Another sniffle. "I haven't been to work since."

"Right. The owner of the Mercedes. He was parked *partially* on the neighbor's lawn. So you must know where the owner lives?"

"I think I do. The car was mostly on what I assume is his property. I mean, I'd seen the car before, okay? Normally, he parks it on his own lawn."

"What's the address?"

"I dunno. But it's an old, small, one-story, middle of the block, west side. It's one of those plain little houses. It's light blue. It's got a faded red trim. What do they call those plain little houses?"

"Craftsman."

"Yeah, Craftsman. And it hasn't got a garage."

"I think I can find it. Thanks."

"You're welcome."

Chip Lyons hung up and dialed the Sickos, Crackpots, Underwear & Mad Bombers squad room. He looked at Marilyn. He said. "What did you say your name was?"

"Marilyn," Marilyn said.

He pointed a finger at her. "Yeah, Marilyn." He got his harness, which he'd taken off, hung over the back of a chair. He checked the Dan Wesson. Montrose finally answered the phone. He asked him, "What are you doing right now?"

"Jesus Christ, where are you?" Montrose demanded. "We're in trouble. We've got a dead Marine in a canyon in Marilou Park. We've got a TOW antitank missile stolen from Camp Pendleton."

Chip Lyons said, "Spook, have you killed anybody yet?"

CHAPTER FIFTY-THREE

Donahoo was waiting in the Murphy. He'd showered first. Presh's turn. He tried to imagine her. She'd be scrubbing off all that gunpowder, he thought, smiling. Hercules 2400. She'd be putting on the eucalyptus. He couldn't believe any of this was happening. The eucalyptus, maybe. But not the rest of it. Hey, guess what, Charlie? There's a miracle in there taking a shower.

The phone rang. He wasn't going to answer. There hadn't been any messages on the machine. This was going to be his first call all day. He wasn't going to take it.

Marie Camargo. She sounded a little drunk. "You're coming to the funeral?"

Donahoo picked up. "Of course. I'm there for sure."

"I put it off as long as possible."

"Yeah. I understand."

"There's something so permanent about burial."

"That's true."

"Tommy," Marie said. "You know what you asked me? If Frank said something to me he didn't say to you? This is about the case."

"I remember."

"Well, how am I supposed to know, he didn't say it to you?"

Jesus, Donahoo thought. He wished he hadn't picked up.

"You can't answer that?"

"No."

"I didn't think you could answer that."

Presh came out of the bathroom. She was wearing his robe. She was smiling. She was beautiful. Her hair was still piled up. She looked like a dwarf in the big robe.

"Marie, listen," Donahoo said, staring at Presh. "He couldn't have told you much. Tell me what he told you."

"He said the case had one track, Tommy. He said it had one track and two trains. Does that make any sense?"

Donahoo remembered Camargo saying something like that. Two trains on a collision course. It didn't make any sense then, and it didn't make any now. Camargo, talking. "What else did he say?"

"That's all. Does it make any sense?"

"It may," Donahoo lied. "It may go together with something else. You never know." He said, "Let me think about it, okay? I'll see you at the funeral. Good night, Marie," He hung up and said to Presh, answering her unspoken question, "The fat, warm Marie. Frank Camargo's widow."

Presh dimmed the light and let the robe fall away. There was one moment when she stood as an unclothed goddess. Then she smiled and slipped into the bed. Her presence was electric.

"Well," she said. "Where shall we start?"

"I'd like to take your hair down," Donahoo said.

"You want to do it?"

"Please."

The big Irish hand reached for the soft silk. Donahoo was thinking something wonderful. *I'm home,* Donahoo thought.

It wasn't eucalyptus. It was lilacs.

CHAPTER FIFTY-FOUR

No time to waste or lose. Chip Lyons led his troops into the gathering dusk of the Balboa Park glide path. Twelve cops in six unmarked police cars, coming from different directions, radio volume turned low, no lights. Main objective, surprise. Patrol cars stationed at major intersections in the event a chase developed. A chopper hovering off the bay for whatever. A quickly assembled army hoping it was ready for any contingency. Chip Lyons way out in front.

Saperstein had given his permission. Saperstein, too far away to take personal command, yelling into the phone from his weekend cabin in Julian, he had said okay, do it. A dead Marine and a TOW missile and you think you know where the killer is? Well, fuck, yeah. Don't waste time calling for SWAT. Don't even think about it. Use who is available and use them now. Use a meter maid if you have to. Go in, kick ass. Every second counts. The guy could be aiming that TOW right now. Saperstein had screamed. "*Get the fucker!*"

Chip Lyons had the house picked out. He had drifted by. A small washed-out blue, faded-red trim house with a big sign, JOSEPH R. FOLEY, REALTOR. He had barely glanced at it. But it was the house. Exactly as described by Minny Mendosa. The clincher was the van they'd found several blocks away. A van with a bad camouflage paint job. The dead Marine's van.

He drifted back. There was a light on now. There hadn't been one before. But there it was now. That didn't mean the guy was home, of course. The light could be on a timer. But he had probably turned it on himself. It was getting dark.

He's in there, he thought. He could imagine the crackpot set-ting up the TOW. He could fire it from...? He studied the house. That attic window?

"What do you think?" Montrose asked. He was riding shot-gun. He was holding it between his knees. He wasn't used to it and he was nervous. If he wasn't careful he was going to blow his face off. He said, his mouth dry, "Is this the place?"

"Yeah, it's the place," Chip Lyons said. He looked at the house, the bay window that took up most of the front, the little attic window stuck in the gable above. The guy could shoot from the house. The planes went right over. "We're going in."

"Jesus," Montrose said. "Hold it. Wait till the other cars get here."

"No. He could be set up. A bunch of cop cars slam in, spook him, he could fire. Who the fuck knows when the next plane is coming. Any minute. We're going in."

"Jesus."

"Bring Him if you want," Chip Lyons said. He got on the radio. He said, "We're going in."

They eased out of the car. Chip Lyons unholstered his Dan Wesson. He motioned. He said, softly, "You take the front, I'll take the back." He moved away. He said, "Take the front, Montrose."

Chip Lyons made a low run for the side of the house. Montrose started for the front. He was like a machine now. He just kept going. He went up on the porch in one huge stride. He kicked down the front door and hurtled inside. He was carry-ing the shotgun low. His finger was on the trigger, the safety off. He fanned through the house. Where the fuck was anybody? He came to the big room that looked like a command center.

Foley was in shock. He was angry, frightened, fumbling. He was leaning awkwardly against his desk, shooting up with mor-phine. Cops, that's all he knew. *Cops.* He'd seen them leaving the car in the street. He'd seen them heading for the house. The cop with the big gun running for the side. The black cop with the shotgun.

He couldn't figure what had gone wrong. The van? Hell, it was six blocks away. How could they connect it to him? The Marine? The sucker was dead.

Foley hurried. The gun, Stryker's gun, was a foot away, next to the phone. The silencer was beside it.

The black cop burst in. He was holding the shotgun low. He screamed, "Freeze! Drop it! Drop it!"

Foley finished. Last drop. He let the syringe fall to the floor.

The black cop was screaming, "Put your hands on your head!"

Foley stared at him. The anger and fright had passed. What concerned him now was how? What had gone wrong?

"Put your hands on your head!"

Foley complied. He heard the other cop coming. He was careful not to move. He could see, corner of his eye, a big gun, held with two hands. It was pointed at him, ready to fire.

"Anybody else?"

"No. Just this guy."

Foley watched the cop with the big gun work. How he looked at him, how he looked at his partner, how he looked at the steps hanging from the ceiling. He had a glass eye. It was obvious.

"I've got him," the cop with the big gun said. Foley could smell his breath as he moved closer. Peppermint. "See what's up there."

The black cop hesitated.

"Montrose," the cop with the big gun said. "Take a look upstairs."

The black cop went up into the darkness. There was a long wait. Then his flashlight blinked on. The light played around the opening in the ceiling. It shifted.

"Anything?"

"Yeah," the black cop responded. "There's a fucking missile launcher here. There's a couple shells. U.S. Marine Corps. It's gotta be the TOW."

"What else? Look around."

"That's all."

"Look around!"

"Okay."

The cop with the big gun pressed closer. He hadn't moved for a full minute, but he was breathing harder. He said, "Who you working with, dicko? I want your partners. Give 'em to me."

Foley shook his head. He hadn't planned for this moment because he never thought it would come. But he always knew what he was going to say. No.

"It would be better, you had partners," the cop was saying. "You can always blame your partners. You can make a deal."

Foley shook his head. No partners. He wasn't going to tell. Marky, Stryker. He'd never tell on them. They were safe.

"You did all this by yourself?"

Foley nodded. He'd never tell, he thought. Never.

"All the killings. The missile up there. Just you?"

Foley nodded. Just me, he thought. He was like a god.

The cop moved closer. He motioned to the pistol on the desk. Foley looked at him. Into the one eye.

"Go for the gun," the cop said.

Foley looked into the eye. It was burning. Hellfire. He thought it was odd. Peppermint breath and hellfire.

"Go for the gun."

The black cop yelled from the attic. "There's nothing else!"

Stryker, he was Stryker, not Foley, reached for the gun.

"No!" Chip Lyons screamed.

Stryker, he was Stryker now, Stryker almost got it. Chip Lyons shot him in the side of the head. Left side, the temple. He slumped to the floor, dragging the phone down. The gun stayed on the desk.

Montrose came down the stairs. He looked at the corpse with the wasted skull. He looked at the gun still on the desk.

"Uh," Montrose said. "Weren't you just a little fast on the draw here?"

"It's the old story," Chip Lyons told him. "Good cop, bad cop. Which are you?" He looked at him cold as ice. He said, "Do you know what a trial costs these days?"

"What a fucking mess," Montrose said. "What a fucking mess." He picked up the phone. He put it back on the desk. He had trouble getting it hung up properly. He had to try twice before he killed the dial tone.

Gomez came in. He was holding a search warrant.

"What the fuck took you so long?" Chip Lyons asked.

CHAPTER FIFTY-FIVE

Donahoo awakened. He was alone in bed. Presh was gone. He pushed up and looked around. The sun was already slanting through the bamboo blinds. Soft bars were scattered across the room, strips of light, strips of dark. Her clothes were gone, too. She's gone, he thought.

Presh. He wondered for a moment if she actually existed. He had never been with anyone who worked such magic on him. God, she was so beautiful, and so smart and funny, he thought. She was wonderful. Tender, caring, giving. Everything about her was perfect. She was just the best lady.

He shook his head. She was, he remembered, smiling, very good in bed, too. She brought all those qualities plus a wild abandon to the man/woman union. She made love with real dedication. Oh, she existed, all right. She was so goddamn alive it almost scared you.

Donahoo pushed off the bed and went into the bathroom. On the way, he picked up the remote control, turned the television on. He kept going.

When he returned, showered, shaved, a newscast had just started. There was a shot of a grinning Chip Lyons. He was saying, grinning, "Yeah. I guess we got him. The Balboa Firefly."

What? Donahoo sat down, feeling strange, a little weak. There was the thought, unbidden, that the Lord giveth, and the Lord taketh away.

The picture switched to a body on a stretcher being hoisted into an ambulance. There was an inset in the upper right hand corner of the screen. A picture of a scowling Joseph R. Foley, Realtor. He was identified that way in the print below.

The newscaster said voice over: "Police believe this man, Joseph R. Foley, a member of the San Diego Board of Realtors, in recent days was responsible for at least six killings, possibly more, in the Balboa Park district. Police had tagged him The Balboa Firefly."

Jesus, Donahoo thought.

Now the newscaster appeared on the screen. "There are unconfirmed reports that some sort of explosive device was removed from Foley's home. The reports suggest it may have been a missile. Police have thus far refused comment."

A missile? Donahoo wondered how the hell a Realtor would get hold of a missile. But then, why not? It was all out there. Every weapon of destruction imaginable. If you wanted it badly enough, you'd find a way, you'd get it.

The TV screen went to the scene the night before in front of Foley's home. The ambulance. The squad cars. Cops everywhere. Gomez. Montrose. Palmer and Cominsky. A grinning Chip Lyons.

Back to the anchor. A Camp Pendleton Marine had been found dead in a canyon in Marilou Park. He'd been shot numerous times. Rumors there might be a connection. Again no official comment.

Donahoo stared at the screen dully. It wasn't registering anymore. He was watching and listening, but it wasn't getting through. He was glad it was over, but he was sorry, too.

New story. Mayor Gordon Fletcher was on the screen. Faye Stuart was in the background. The Mayor was talking about a project called Pilgrim Restores America. Donahoo found himself tuning in about the middle of it. The Pilgrim Tobacco Company had quietly bought up a large section of Golden Hill. Now it was putting it back on the market, at cost, for restoration. Pilgrim's seed money investment—its corporate good citizen leadership—had taken the risk out of restoring this section of

Golden Hill. The rehab could be done all at once. There'd be no gamble. No chance of someone restoring a building only to have slums remain all around. Mayor Fletcher beamed. "San Diego salutes Pilgrim Restores America."

New picture. Grayson Grenier III, president and CEO of Pilgrim Tobacco, being interviewed by several reporters. Grenier was all aglow, too. He said his company planned similar projects. He said it hoped to be a continuing example to other large corporations. It intended to show the way with Pilgrim Restores America. It would go into cities unannounced. It would quietly buy up strategic areas in slum neighborhoods. It would release them, all at once, for restoration by others, or, in some instances, it would do the rehab itself. He personally might do it for a particular project. A reporter asked where the next project might be. Grenier smiled. He said, big smile, a big Chip Lyons smile, "That would be telling."

Donahoo snapped off the television. A lousy day for him, but a great day for San Diego. Balboa Park gets saved. Golden Hill gets restored. Two kick-ass things happen. The same day.

Something made him turn the television back on. Grenier was gone. They were already talking about something else. He snapped it off again. Two things, he thought. What Frank Camargo had been worried about. One track, two trains? Golden Hill, that was one. The other was…Donahoo shook his head. Was that possible? Fuck, it would work, he thought. The guy sets himself up as a hero. He gives himself carte blanche to quietly buy up property in distressed areas. The operative word is *quietly*. He has to do it secretly. If the cat's out of the bag, everybody starts doing it, nothing changes. So he has to do it secretly. Donahoo asked the question aloud. "And it's not his fault whatever happens later? You can't blame him if the land unexpectedly increases a hundredfold in value?"

He picked up the phone and dialed Police Headquarters and asked to talk to Saperstein. There was a long wait. Saperstein wasn't available. He called Lewis. Same thing.

He called Chip Lyons and got Montrose. He asked to talk to Lyons.

"He's gone," Montrose said. "Day off. Victory dinner. He's picking his teeth somewhere."

Donahoo had to tell somebody. He told Montrose. He said, "Listen, what if there were two missiles, Montrose? Two guys, two missiles, and, last night, you got half of the equation?"

Montrose said, "Well, like you're fond of saying, we could do this all morning, Sarge. What if? What are you telling me? Do you have something or not?"

"I've got a theory. The Marine found dead in Marilou Park. Have you got an approximate time of death?"

"We've got a good guess. A motorist says he saw a couple guys heading down into the canyon about six forty-five Friday. There was a van, camouflage paint, off the side of the road. So that figures to be the victim and his killer."

"When the mystery prowler was trying to plug me?"

"Yeah?"

"Camargo was right. Two trains."

"So?"

"So let me talk to Gomez."

"He's not here."

"Palmer."

"Sarge, there's nobody here," Montrose said. "The whole squad's got the day off. I'd be off, too. I drew the short match."

"Jesus Christ."

"Take it easy."

"Yeah."

Donahoo hung up. He'd heard that before. The bus, the ocean, the whorehouse. He looked around for his clothes.

Grenier opened the storage unit in Old Town. The Jeep Wrangler was waiting like a shiny red new toy. It was the way Valesy had left it. All ready to go.

Well, Grenier thought. Now or never. He quickly closed the door behind him and then lit the big battery-powered lamp. He had discussed this with Valesy many times. He knew the routine. He went through it. He removed the ragtop. He unzipped the canvas bag. He swung the launcher around on its swivel. He loaded a round, aimed. It was easy. But could he do it? Grenier practiced with the launcher, thinking about his dinner with Faye Stuart, and how, after a few drinks and very little prompting, she did mention some of the inadequacies at Lindbergh Field. He had casually remarked that it seemed like a small airport for a major city and she had quickly volunteered that special arrangements had to be made before it would accept a jumbo. If notified in advance, they would close the taxiways, permitting a plane as large as the Boeing 747-200B to land. They were used mainly on charters and to handle overbookings. Later he'd made a few phone calls. The 200B could carry 452 passengers, an operating crew of three or four, and, at capacity, nine flight attendants. American Airlines Flight 5328 from Los Angeles was coming in this morning using a 200B. It was fully booked. It was due at 11:33.

He practiced for half an hour. He got faster all the time. He was ready. He put things back together. He turned off the lamp and opened the unit door and drove outside. He locked up and looked into the sky. It was a nice day. A few puff clouds. Grenier did the arithmetic again. On the plane, passengers, crew, 465 people. And, when it came down, a lot more people on the ground. The death toll could reach 500. It could hit more than that. The worst single plane disaster in history involved a Japan Air Lines Boeing 747 that crashed into Mt. Ogura in Japan, August 12, 1985, claiming 520. This one could go higher. This could be the worst. He shuddered.

It was easy, but could he do it? Well, yes, Grenier thought. Three hundred, 400, 500. When it got that high, what was the difference? When it got that high, it was like stepping on bugs. He got back into the Jeep. He drove out of the storage yard and headed for the I-5. He glanced at his watch. He'd be in the glide path in five, six minutes. He looked to the sky again. Somewhere, headed this way, his way, an airliner had his name on it.

He reached under the seat for the pistol he knew was fastened there. Valesy's spare Browning Model 1935. He pulled it out and put it on the seat next to him.

Donahoo pushed into Madam Zola's. Presh was bent over her crystal ball. A stout woman in a flowered dress and a derby straw hat was listening intently.

"I see a tall, dark stranger," Presh told her.

The woman said, "You're sure he's tall?"

Donahoo said, "You've got to get outta here."

Presh glanced up at him, her smile fading, becoming a frown.

"Please," Donahoo said. "Trust me." He went around the counter and grabbed her by the arm. "I mean it. You've got to leave. Now."

She started to struggle. "What's the matter with you?"

"Presh, just come, okay?" he demanded. He told the woman, "You, too. Get outta here. Get in your car and start driving."

American Airlines Flight 5328 out of Los Angeles, 466 on board, including crew, left Miramar Naval Air Station's control and was handed over to San Diego Approach Control.

San Diego confirmed. "American 5328, contact San Diego Approach Control, 124.35."

"Good morning," Capt. Hughie Bishop, the pilot, responded. He was handling the radio. He wasn't at the controls.

First Officer Kenneth Jackson, who was piloting, began a slow, careful turn toward Lindbergh Field.

American off-duty Capt. Jim Pantages, riding in a cockpit jump-seat, leaned in closer, chuckling. "Okay. Kelly says, 'Hung Jury,' and before anyone else can think, Margellos says, 'Twelve of the luckiest men in America are empaneled for the Mike Tyson retrial.' Margellos said it that fast. Without fucking thinking."

Second officer Lou Calvelli, the engineer, gave him a quick, disbelieving look, then turned back to his instruments.

Bishop said, "Approach, American 5328 out of nine five, descending to seven thousand, the airport's in sight."

"What are we doing here?" Jackson asked. He hadn't been listening. "Movie titles?"

"Yeah. I give you the title. You give me the plot."

"American 5328," San Diego Approach Control said. "Cleared visual approach. Runway 27."

"Here's an example," Pantages said. " 'Africa Screams.' Ted Danson drops his pants."

"Margellos again?"

"Yeah."

"Thank you, cleared visual approach, 27," Bishop radioed.

"How about this one?" Pantages said. " 'Nothing But Trouble,' Sonny Bono's multicolored sweater is mistaken for a piñata and he is beaten to death by five-year-olds at a birthday party fundraiser in Mecca."

There was a garbled transmission from San Diego Approach Control.

Bishop: "Sir, was that for American 5328?"

San Diego Approach Control. "No, that was for the company, sir."

" 'Raising Arizona,' " Pantages said. "Raising the Titanic wasn't enough trouble."

San Diego Approach Control: "American 5328, traffic one o'clock, one mile northbound."

Bishop: "Okay. We're looking for it."

San Diego Approach Control: "American 5328, contact Lindbergh tower now, 133.3. Have a nice day."

Donahoo pushed Presh into his Olds. He held her there for a long moment. She was strong and she was resisting.

"Do this for me, once," Donahoo said. "Blind faith. Just once. Trust me." He finally released her. "Once."

"Once," she said.

Lindbergh Tower: "How far are you going to take your downwind, 5328? Company traffic is waiting for departure."

Bishop: "Ah, three, four miles."

Lindbergh Tower: "Okay."

There was additional radio conversation between the tower and the waiting aircraft.

"... taxi into position and hold."

"... position and hold."

Lindbergh Tower: "American 5328, cleared to land."

Bishop: "5328 cleared to land."

Donahoo jammed the Olds up Kalmia. Maybe he didn't know the future, he thought. But he had a premonition. If it was going to happen, it was going to happen today, it was going to happen soon. Camargo had been right all along. Not two trains, maybe. But two missiles.

He said, "I *think* I know this. There's a crackpot around here. He's got a rocket. He's after a plane."

"Then *tell* somebody."

"I have. And I will. But first I want you out of here."

The Olds, big as it was, took to the air as he left Kalmia's sharp incline, crossed the sudden flat that was Albatross.

"You are going to get us killed," Presh told him. She wasn't afraid. She was still angry.

Donahoo didn't answer. Out of the corner of his eye, he had seen the red Jeep Wrangler, parked at the intersection of Albatross and Ivy. He started to turn in midair.

"Tommy!" Presh yelled.

The Olds landed with the wheels angled. Donahoo barely kept control. He could see the Jeep Wrangler very clearly at the other end of the block. It was out in the middle of the street. Something was mounted on the roll bar. It looked like a big camera, telescopic lens.

Donahoo's stomach went to a knot. "There he is. He's ready to fire."

Presh closed her eyes. "Do what you gotta do."

Donahoo floored it. He thought, inanely, that they ought to be in a department vehicle, that they shouldn't be doing this to his Olds.

"Your belt on?" he asked.

Presh buckled up grimly. She still had her eyes closed.

Grenier had moved into the backseat of the Jeep Wrangler. He was loading a round in the launcher. He was aiming it into the sky.

"Hold on," Donahoo said. "I'm gonna ram the sonofabitch."

"Okay."

Grenier saw him coming. He swiveled the launcher back out of sight. He ducked down with it.

Donahoo headed for him with the gas pedal on the floor. He closed his eyes and rammed the Jeep. It rolled over like a garbage can and landed upright. Grenier, dazed, bloodied, rose from the backseat with the launcher, resumed his former position behind it. He was still going to fire.

Presh screamed: "Stop him."

Donahoo struggled out of the Olds. He could barely move. He was hurt, his chest seemed crushed, his right arm felt like it was broken. He went for his gun and it fell from his grasp.

Grenier was aiming. There was the rumble of an approaching airliner.

"Tommy!"

Grenier fired. The Spigot left with a whoosh. Two thin guide wires trailed behind it. Donahoo threw himself into the wires. He rolled around in them desperately.

The missile veered, corkscrewing the sky, looking for a target, hunting. It found the airliner again. It started after it.

Jackson: "Did you see that?"

Bishop: "Gear down."

American Airlines 5328 shuddered with a loud impact
   and explosion.

Calvelli: "What the fuck?"

Jackson: "I'm losing control."

Bishop: "What have we got here?"

Jackson: "We're in trouble. We've been hit."

Bishop: "Huh?"

Jackson: "We've been hit by something. The tail's gone."

Bishop: "Tower, we're going down, this is American."

Calvelli: "Oh, fuck, fuck."

"Soo Boo, I love ya," Pantages said.

The Boeing 747-200B jetliner roared across the glide path. Most of its tail was missing. For an instant, the huge plane faltered, almost fell out of the sky with the shattered pieces of metal it was dropping. Then, at the last moment, it righted itself, held altitude, kept going. It flashed across the I-5 Freeway. Lindbergh Field was straight ahead. It was going to make it.

Donahoo pushed to his feet. He was in the tangle of wires left by the Spigot's missile. He looked for the Python. He couldn't see it.

Grenier loaded his second round. He swung the launcher around. He aimed it at Donahoo. He wiped the blood from his eyes. He fumbled with the firing mechanism.

Donahoo waited. He was too hurt to move.

The Browning Model 1935 was in the street. It had fallen out of the Jeep. Presh picked it up. She pointed it at Grenier.

"Kill him," Donahoo said weakly.

Presh said, an anguished cry, "It's not the same."

"Kill him."

She fired. The slug caught Grenier in the middle of his forehead. He slumped dead over the Spigot.

Presh dropped the gun. Madly, she went to Grenier, pulled at him, tried to revive him. She came away with blood on her hands.

"Oh, God, I've killed him!" she whispered. "God, I've killed somebody." She was crying now. "Tommy! Jesus Christ, he's not a bottle, he's a human being. Who *is* he?!"

Donahoo limped painfully to her. He kicked the gun skittering to the gutter. He took her into his arms. She clung to him.

"It's not the same," she said, sobbing. "I hate guns. I *hate* them." She said, barely able to speak, her body shaking, "I never killed anyone before."

Donahoo held her. Very few of us have, he thought. He didn't know what to tell her. He didn't know what it was like to kill, had no idea. Anything he said might be false. He stood holding her in his loving arms, the only thing he was sure about right now, the only truth he knew.

"I love you," he said.

CHAPTER FIFTY-SIX

Nobody could remember the last time Saperstein had been in the Sickos, Crackpots, Underwear & Mad Bombers squad room. Then they decided that he had *never* been there. He was there now, though.

"Let's reconstruct," Saperstein was saying for the benefit of the whole squad. Donahoo, and Gomez and Montrose, and Cominski and Palmer. Lewis, too. He was there. He'd brought the bottle of Old Crow. It was against regulations, but Lewis didn't much give a shit, not today.

"What happened," Saperstein was saying. "Joseph R. Foley, Realtor, devises a plot to get rid of Lindbergh Field and recoup his real-estate losses in Balboa Park. He becomes, in his madness, this is in the diary we found …"

Saperstein paused to pour himself some more of the Old Crow. The moment gave him the opportunity to assess his audience. He looked around. "… an unholy trinity." He said, "We can reconstruct some other time."

Lewis, very quietly, he raised his glass, he said, "Cheers."

Saperstein didn't hear. He was kind of full of himself today. It wasn't official, but the word was out. The special commission that had been looking all over the country for a new police chief had found one right under its nose. The new Chief was going to be Walter Saperstein, presently Assistant Chief, Detectives.

"One thing more I do want to say," Saperstein was saying, "publicly, I owe you an apology, Tommy. I think I ought to point out that both of your adversaries, Foley and Grenier, both had such a high opinion of you, they both wanted you out of the way. Foley wanted to kill you. Grenier wanted you under suspicion. I'm sorry I didn't recognize that at the time. I was wrong and I am sorry." He said, "Publicly."

Now Donahoo looked around. In front of five other guys? This was publicly? But it was in the presence of the men who mattered to him. So he accepted. "Okay."

"I also want to thank you," Saperstein said. "You did a hell of a job."

"Hey, it was luck," Donahoo told him. He was quoting. "Just a shuffle of the cards."

Saperstein ignored that. He said, "We've got some changes coming. There'll be guys moving up, filling vacated slots. We're gonna need a new lieutenant. You interested?"

Donahoo didn't think about it. "No. I don't want to move up."

Saperstein considered. He had some plans for reorganizing the department. "You want to move anywhere?"

"I want to move to Coronado."

"Well," Saperstein said, "I don't think I can help you there, Tommy."

Donahoo said, "No, I guess you can't."

Saperstein was already talking to Montrose. He said, "Why do they call you Spook?"

CHAPTER FIFTY-SEVEN

Frank Camargo's funeral. Donahoo thought it was something. They were putting him down at Mount Hope Cemetery, on Lincoln Drive in the tombstone section, in the shade of a big pine tree. Dead slap middle of all the shit he hated. LOCK YOUR PURSE/VALUABLES IN TRUNK. BEWARE OF ANY SUSPICIOUS INDIVIDUALS. IF POSSIBLE DON'T VISIT ISOLATED AREAS ALONE. Camargo, looking ahead, had bought the plot in better times, when they didn't have to put up signs like that. Then, you could put flowers on a grave without getting knocked on the head for your trouble. You could come out of a cemetery alive. Still, if a guy could only stand up, they hadn't yet stolen the view.

Donahoo stood watching with Presh Carling, listening to the usual funeral stuff, the pomp and the ceremony, the grief.

"I wish they had valet parking, Mike. When are they ever gonna get that? Valet parking where you really need it?"

Donahoo was mostly listening.

"I didn't expect this big of a turnout. He never drank with the guys."

"Yeah, well, you know, Jamie, they want to make sure he gets buried."

"Camargo, what do you think he died of, really? Dumbness?"

"Naw. He got his arm caught in a can redeemer. That tight spick. He had to go home? He didn't wanta buy you a drink."

"My all-time favorite: Frank, he's got this case, there's two brothers, they're identical twins, one charges the other with assault, robbery, grand theft auto. Later, the accused comes in, withdraws the charge."

Donahoo was listening and taking names.

When it was over, shots fired, flag folded, placed on top of the shiny casket, Frank Camargo lowered into the ground holding the *Union-Trib* and the story, quoting Donahoo, of how he, Frank Camargo, something a lot of people didn't know, was a real smart cop. He named the case. He solved it. And...

"We all go back to dirt."

"All part of the Lord's plan, Ray."

"Ashes to ashes, dust to dust."

"You can think of something better?"

"So this guy comes in, and he says, 'How do I find Saperstein?', and Lewis, he says, 'Pull the string on the Tampax.'"

"Duran and Fitz. They get this whore, she's gonna take on both of them, a ménage à twat. Duran, he's a winner, but Fitz, he can't get it up. So they're playing good cock, bad cock."

... when it was over, the bunch of them, what they were saying now, they were all going over to the Mad House sports bar in El Cajon.

"You coming, Tommy?" Chip Lyons wanted to know.

Donahoo shook his head. No, he and Presh, they were going over to the fat, warm Marie's. They were going to have some cookies.

In New York, Ruby Slippers got a call from Grayson Grenier's attorney, Kilpatrick. He had the usual kind of papers for her to sign. No claim on Grenier's assets. No claim on his estate.

"Fuck you," Ruby said sweetly. She was going for it all.

Near Alamos, Mexico, Larisa Krasnitskaya, effective woman, walked out onto the land with her mozo, Juan. She picked a place.

"This looks like a good spot," she said. "We will dig the well here."

Her son, Mikhail, had a jumping bean in his open palm. It jumped out, fell to the ground, and he couldn't find it. He didn't cry, though. There were more.

Alamos is the jumping-bean capital of the world.